THE DRAYTON CHRONICLES

TONY BERTAUSKI

BERTAUSKI STARTER LIBRARY

FREE!

* * *

bertauski.com

* * *

Drayton once believed he was a vampire.

He doesn't know what he is. Or why he has lived for thousands of years. He takes not his victim's blood but the silky essence of their soul during their last breath. Often mistaken for the Angel of Death, his victims sometimes ask for forgiveness. Sometimes he delivers. After all, he is not without sin.

DRAYTON, THE TAKER

BOOK 1

Sometimes, Death delivers.

1

---

unk-ass bitch.

Blake ignored his Thoughts. When you hear something like that a million times, it loses meaning. Or it sinks in so deep you don't even notice it, like a clock ticking on the wall.

The Thoughts lived in Blake's head from the very beginning. When he was five, he talked back to them. He'd be up in his attic room playing games with them, like Chutes and Ladders. They were friendly, told him he was smart. That he was a good boy. The Thoughts were Blake's best friend. His parents figured it was just an imaginary friend. That it was normal. Healthy, they said.

But the Thoughts changed when Blake was eighteen, wanted him to do things he didn't want to do. Wanted things he shouldn't want to do. That's when Blake started ignoring them, but he'd lived with them all his life. And they didn't like being pushed aside. He tried to make them go away with booze and dope and sometimes that worked, but they always came back. Some say Blake Barnes just up and went crazy one day. If you asked Blake, he'd tell you he just couldn't take it anymore.

Motherfucker.

Now he was on his back. Snow had drifted over him. He was

beyond cold. Shivers had racked his body like electricity, but that was over now. They ended... he couldn't remember how long ago they ended. How long had he even been lying in the snow? Two hours? Eight? Funny, he didn't know that, either.

Blake had maxed out his credit cards buying climbing gear in Portland. The debt collectors could kiss his ice cold ass. He also bought a Range Rover. It had in-dash GPS, satellite radio, seat warmers and a dashboard that talked. *Fucking classy.* He drove up to Mt. Hood and left it at the Timberline Lodge with the keys in the ignition for some lucky bastard. Finders keepers.

The sky was gray when he left the automobile running in the parking lot. The top of Mt. Hood swirled with clouds driven by searing wind that could clean the chrome off a set of Craftsmans. He had started the climb without seeing a single person. Nobody in their right mind would climb in that weather. Unless they had the Thoughts living in their head.

About a thousand feet up, Blake passed two retreating climbers crusted with snow. They warned him. Called him crazy. *Me? Crazy?* One of them grabbed Blake. "It's suicide, man. You got a death wish?" The climber tried to force him back with them until Blake connected with a right hook above the guy's ear. Pain lanced the back of his hand. He broke a knuckle, but it was a sweet punch. Put that asshole on his back. Made the Thoughts giggle.

"Go on, kill yourself," the guy said.

We will.

Five hundred more feet up the mountain, the blizzard was all around him. The wind had scrubbed his cheeks raw and flattened his lungs. He thought maybe he remembered the sulfuric smell of Devil's Kitchen, maybe even made it to the base of Hogsback Ridge before time got hazy on him. Or maybe he fell down after he clocked that climber.

It won't be long now.

Freezing to death ain't so bad, really. At first it sucked, sure, but after the body ate up all its energy, there was nothing left to shiver and everything went numb. It was kind of pleasant, really, like half a dozen pills. The Thoughts were still muttering because those mother-fuckers never shut up, but even they were getting drowsy. Maybe they would go to sleep for once. That's why Blake took the trip, after all. To shut their ass up.

A hang glider appeared in the snow. Blake had been comfortably numb for a long time, even thought his eyelashes had crusted over, but there it was, a goddamn hang glider. He found the strength to sit up. The wind was still blowing, but wasn't so cold. In fact, it was sort of balmy. He climbed on quite nimbly, pushed off the side of the mountain like he'd hang glided all his life and soared out of the storm and away from Mt. Hood. Away from the Thoughts.

Below was a thick green forest and above puffy skies. White cotton tore off the clouds, snagged on the glider and stuck to his face. It tasted like cotton candy. *Vanilla-flavored.* He went in and out, poking holes in the sides of the clouds, harvesting light, fluffy goodies in his outstretched hands and shoving them down his gullet like he seven years old again, walking through the fairgrounds.

Blake saw his house. It was nestled in the woods below, smoke leaking out the chimney. He bought the cabin ten years earlier for next to nothing because everything was cheap in the middle of nowhere. And that's where Blake wanted to be, miles away from everyone and everything. Trees didn't talk back. And if an animal got in your business you could stick a gun up its ass and blow the lunch out of its mouth. No law against that.

Blake mixed with people like ketchup and ice cream. Too bad he couldn't outrun the Thoughts. In fact, they just got louder now that they had Blake all to themselves. Wanting this, wanting that, go here, do this, you fuck. You fat, disgusting, perverted fuck. They whispered when he hunted so as not to startle the deer. They shut up when he made the kill and dressed it right there. They hummed, like that fat Willie Wonka kid swimming in chocolate. Sometimes they told him to do things to the carcass, like cut the eyes out and piss in the skull. Blake refused. That was sick. But then they wouldn't shut up. So, you know.

They listened to pain. Like when he put a hot iron on his leg, oh, they listened, all right. Once he hung himself from a doorknob and jerked off until he blacked out. They shut up for the rest of the night. He hung himself from the doorknob a dozen more times, but they got bored after a while, so he pounded ten-penny nails through his hand, pulled a molar out with pliers and even peeled a fingernail off his little finger. But they always got bored. That's when Blake came up with the Mt. Hood idea.

Blake was afraid seeing the cabin might wake the Thoughts up. He might be insane, but he wasn't stupid. He knew he was hallucinating. But just to be safe, he steered away from the cabin. He just wanted to go to sleep, drift off in a nice and numb blackness, go back to that feeling when he was tiny, suckling on his momma's satisfying tit. Everything was going to plan and he didn't want the Thoughts fucking it up.

Blake turned the hang glider for Las Vegas. He hadn't been to Vegas in years. In fact, the last time he'd been to Vegas was… well, right before he moved to the cabin. He took all the money and played blackjack, craps, and slots. Stuffed his winnings in women's panties. Sade was a plastic-titty stripper. He must've shoved a thousand dollars down her shorts that week. She didn't really thank him, either, besides grind his lap until he shot a load in his pants. For shit sake, a thousand bucks should've at least got him a hand job. The Thoughts wanted Blake to teach the whore a lesson, something along the lines of pissing in her skull. That's why Blake left for the country. *Ketchup and ice cream.*

The Vegas strip illuminated the sky. Blake brought the glider down, figured to make a landing and hit the first club running. He could hear the traffic, wondered if a shot of whiskey would buzz him up, even if it was imaginary. Hell, he could do all the coke he wanted. He could teach Sade a lesson, too. You know, chop her goddamn head off. Nothing illegal about pretending to do that.

The Vegas lights flickered. He'd have to hurry if he was going to get to Sadie. No telling how long the hallucination would last. He never believed there was life after death, so he needed to do it before his body froze solid. The glider spun, aimed at the hood of a BMW pulling in front of the Bellagio. He'd impale the car, maybe the driver, too.

But he didn't spear the car. Didn't even land on the strip. The pavement turned to black water and the police sirens sounded like insects. City lights dimmed and the sun was setting on the far end of a marsh. Blake crashed in a wetland.

No.

Not only did the dream get off track, he landed in the Lowcountry, the last fucking place on Earth Blake wanted to be. That was the whole goddamn reason he went to Oregon. He took an oath never to set foot in South Carolina again. He was born there but for shit sake he wasn't going to die there, even in a dream. He tried to get the glider running again, but the pluff mud pulled at his feet. Blake went face first into the mud, sucking him down into the smelly, wet ground. Fuck it, he wasn't going to die in a shitty hallucination.

His eyelashes crunched as he opened his eyes back on the mountain. Snow had completely covered his face. He wasn't numb anymore. He was smoking ass hot, in the last throes of hypothermia as the blood vessels constricted. He pissed all over himself, too.

Why the hell did he have to end up in the Lowcountry? That hallucination was going just fine but ended like his whole life had gone. Just shitty. Blake couldn't catch a break. He was born with the Thoughts and he'd die with them. For once he just wanted to feel happy, but he couldn't even do that right. The Thoughts were right, he deserved to die like a pig. And he deserved to die more painfully. The Thoughts wanted him to shoot his balls off or stick his head in the fireplace. Freezing to death was too easy. But it wasn't too late.

Blake pulled himself up. His piss-frozen pants crunched. Blake fumbled at his coat, trying to undo it but his fingers were like wooden pegs. He wanted to feel Death's hand around his throat, wanted to feel Death rip the last breath from him like a bullet or pull his guts out with cold hands. He deserved that for the shit he'd done.

The Thoughts woke up, adrenaline dumping into his flattened veins. *That's the spirit!*

A black hand touched Blake's stiff fingers.

Blake's eyes filled with water. He blinked several times. Was he hallucinating, again? Yeah, he must be still laying in the snow, dreaming he stood up trying to take his clothes off. He blinked again. It didn't feel like a dream, though. Maybe he was wrong about the afterlife. Maybe he was already dead.

He was going to fall but the black hand held him steady. A boy stood in front of him, dressed like it was July. His black shirt fluttered violently in the wind.

"Am I dreaming?" Blake asked.

The boy shook his head. His lips moved, but Blake couldn't hear him. His skin was thick, but not wrinkled. Maybe he wasn't a boy, but something about his eyes, his clear blue eyes, looked innocent. Blake was lying in the snow, for real this time. The boy hovered over him, his nostrils flaring. The boy's touch was somehow colder than the air.

"Are you an angel?" Blake asked.

The boy spoke into his ear. "Of sorts."

An angel. Of course, he was the Angel of Death. Blake hadn't thought it would be so literal, an actual boy coming for him, but then again this was his first time dying. Somehow he pictured Death wearing a black cloak riding a fire-spitting black horse. Big fangs. The stink of death preceding him like a rotting corpse. Turned out Death was a boy with a respectful disposition. Who would've guessed?

The boy took Blake's hand away and unbuckled the top of his coat. The wind rushed inside, down his neck and over his chest. He couldn't feel much, though. Numbness returned. The boy massaged Blake's chest. It began to hurt.

"Don't save me."

The boy continued to rub.

"I don't want to live." Blake grabbed his arm, tears swelled in his eyes. "I don't deserve it."

The boy didn't blink. Blake somehow knew he was wasn't trying to save him. He was beyond saving. The boy was helping him die. Of course, he was. He was Death. The boy continued rubbing as if it were a ritual. The Thoughts in Blake's head faded. *Goodbye, fuckhead.* He saw the Lowcountry marsh again. The sun had nearly set on the horizon, only a sliver of the orange disc left. Blake felt the sticky mud wrap around his ankles. He saw the messes he left in South Carolina. The people he hurt. The things he'd done.

Blake's lips hardly moved. "Do me a favor."

The boy looked annoyed.

"Find my family. Tell them… tell them I'm sorry."

The boy hesitated, continued rubbing. He heard. Blake knew the angel heard. Blake imagined the Lowcountry wetlands as if to draw him a map. He imagined the house he left behind ten years ago, where his family still lived. The boy flinched like the thought stung.

The boy nodded, imperceptibly. He nodded because he understood.

Blake's breaths were numbered. The boy's hands got colder. It felt like he was breathing through his chest, now. Like his breath was going directly into the boy's palms. His chest continued to expand like he was still breathing, but it was getting slower. Shallower. He couldn't feel his heart anymore. But at least the Thoughts were gone. For once in his life, gone for good. Blake was right to bring them to this mountain. For once, he got something right.

Blake Barnes passed from life on Mt. Hood. His last breath leaked from him. His body was below him. The boy hovered over it, his hands pressed on his sternum like he was about to administer CPR. The wind had no effect on Blake, passing through him on another plane. Up, he went, the body far below. The mountain faded and Blake was going wherever dead people go, but not before he heard one last thing. It could've been one last Thought come to haunt him, but it sounded more like the boy pressing close to Blake's body.

"Thank you," the boy said.

And just before the mountain and the snow and the world faded, the boy took from Blake what he came for.

2

Annie was starting the midnight shift at the Waffle House. It was her second shift that day. She wiped her hands and grabbed the coffee pot to make the rounds. Ernie Crites, a fat man that spent half his life wearing out the stool near the cash register, smiled at her with eggs stuck in his bristled mustache. Ernie started a conversation while she topped his coffee mug. Something about bowling. Ernie was a good tipper, so she listened. She was nodding, but she was looking to the end of the counter where a kid stared into his cup. Ernie noticed. He tried to change the subject, talked about what Annie was doing when she got off her shift.

Annie walked off, mid-Ern-sentence, and filled the kid's cup. "Need anything else?"

The kid snapped out of his thoughts, noticing Annie with steam rising out of the coffee pot. She hadn't seen him around. He exuded charm like a fragrance. Annie leaned against the counter, wondering if he was older than she thought. His skin was dark, like it had been exposed to endless sun. She could feel the warmth radiating from him.

She was going to ask if he was new in town; she hadn't seen him at the Waffle House. But then she forgot what she was doing. His eyes were mostly pupil, outlined by a sliver of blue, like the black was swallowing the irises. She could see her reflection in them, in a three-dimensional sort of way, like they were liquid pools. She leaned in a few more inches, studied the details of her reflection. The Waffle House disappeared around her. There was no sound. Only her reflection.

Annie jerked backed, shook her head. It felt like she was doused with ice water.

"You sleeping on the job?" Ernie the fat man said, bouncing as he laughed.

Annie frowned. The young man stared back into his cup. She picked up the coffee. Steam was no longer rising from the pot. She put it back on the hot plate. *Who screwed with the air conditioner?*

The kid finished his coffee and slid the cup across the counter, placed a crisp bill on top and started for the door. Ernie spun on his stool and stuck his foot out. The kid politely stopped. Ernie mumbled something to him. The kid didn't respond. Ernie stood, pulling his belt up under his belly, snorting a layer of phlegm back in his throat. He was going to sort out some business with this shit. Maybe because he was black, maybe because he blew off Annie. Or maybe just because.

Annie was fishing forks out of a basket but noticed Ernie grab the kid. Annie had never accepted a ride from him, but that didn't stop him from trying. And if she didn't get over there, there'd be a fight. They'd thrown Ernie out of the Waffle House for protecting Annie's honor once before. If he wasn't careful, he'd have to eat his midnight eggs down at the Huddle House.

But Ernie stopped working his belt back and forth. In fact, he froze like he forgot what he was going to say and went back to his plate. The kid walked off, opened the door for a customer and left.

Annie took Ernie's plate and wiped the counter. "How many times I got to tell you, Ern?"

"What?"

"You hassling customers."

"I don't know what you're talking about."

He wiped his mouth and threw the napkin on the plate. She couldn't tell if he was joking or just dumb. She cleared off all the abandoned plates. When she reached the end of the counter, she pulled a hundred dollar bill off a coffee cup. She snapped it tight and held it up to make sure she read the zeros right.

"Where'd you get that?" Ernie asked.

"That kid left it."

"What kid?"

She folded the bill in her pocket. "The one sitting here drinking coffee, that's who."

Ernie shrugged, jammed a toothpick between his teeth. *He is dumb.*

Annie could see the kid through the humidity-streaked windows. He crossed the street. No luggage. No backpack. And in no hurry.

3

———————————————

*T*ea was a full sensory drink, just not Waffle House tea. Drayton had been in Europe for the past century and developed an appreciation for Earl Gray. But now he was in Charleston, South Carolina, the breadbasket of the South. He figured if Americans could make decent tea, it would be in the South where a plantation was within walking distance. The Waffle House waitress couldn't hide her smirk when he'd asked for Earl Gray. She offered him sweet tea. *An abomination.* Drayton ended up staring into a mug of coffee, instead.

Annie had worked at the Waffle House for six months. She was a big reason Drayton was there, she just didn't know it yet. That would come soon enough. Drayton made the mistake of looking at her when she filled his cup and she was quickly drawn in. He didn't try to mesmerize her. The simple-minded did it to themselves. He dropped the temperature around her to break the trance. It was a simple energy trick he learned centuries ago. His body became an energy sink, absorbing vibrations from the molecules around him. He could become an instant blizzard with a thought. Or a ferocious fire if he gave the vibrations back.

Drayton wanted to reach the coast by sunrise. He encountered a little problem with Ernie. *Sit down. Forget.* Ernie didn't hear Drayton's thoughts, he felt it. Ernie did like everyone who felt Drayton's thoughts. He sat down. He forgot.

When day broke, Drayton was somewhere south of Charleston on a dirt road watching the sun rise above the wetlands. The light danced in the murky water that wandered through the reeds. Mosquitoes landed on his arms and probed his midnight skin for blood, finding none. Maybe he started his existence with white skin, he couldn't remember that far back. Either way, centuries of exposure to the sun had blackened his flesh. No matter what color it was or had become, there had never been blood under it.

It took six months to walk from Mt. Hood to the Lowcountry, but it wasn't exhaustion that weighed on Drayton. Blake Barnes was insane, no doubt. His personality was split in two, one side feeding on the other. He heard voices and couldn't take it. Maybe if Blake lived another couple hundred years he would've understood his insanity. His thoughts would've died out with understanding. After all, it took Drayton two hundred years to understand his own dysfunction and find peace. Humans didn't have that luxury.

Drayton didn't murder Blake Barnes. He only took the last few moments of his life. He showed no prejudice – fat, skinny, black, white, republican, democrat – he took from them all. They often mistook him for the Angel of Death, but Drayton wasn't sure *what* he was. Maybe he was Death and no one told him. He just knew he'd lived so long he couldn't remember when, where, or how his life began. Or why.

Tell my family I'm sorry.

Drayton didn't have to honor Blake Barnes' request. There was a time when he ignored all last requests but figured he owed his victims something for taking the last of their life, didn't he? He hated to call them victims, but that's what they were; they were all victims. The essence he craved was a silky energy that penetrated every human being. He could absorb it just being near them, leave a man, woman or child an empty shell. It wasn't like the old days when he tore out their throats and devoured them as they begged and pleaded. Back then, he ignored them, even laughed at their helplessness. That was how the whole vampire legend started. But Drayton didn't have fangs or hide from crosses. He didn't know what he was. He only knew he craved the human essence. But now he only took it from their last breath.

Even still, they were all victims, whether Drayton thanked them for their involuntary gift or not. He honored requests for a reason. *Atonement.* But if he got honest, drop dead on your knees honest, he did it because he wasn't really sure what happened to the victims after he took their essence. If Drayton died like them, would he go there, too? He wasn't human, not really. But did he have a soul? And if there was a God, like a bearded man looking down from heaven, Drayton figured he would have plenty to atone for. There wasn't a lawyer alive that would defend him. Nor should they.

Drayton didn't really care if there was an afterlife. He'd sent millions of people to the other side and had yet to see evidence of heaven or hell. If there was, so be it. He didn't ask to be born. He didn't want to live and live and live. He didn't atone so that he could go to heaven or avoid hell. He atoned because he believed there was a balance in the universe. He atoned because that was the order of things.

When the sun had fully risen above the horizon, Drayton started down the dirt road. About noon, he was near his destination. A mud-spattered truck roared past him, close enough the side view mirror nearly clipped his ear.

Almost there.

4

———

*A*aron Towgard buzzed the dumbfuck walking down the road with the mirror. Came a little close, thought he might've hit the guy. He didn't want to kill the asshole, just fuck with him. Dipshit looked lost so why not?

That happened first thing that morning. Now it was almost 1:00. The hunting dogs were boxed in the back. Aaron's little brothers fought over the radio. He didn't have time to take any of these idiots home. He was told to pick the check up at noon and not a minute later. He'd dicked around all morning and now he was fucked.

He about took out a line of mailboxes thinking of an excuse to tell his old man, but then he turned the corner and, what'd you know, there was ole Bo closing up the mailbox. Today was his lucky day. Bo always managed to avoid Aaron at school, but there was nowhere to hide this time.

Aaron locked up the front tires and stopped inches from the mailbox. Bo jumped in the ditch, falling against a pine tree. The dogs yapped. "Shut up!" Aaron stepped out of the truck. His brothers started climbing out. "Get back in the truck."

Aaron pushed his long, sweaty hair under his hat. "Hand me the check, Bo."

"It's in the box."

"I know where it's at, you shithead. Hand it to me."

"If you want the check," Bo said, "you know where to get it. I'm no delivery boy."

"You're a delivery boy if I say you are."

Bo plucked his white t-shirt nervously, then started back down the private drive.

"I'll let the dogs loose," Aaron said. "They'll give your horses a run all day. They ain't going to make it long in summer heat like this, you know."

Aaron was talking straight. How many times had they snuck on their property to fuck with them horses? Shit like that was fun.

"What?" Bo turned, put his arms out. "You want me to come over just to hand you the check?"

"Disrespecting me is disrespecting my daddy. You don't want to piss off big daddy." He jabbed at the mailbox. "Now deliver the mail, fucknut."

Bo heaved a stick into the trees, cursed under his breath. He yanked out an unstamped envelope and slapped it in Aaron's hand. "Erica wouldn't be impressed."

Bringing up Aaron's ex-girlfriend hurt worse than a boot to the nards. Bo knew that. He also knew it was better to leave a hornet's nest alone but sometimes you just wanted to see what was inside. Aaron snatched his skinny wrist before he could turn away.

"This got nothing to do with that whore."

Bo tried to pull away. Aaron yanked and twisted in one fluid motion, throwing Bo into the truck. He cranked his arm up his back and ground his face into the muddy hood. The horn blared. Aaron's little brothers bounced on the seat.

"You're a little bitch." Aaron slapped the crumpled the envelope on Bo's face. "The next time you ruin my check I'll take the change out of your ass."

He tossed him on the road. Bo wiped the mud off his lips and started to get up. Aaron planted his boot in the middle of his chest.

"You get your jollies from this?" Bo said.

Aaron grabbed Bo's flailing hands and pulled him against the bottom of his boot like stretching a bow. He snerked phlegm to back of his throat and let a snotwad hang off his lip. Bo shook his head side to side. The tobacco-speckled hocker rolled off in slow motion, stretching on a slimy string. Bo twisted and squirmed. Aaron pulled tighter, dropping the payload on Bo's shaved head.

"Let's have some jollies," Aaron said.

He was all set to pull Bo up by his ear. Aaron could swing him around like a doll all day long because shit like that was fun. But then his stomach tightened. An involuntary knot twitched inside, like the feeling he got when his daddy stormed red-faced into his room.

The dogs felt it. Something was in the woods. Maybe Annie was coming down the drive with a rifle. Was she hiding in the trees? He rubbed his chest, could feel the crosshairs on him.

"Who's out there?" Aaron walked to the edge of the road, looked through the trees. "Annie? If you out there, I wasn't going to hurt him. Bo just got a little mouthy. Come on out."

Bo stood with a big muddy print on his white shirt, looked dumbly past the truck. Someone was a hundred yards down the road. It was the guy Aaron buzzed first thing this morning. Each step he took shook the knot in Aaron's stomach that was now the size of an orange. Cold sweat broke across his forehead and the knot broke open like a foul egg, spilling fear.

Aaron puked his breakfast all over the road. Grits and eggs and gravy splattered like a bucket of mud. He put his hands on his knees, strings of spit draining in a puddle of vomit. He puked until there was nothing left but thick, green slime. His little brothers didn't honk the horn. They didn't tell him to get up and kick the guy's ass. The dogs didn't make a sound.

A well-worn pair of boots stopped inches from his fingers. Aaron wiped his mouth with the back of his hand. Still on his knees, he rose up straight and proud. It wasn't no guy walking down the road, it was just some black kid. Couldn't be no older than a sophomore.

"Who the fuck are you?" Aaron said.

"You should go home and rest."

"You ain't no doctor." Aaron spat vomit-flavored snot. "What you are is lost. And you got no business here, so get on your way."

The kid looked up into the trees as if reading a street sign. "This is where I'm going."

He spoke with a strange dialect, like he'd mixed Spanish and good old American. But underneath it was a Southern flavor—the twang of home-cooked country talk—just diluted many times over.

"You mistaken, son," Aaron said. "This ain't your stop. This is nowhere you want to be."

Aaron slowly straightened his hat. Nothing made a sound, not the dogs or bugs or wind or nothing. Aaron would show them what an enforcer does in a situation like this.

Aaron feigned sluggishness when he stood and wiped his mouth. He turned like he was going to the truck. With his hand already up, with his hips turned, he would strike like a cobra. In a single, swift motion, he balled his fist and started toward the kid like a power hitter, would knock this smug dickweed over centerfield.

But his hand didn't move like it was supposed to. His momentum stopped. The muscles along his back tightened like 240-volts had been rammed up his ass.

It was moments later that he could see again. He was on his knees, square in the puke. The kid had him by the wrist, still next to his ear. The kid gripped him by the neck with the other hand, pinching nerves that screamed to the bottom of his feet. Panic swept through Aaron's belly, slamming into his balls.

"Get along, boy," the kid said.

When Aaron could feel his legs again, he stumbled to the truck. His brothers stared out the window, mouths hinged open. He put the truck in gear and trenched the sandy road on his way out of there. A rubbery nutsack swung on the back bumper. In the rear view mirror, he was white and pasty. And the truck was starting to stink something fierce.

The deer hunter was stepping on a boy in the road. Drayton knew a thing or two about hunting. He didn't need a bow, knife or rifle. *Come, fear. Fill the belly.* The deer hunter's body obeyed, dumped adrenaline into the blood stream. Ernie just lost his appetite, but Drayton pushed harder on the deer hunter. Drayton could bring a cold killer to tears. A redneck teenager? He'd shit himself.

He was throwing up bile. Drayton showed mercy, let him up. Maybe it was a mistake. The boy didn't think of it as mercy, but an opportunity. He wasn't accustomed to losing a fight. But like most street fighters, he believed real pain was meted out with knuckles. Pain was delivered through the nervous system. Why swing a fist when pressure was more direct?

Drayton squeezed the boy's radial nerve below the elbow. The shock overwhelmed him. Drayton gave him time to recover, then pinched his brachial plexus near the base of his neck and introduced him to raw pain. He was a believer after that, at least his shorts were, and spun his fat tires to get away.

The victim picked at his shirt on the side of the road, breathing through his mouth while the obnoxious muffler faded down the road. He was one of Blake Barnes' boys.

"Who are you?" Bo asked.

"Drayton."

"You know where he's going, Drayton? He's going right back to his daddy's house and tell him everything." Bo picked at his shirt faster, not letting it fall to his chest before he picked it again. "I mean, don't get me wrong, I appreciate you showing up and everything, but you just pissed off a big dog. I ain't shitting."

"I'm looking for a place to stay."

"I, uh…" He studied Drayton's face, the thin lips, and deep, black eyes. He couldn't remember what he was saying. Drayton took the opportunity to calm the boy's nerves with a thought, to slow his heart and cool his sweat glands. When he stopped picking his shirt, Drayton looked away.

"Your home is a bed and breakfast, is it not?" Drayton asked.

"Uh." Focus returned. "We haven't had anyone stay in a year, but yeah."

"Today's your lucky day."

Bo looked him up and down. "You live around here?"

"I'm afraid I'm from out of town."

"You visiting family or something?"

"I could use a place to lay my head," Drayton said. "If I could see your quarters?"

Bo drifted back into his eyes, again. Drayton looked away, repeated the question. Bo shook his head, then nodded. He started down the shady drive, toeing the strip of stringy weeds growing between two sandy tire tracks. They walked for a full minute before they reached the end. Bo suddenly turned around.

"Thanks for what you done back there." He walked backward, stuck out his hand. "My name is Bo."

Drayton considered his extended hand, thought twice, then shook it. His hand felt cold as well water in December. Bo shook back, had a strange look melt on his mug but didn't comment. He wiped his hand on his leg and walked around the bend. An old house sat on columns of brick pillars, the white paint peeling off the walls. Brown fences, paint peeling just the same, were beyond the house and several paddocks filled with horses. Massive crape myrtles with sinewy, peeling trunks grew in the open, pink blooms poking through thick layers of Spanish moss. Further back, live oaks reached out from the surrounding trees, their branches ancient and flexing. There was a barn to the left. A wooden fence stretched between the barn and the house, a few of the boards hanging. Drayton dragged his feet through the tall grass. The smell of horse manure filled the humid air.

"Listen, I got chores," Bo said. "You can go wait on the porch and get out of the sun if you want. Mama will be home any minute. She'll get you set up in a room."

Bo went inside the barn. A tractor sputtered. An old quarter horse stuck his head out of one of the stalls, sniffed the air as if feeling Drayton's eyes on him.

The frilly curtains dropped on one of the house windows. They were faded, almost yellow and nearly transparent. A shadow passed inside. Drayton climbed the wide steps to the porch wrapping around the house and peered inside. Someone moved to the kitchen in the back, disappeared around the corner. Drayton sat on one of the rocking chairs weaved from grapevine and bended saplings beneath a ceiling fan that pushed the heat around but not the flies.

All the horses were looking at him while they ground hay side to side between their teeth.

There was a boy sitting on the porch talking to Bo. Annie thought he looked familiar, but she hadn't slept yet. This time of day played tricks with her eyes, so Annie stopped the car and viewed the kid like she did everyone. A potential threat.

She threw the car in park and let the air-conditioner blow on her face. The car was the only reprieve from the South Carolina heat. She adjusted the vents, listening to the belts squeal and studying the slow-rocking boy. His skin was unnaturally dark. Most African-Americans were brown-skinned. This kid was pure black. He didn't look up, just sat rocking in her grapevine chair.

Bo ambled through the long grass pointing back. Annie turned the car off and got the groceries out of the back seat, handing a bag to Bo. "He's looking for a room," Bo said.

"Where's his parents?"

"He's just visiting, says he's by himself."

The kid was still looking down when she stepped on the porch. She didn't trust people that couldn't look her in the eye, but he did it in a way of respect, like he wouldn't dare challenge the old silver back for control. And Annie had plenty of silver hair.

A high school kid looking for a room? Hardly seemed right, but Annie was on her own when she was about the same age. She knew what it was like to scuffle.

She couldn't shake the feeling she'd seen this kid before, but nothing was catching. "You wait on the front porch," she said. Drayton sat in the rocking chair without a single word. Annie went inside, but not before looking back and saying, "And don't be snooping around this farm, you hear? We'll be out in a minute."

7

There was shouting inside the house. Something fell. Bo was explaining. The shouts turned to murmurs. *We need the money.* That was the trump card. Although Annie was the only one arguing otherwise, even she couldn't over play that one. *They needed money.*

Drayton suggested with a thought that Annie forget she'd seen him at the Waffle House, otherwise this would all be too suspicious. He looked innocent enough, but plenty of good predators do. And Drayton was the greatest predator of all. If they knew what he was, there would be no room available, end of discussion. Not like that would matter.

He rocked silently, watching the shadows creep across the yard. The horses grazed, occasionally looking at Drayton. There was something comforting about the scene. He explored his memories to see if he had been here before. He could remember back a hundred years like yesterday, but after that the memories got fuzzy like long-past ghosts of another life, like an old man remembering the thrill of a first kiss. Try that when you're a thousand years old. Or however old he was.

The screen door smacked against the wall and clapped back in the door frame. Annie carried a big leather book and sat on a porch swing opposite Drayton. She opened the ledger on her lap and tapped her pencil. She bounced the tip off the page with an erratic, nervous beat. "You got a name?"

"Drayton."

She scribbled in the book. "That's your birth name?"

"That's a nickname."

She slowly flipped the pencil and erased her last entry. "I need your birth name."

"Drayton will do."

"You don't understand, young man. I need your birth name because I'm going to do a background check on you to find out if you're a psycho. I don't take kindly to crazy people in my house. Now, I'll ask one more time."

Drayton's birth name was probably the only thing he remembered from the early days. He didn't want to forget it because someone gave it to him, even if he couldn't remember where it came from or who gave it to him. He didn't use it often because, quite frankly, no one cared for foreigners in America these days. Nor did they care for funny names.

"Nassfau."

Annie scribbled in the book. The pencil remained poised over the page as the silence stretched over long moments. "You've got a last name, don't you?"

"Rauttu," Drayton said. "Nassfau Rauttu."

"Let me see an ID." She looked over her wire glasses at Drayton, sprigs of kinky gray hair around the frames.

"I don't have identification."

Annie narrowed her eyes, rethinking the whole thing. Yeah, they needed the money, but what good would it do if he caved her skull in. She had enough people trying to hurt her in her lifetime. Drayton let her look deep into his eyes. She fought the temptation, like everyone did, but soon found herself soaking in his soothing glance. It allowed him the opportunity to see inside her.

She was tough as weathered rawhide, unyielding as an oak. But she was mortal. He detected something all mortals shared in common, something found on battlefields. She was dying and didn't know it. A tumor in her brain. He took a short whiff. The tumor was small, just forming. She had plenty of time, two years, maybe three, before it would start affecting her memory and balance. It was hard to tell, so many variables. There was no sense in telling her, she was better off living life in this moment than worrying out her fate. And, judging by the wrinkles around her mouth, there was plenty to think about already.

Drayton looked away. Annie blinked quickly, tears forming in her eyes. She composed herself, writing the word slowly.

"Rauttu?" she said. "You Chinese or something?"

"I have some Chinese in me." Drayton grinned so faintly his lips barely moved. "Drayton's actually my middle name," he said. "If you want to write that down."

"Well Drayton may be a Southern name, but it don't make you so." She turned the pencil over, erased the last name and cursed under her breath, adding the middle name. "Nassfau Drayton Rauttu."

"You can call me Drayton."

"All right, Drayton. How many nights you want to stay?"

"A week. Maybe longer."

Annie raised her eyebrows. "What'd you plan on doing here for a week?"

"Rest."

She looked around the yard, wondering what the hell a teenage-looking kid would do out there for kicks.

"That'll be $300 with a $100 deposit." She went back to scribbling in the book. "I don't take credit cards and I don't take checks. So if you plan on paying with either, then our business here is finished."

Drayton peeled four bills off a roll of money and placed them on her book. She stopped scribbling, watched him put the roll back in his front pocket. Judging by the thickness, he could rent the room for months. Maybe years.

"Tell me something, Drayton." She stared at the bills, untouched. "Why are you here?"

"I have business."

"You dealing drugs?"

"No, ma'am. No drugs."

"Then what's a boy like you doing with a wad of cash like that."

"I've invested well."

"Then what's your business?"

"It's hard to say. I'll know soon enough. In the meantime, your hospitality is appreciated. It's hard to find courtesy in this day and age, you know."

She watched the bills as if they'd sprout teeth and tear through her faded floral blouse. The ceiling fan made them tremble on the page. She gently placed her hand over them to make sure they didn't sprout legs, too.

She creased the bills in half and slid them into her pocket. "You have a room for one week, Drayton. If I see anything I don't like, you will leave my property with no refund. Do we have an agreement?"

"Indeed, we do."

Annie snapped the book shut. "Come along to see your room."

He took his time going into the house. No sense in rushing. Delivering Blake Barnes' message wasn't about words. He couldn't stop by and tell them their deadbeat, runaway husband and father says he's sorry. It wasn't about that. Drayton had to deliver the message, and sometimes it took a while to figure out what exactly the message was.

8

Drayton followed Annie past crooked pictures with dusty glass and family faces. Annie and her two boys and daughter. The daughter was the oldest, but she'd moved out a year earlier. The youngest boy, Drayton had yet to meet. The hallway ended in the kitchen with peeling wallpaper of flowers and stripes and a small table with aluminum legs. Annie was already climbing the steep steps to the right, her footsteps clobbering each tread. At the top, a short hall went left and right, each ending at a door. Annie went left and turned the glass doorknob.

The ceiling inside was slanted. The books on the shelf were bloated from the humidity. Annie asked Drayton about his luggage. He didn't have any at the moment. She curled her bottom lip, stared, then decided it was an argument she didn't have the energy for.

"Well, if you get any luggage, you can put it in those drawers." She pointed at a bureau in the corner with a metal fan on top. "For your information, I don't do your laundry. If those are the only clothes you plan on wearing, you're going to have to wash them yourself. The washing machine is downstairs but the dryer don't work. In this humidity, it'll take a day and a half for them to hang dry. I don't mean no disrespect, but if you start stinking to high heaven, you'll have to sleep in the barn and that bed cost the same as this one."

The day had gotten up to one-hundred degrees, but his shirt was still dry. Doesn't matter, a man can still smell underneath a dry shirt. The how and why his stink didn't reach her nostrils didn't seem to bother her. Wasn't her problem, really.

"I serve supper at 6:00, but I'm running late today. You're welcome to make yourself at home up here or wander around the farm, pet the horses or whatever you plan on doing. Riding is off limits. I got an old mare stabled that you can take on the trail, but not until it cools off and not without one of us going with you. And you'll have to sign a waiver. Understand?"

He nodded. Drayton listened to her descend the stairs. Pots and pans clanged below. She spoke quietly with Bo for some time.

Drayton had been in prison hot boxes in the Middle East cooler than that attic room. He stood at the window, contemplating Blake Barnes' message. The day moved on and Drayton was still at the window. Annie knocked and told him supper was ready. He politely declined without opening the door, said he would like to rest. Then he watched the sun set. He listened to the house and the years of memories that penetrated the walls.

When night fell, a television muttered from downstairs. Then music. Eventually, it was quiet. There was only the sound of tree frogs. Peace fell over the house. Those inside slept like the dead. Their slumber was deep and filled with dreams. Drayton stood at the window like a sentinel, as still as the night.

When the sun was near and the black sky turned gray, he walked downstairs without a sound, found several boxes of tea in the cabinet. Among them Earl Grey. He prepared a cup and went outside. He sat at a tiny cast iron table on a similar chair, both peeling black paint beneath a sprawling live oak. He savored each sip, watching the sun rise above the trees.

9

$\mathcal{A}$nnie would rather starve than take a risk. She blamed her ex-husband for her conservative nature. Letting the kid in the house, a stranger, was the riskiest thing she'd done since Blake left. Starving is one thing, but letting a serial killer in the house was another. When she saw Drayton on the porch, she had every intention of marching his ass down the road, even if that meant a loaded shotgun. Don't know what stopped her.

She lay in bed that first night staring at the ceiling wondering if she made a mistake. That floor hadn't creaked once since she led him to the attic room and those boards whined even when you thought real hard. He must've gone right to sleep because it was dead silent. *Don't say dead.* Annie wondered if she would sleep at all thinking about it. That money would only last a few weeks. Then what? That boy could be a lifetime of trouble.

She rolled back and forth, thinking the risk just wasn't worth it. She was about to get out of bed and sit at the foot of the steps, just in case he got any ideas. But sleep rolled over her like a rogue wave.

Annie didn't own an alarm clock. She woke every morning at 4:00 AM, no matter what time she went to bed. She would lay there for half an hour and pray for her children, then get up to make breakfast. Annie hadn't been late for the morning in twenty years.

She was late that morning.

The horses were whining. Annie blinked. The sun pierced the room in flat lines through the blinds. The clock read 8:30. She sat up, checked her watch. Still 8:30.

She came storming out of her room pulling on a robe. The house was silent. Annie leaned over the kitchen sink, looked out the window. The horses stretched their necks over the fence, pawing at the ground. They hadn't been fed.

"Bo!" She fired up the stove. "Time to feed!"

Bo stumbled into the kitchen, rubbing his eyes. He stared at the clock, pulled on his boots. The back door slammed. The horses were waiting at their stations.

Annie melted butter in the pan. She'd let Young, her youngest son, sleep until breakfast was ready. He was a late sleeper anyhow. Probably slept right through the shouting. She had dreams that night. *Dreams.* Something about a park and the water. There was a sailboat, too. She could still feel the breeze on her face and smell the ocean.

The butter crackled in the pan. She broke open four eggs and noticed the tea pot was out. It was still warm. Bo walked in a hurry with stainless steel buckets across the backyard. Off to the right, under the largest oak on the property, was the boy. He sat at the iron table with his legs crossed, a teacup on one hand and a saucer in the other. He watched Bo dump buckets into the feedboxes and the horses stuff their heads inside. He sipped his tea elegantly, lifting the cup to his lips with his little finger poised outward. She'd never seen anyone drink tea like that, except on television maybe. It was like royalty.

She hated to say it, but until she saw him out there, she'd forgotten about him. And Annie never forgot about anyone when they were on her property. She always said she could smell people on the other side of her twenty acres and that boy slept upstairs while she slept like the dead.

The eggs spattered.

Don't say dead.

1 0

Bo woke up late on the second day, too. This time it was after 9:00.

He was thinking he never slept like that before, or dreamed like that, either. Drayton had been there two days and pretty much stayed in his room. Hadn't come down to eat, piss or nothing. He just drank that tea the other morning and that was it. It should've been creepy, but for some reason it wasn't. Maybe all the sleep Bo was getting just put him in a good mood. Mama certainly was.

The kitchen was empty, too. Except for the tea kettle, the counters and stove hadn't been used. Mama must've been sleeping in, also. That was a world record, her sleeping in again. Since it was Saturday, he didn't bother waking her for work.

The horses didn't seem too upset. None were tromping around the pasture. In fact, they were already grazing at the round bale. The little table under the oak was empty. Drayton must've been back in his room already. Bo figured that maybe Mama got up and fed. Good moods can do that. He went out to the feed room in the barn and heard the buckets clanging around. It was Drayton, cleaning out the steel feed buckets

Bo pulled a Coke from the tiny fridge under the sink. "Morning."

"It is," Drayton said.

Bo popped the drink and took a sip while Drayton went about cleaning. Shit, if he wanted to kick in around the farm, Bo wasn't going to stop him. He went out to the barn to start hauling hay and dragging fields. The tractor spit black smoke from the straight pipe pointing out of the front hood. He pulled the long trailer loaded with bales of hay out of the barn and around the first corner of the fence. He sat back in the seat on his first stop and chugged the rest of the Coke and belched louder than the tractor. He twisted the can and crushed it, putting in the small toolbox next to his seat. He noticed a bale had already been thrown out and broken for the horses. When he turned back, Drayton was climbing back on the trailer. He nodded to Bo to go ahead.

Bo did just that. He drove and Drayton bucked bales. They got chores down in half the time.

A black Hanoverian horse came to the fence sniffing at Drayton. His lips flapped and he snorted. His coat was radiant. His eyes fearless. Drayton had ridden many like this one through battlefields. He was a warmblood, his descendants trained for war. A magnificent beast.

Drayton stepped out of the mid-afternoon shade of the live oak and offered his hand to the horse. It snorted and blew warm air from its nostrils.

"His name's Blackjack."

Drayton eyed the young boy in the wheelchair that pulled up beside him. The grass was pushed over in tracks leading from the house.

"My mom's horse," the boy said.

"Beautiful horse," Drayton said.

The boy pushed thick glasses up his nose, held out his hand. "I'm Young."

Drayton shook his hand, nodding imperceptibly.

"Bet you didn't know my mama had another son." Drayton tipped his head. He did, but acted otherwise. "Bet you didn't know I was in a wheelchair, did you."

It didn't take an immortal to know that. A ramp led up to the back door. But Drayton shook his head, nonetheless.

Drayton heard Annie talking to Young at night, heard the rubber treads of his wheels squeak on the hardwood floors. He even sensed Young watching him through the downstairs window, the curtain drawn just enough, when Drayton was outside. Now that he had a good look into the boy's eyes, he could see he was fifteen, bound to a wheelchair all his life. Drayton sensed the disease that ravaged his immune system, degraded his muscles. In fact, he was supposed to be dead already but was too stubborn to do so.

"You don't exist," Young said.

"Pardon me?"

"I've been researching you." Young pulled a laptop from the saddlebag alongside the wheelchair and flipped it open. "You don't exist, at least not by the name Nassfau Rauttu."

"You can't afford air conditioning, but you have a laptop and Internet?"

"In case you haven't noticed, my legs don't work. There are government programs that take care of me." He tapped his keys as if case closed. "You either lied about your name or you're hiding something, I can't find anyone named Nassfau Drayton Rauttu in the last hundred years."

"Depends on how you look at it."

"Are you a liar or have I met my match?"

"I'm neither hiding nor lying," Drayton said. "I don't exist."

Young waited for a follow up. When there was none, he pulled a broken radio antenna from the saddlebag and poked Drayton's leg. "Lie number one. You *do* exist."

"I was speaking metaphorically."

Young seemed to get off track and told Drayton all the horses names and what their owners were like. He didn't like half of them because they felt sorry for him. He didn't usually talk to people, especially strangers. But then the sun tracked further across the sky until there was no more shade where they were standing. Drayton hadn't said two words. Young was back to the horses when Drayton asked him if he ever rode one. Young said his daddy used to put him on Imelda and walk him around the pasture. Young got quiet after that.

He spun the chair around, looked over his shoulder to make sure Drayton wasn't looking. Young typed loudly. He looked over his shoulder once or twice, as if comparing Drayton's face to a picture. Young smacked the keys then abruptly snapped the laptop shut. He let go a long frustrated breath. "I accept the challenge."

Drayton raised his eyebrows.

"You exist, therefore you're out there. I'll find out who you really are."

"Very well."

Young wheeled over to the ramp that led to the back door. He stopped in the doorway, pointed two fingers at his own eyes and then at Drayton.

A smile touched Drayton's lips.

12

"You invite that boy to supper," Mama told Bo after watching him help with the hay and drag the fields. Then they spent the next day mending fences. Except for a pot of tea on the stove every morning, they hadn't seen him eat a thing. "Don't take no for an answer," she said.

But when Bo tapped on the bedroom door, Drayton spoke without opening it. "Pass along my regrets," he said. "I'm a bit tired this evening and would like to retire."

He didn't look tired when they were working. Bo had soaked through two shirts finishing that fence and Drayton had yet to sweat. Not sure what kind of a person works in heat like that and doesn't sweat. Must've been some sort of deformity, no sweat glands or something.

Later that night, a boarder called. She forgot her camera in the round pen. She'd been filming that day and asked if Bo could bring it in so it didn't get rained on. He broke away from the Braves game and found the camera hanging from the post. He admired the sleek design, the way the digital panel flipped out. He turned it on, switched it to night mode and panned around the pasture while he walked back to the house. He zoomed in on the kitchen window where Mama was cleaning up, then swooped toward the second floor. Drayton was standing at the window.

Bo looked up from the camera. The window was empty. He had to be imagining things. Besides, the floor hadn't creaked once since he *retired*. Bo didn't want to make a big fuss out of it. As long as Drayton helped with chores and paid his mama, he could stare out that window until he passed out. He went back to the Braves game. Forgot all about it.

13

On the seventh morning, Drayton watched the sun come up from his table as he did the previous six. He took careful sips, savoring the aroma of Earl Grey, even if it was old and stale. It was still a gentleman's drink.

But his time as a gentleman was drawing to a close. He sensed a resolution to Blake Barnes' request was near. He was enjoying his time on the farm; the scent of mowed grass, the horse feed and manure was refreshing. The hard work was satisfying and the family needed the extra pair of hands. But that wasn't what he had come to do. He would like to stay much longer, but it was no place to be when the hunger returned. Certainly not around the family.

Perhaps he would stay a bit longer if the opportunity presented itself. But that, also, he sensed would not happen. Yes, he would have to leave the farm soon. The ache was beginning to gnaw at him. It was a hollow pain, a yearning that was ancient. One might call it hunger, but it had nothing to do with satiating an appetite. It had more to do with his existence. The longer he denied the ache, the hollower he became. He did not fear the pain that came with it, for Drayton learned to deal with physical pain centuries ago. What Drayton feared was the instinctual reactions that came with it. His desire to live, to exist, was innate. Over that, he had no control. And when the ache became strong enough, he had no control at all. A gentleman, he was not.

Still, there was time. And the resolution was near.

al Towgard was a man of his word. It was touching one-hundred degrees for the seventh fucking day in a row. He hated doing business when it was that hot. Hell, half of Charleston hated doing anything when it was that hot. They might be in the South, but contrary to satirists, they weren't stupid. He never once fucked his sister, nor did he know anyone who had (fucked their own sister, that is). They weren't inbred, they didn't own slaves, nor did they all fly a Confederate flag. Hell, if they thought the South was so goddamn stupid, how could anyone explain all the presidents of the United States coming from the South. (Forget Jimmy Carter, he *was* a dumbass.)

No, Hal hated doing business when it was hot enough to boil shrimp on a tin roof, but he had business to attend and business was his word. Cockroaches were a part of the Lowcountry. Sometimes you just learned to live with them, other times you had to grind them under foot. *Snap, crackle, pop.*

His pits were soaked before he got in the Chevy Silverado, squeezing behind the steering wheel. He tongued his mustache then wiped his bald head with a handkerchief and shifted ten ways to China trying to squeeze the hanky back in his pocket.

Aaron stepped into the garage talking on his cell. The little dumbass didn't close the door all the way. Hal could feel the meter spin as cold air was sucked out of his house. He pushed a button, rolled the passenger window down.

"Close the fucking door."

Aaron took his sweet ass time doing it, that cell attached to the side of his head. He damn near stopped on the last step. Talking. Hal punched the horn. It echoed inside the garage. Aaron swung his foot off the last step with sweet ass luxury. Hal was about to go through the windshield. Hal Towgard, waiting on his son. When Aaron pulled open the passenger door, Hal tore the cell off his head and rifled it against the wall. It dented the sheetrock and skittered beneath the truck.

"Get in the back," Hal said.

Aaron held an empty hand to his face. Rage boiled under his blank expression, flickering past his eyes. He pushed it down – all of it – and slid onto the back bench. Hal adjusted the rearview mirror and watched the boy. One sign of defiance and he'd dent the sheetrock with his head. Hal backed out of the garage and something crunched under his tire. Aaron slunk in the corner looking out the window. He kept it pushed down, he did. Kid wasn't as stupid as he looked.

People didn't understand that politics is politics. It was no different no matter where you were. Washington. New York. The country roads outside Charleston, South Cackalacky. It was all about control. People needed to be controlled. They craved control and, thankfully, there were people like Hal Towgard to give it to them. There were different ways to do it. The trick was finding what worked. Aaron dared a glance in his father's direction, slunk lower in the seat and stared hollow out the window.

Fifteen minutes later, Hal turned down the last country road. One of his tenants needed a Come-to-Jesus talk. A cockroach problem was brewing and he liked to stay ahead of things. He turned onto the long winding drive and eventually down a wooded driveway. Hal pulled next to Annie's piece of shit car and gunned the accelerator. He didn't honk. He didn't need to. People knew when Hal Towgard arrived. They felt it in their bones. And if they didn't...

Snap, crackle, pop.

15

A truck eased up to the house. Bo stopped measuring beet pulp in the feed room and looked out the window. He passed the steel bucket to Drayton without a word. A man climbed out of the brand new Chevy, his belly covering half his belt buckle.

The front door rattled and Annie was down the steps.

"I come to check on y'all." Hal wiped his head with a handkerchief and tongued his mustache with the tip of his tongue. "Aaron said he got in trouble over here and I wanted to make sure no one was hurt."

"No trouble, Hal," Annie said. "You can move along now."

"You got company, Annie?" Hal looked past Bo toward the feed room.

Drayton stood in the doorway, looking at the devil Blake Barnes left behind. *Tell them I'm sorry.* For leaving? Or to fend for themselves?

"None of this is your business, Hal. Kindly get your truck off my property."

"Annie." Hal worked his lips as if chewing on which words to spit. "I'll get off *my* goddamned property when I'm good and goddamned ready."

"This ain't your property as long as I make payments."

"And if one of those payments were to... disappear." He twiddled his porky fingers. "I'm letting you live here, Annie, we both know that."

Annie's hands worked at her sides, opening and closing.

Hal hiked up his belt, shifted his weight like he had to fart. He plucked a strand of foxtail from the ground and minced it between his front teeth. He took a deep breath, looked into the trees as if to tell God to turn down the thermostat. He twisted the foxtail between his fingers. Bo stepped back and Hal kept walking, would've knocked right into him had he not.

"Two days ago my boy comes home with your check and a load of shit in his pants." Hal looked down on Annie, the foxtail dangling toward her nose. "Now what do y'all know about that?"

"He-he-he was pushing me down in the road, Mr. Towgard," Bo said. "Aaron came to pick up the check and wanted to fight."

"Did you fight him?"

"No, sir. I didn't want to fight, but he wouldn't listen."

"You saying my boy shit his pants for fun?"

"That's enough, Hal!" Annie squeezed between Bo and him. "Your boy makes plenty of trouble and if he got a little back, he had it coming."

"Your mama fight your fights for you, boy?" Hal swung an open hand at Bo. Annie caught his forearm with both hands and it almost knocked her over. Bo was huffing, squeezing his fists at his side. Annie shoved at Hal but his massive frame didn't budge.

"Don't start making threats, Hal."

"I'm not making a threat, I'm laying down the rules."

"What do you want?"

He lugged himself back to the truck after glaring at the two for a good several hot seconds, laughing as he went. "I'm making sure y'all are safe. I'm making sure no one gets hurt. My job is to stop trouble before it happens, even if I have to make a little trouble to do it." He pointed at the feed room. "Boy! Come here."

Drayton did not respond. He observed the moment, then casually pushed off the doorframe and started across the grass. He walked like a person with all the time in the world. A person that had no beginning. That had no end. Just walking. Bahiagrass seed stalks whipped his legs, but his pace was so casual it seemed like space was growing.

Hal's tongue ran back and forth along his mustache. When he could wait no more, he took the last two steps. Drayton stopped before they collided.

"You from around here, boy?"

Drayton kept his eyes cast down.

Hal moved closer, his voice rattled deeply. "Here in the South we have manners, son. When an adult speaks, you answer 'yes, sir'. So let's try this again. You from around here?"

There was no bitterness or edge in Drayton's voice. He simply said, "No, sir."

"My boy tells me you were interfering with his business a few days back. Now boys will be boys, son, that's a fact. But you got no business in my business, you understand? I forgive once, but cross me again, and you'll see a real monster, son. One with teeth, claws and shitload of guns. One that eats everything on the farm until there's nothing left. Horses, included. You understand what I'm saying?"

Drayton didn't respond.

Hal backed up a step, his hard eyes bearing down. "Understand, son?"

"Yes, sir."

"Lift your eyes, boy, and behave like a man. Look me in the eyes and answer the question again."

Drayton focused on the third roll of Hal's neck, the red bumps where he shaved. Hal's heart pulsed beneath the collared shirt sticking to his chest. Drayton closed his eyes, took a deep breath and breathed in the man's foul essence, tasted the pain that hid deep inside. His forgotten memories were an iron maiden. His anger encased him like a tomb.

Hal's father beat him. He felt his father's rings often. He learned to patch himself up and he learned not to cry. His father was raising a man, not a pussy. He watched his father beat his mother, too. He stomped her in the kitchen. Called her a whore. An ambulance took her away while Hal's father sat in the living room with a scotch and water.

No pussies here.

Hal's anger hid his sadness like a glacier, a layer that would take centuries to melt. Drayton did not judge this man. After all, it took Drayton that long to resolve his own madness and rage.

Drayton opened his eyes, lifted his gaze to Hal's. With a thought, he removed the ice, exposed Hal's pain and fear all at once. Showed him the depth of his neglected soul. Revealed the insatiable sadness he had avoided all his life. The things he did not remember. The things he did not feel.

The things he cared not to see.

Hal's tongue stopped working. His chest heaved once. Twice. The color on his cheeks drained away under a sheet of sweat. Hal took a step back, clutched his chest.

Aaron jumped out of the truck. "You all right, dad?"

Hal concentrated on breathing, yanked his arm away from his son. Aaron retreated slowly, unsure if his father would fall over in the next second. Hal wiped his whole head and all his chins. Twice. His mouth worked rapidly, but words could not make their way out, only the gummy sound of his tongue working for saliva. He felt his way along the hood, still trying to speak, and got into the truck. His pasty, color- less complexion was evident through the tinted window. His mouth still working. He backed the truck up, nice and easy. He didn't spin the wheels and throw dirt and rocks, he just pulled out.

They watched him roll out of sight in disbelief. Hal Towgard had never left without the last word.

"Don't y'all have to finish feeding?" Annie said.

They returned to their chores. No one spoke a word. But they all knew things had just changed forever.

16

Hal stopped at the end of the drive, stared straight ahead at the reflective blue marker pinned to the water oak across the road. The truck idled in place. He gripped the steering wheel with both hands. The rubber material twisted under his sweaty palms. He just needed to catch his breath, but no matter how hard he tried, the next breath came a little faster, a littler shallower. The boy's eyes... they were...

Once, when Hal was seven, he went to open the gate to the pasture. One of the wires was hot, but he'd seen his dad grab the other wires a hundred times. They weren't all hot. But when Hal touched that wire, a jolt rattled through him, shook fingers, toes and nuts all at the same time. He tried to let go but the wire had him now. It grabbed back, sucked his fingers around it tight.

The boy's eyes were like that. They were a hot wire. They wouldn't let go.

Only they didn't deliver a jolt. It was sickness that rolled in his stomach. It was cold. Spoiled. Rotten. It reached up and clenched his heart. He tried to look away, but couldn't. He felt colder. *Foul.*

"You all right?" Aaron sat up in the back seat.

"Fine, fine."

Aaron didn't move. Hal waved him off and turned left. He flipped the A/C off.

17

Drayton cleaned the last steel bucket and placed it in line with the others. He dried his hands and hung the towel on a hook. Everything was in place. He was just about finished. The sun was down and the sky dimming. Drayton stepped outside the feed room. The horses were lined up at the fence, watching him. Each of them nuzzled his outstretched hand as he passed, bowed their heads.

Drayton watched darkness settle while dishes clattered inside the house. The light cast out from the kitchen. Annie was busy at the sink. They'd asked him to join them for dinner, but Drayton politely declined. He needed to move on. Food did nothing to quell the ache and it had been several months since he truly fed. The time was near. After that, maybe he would spend some time in a city where feeding was easy. Plenty of dying in the city. Maybe Charlotte, this time.

The horses pushed each other to get their turn with Drayton. Bo was coming from the house. Drayton sensed the cool silkiness of his essence flowing as he neared. He kept himself centered to avoid absorbing some of it. But it felt so good. The horses felt the flare of his instincts, reared up and fled across the pasture. Drayton gripped the fence, eyes closed, bringing control to his body.

"What's with them?" Bo rested the heel of his boot on the lowest rail of the fence.

"A little spooked."

"Yeah, well, supper's still waiting for you. Mama told me not to ask this time but to drag you inside. She wants to apologize for Mr. Towgard's behavior, or something."

"No need. Your hospitality is much appreciated, but I must excuse myself, once again."

"She ain't going to like that much, Drayton. She'll come out here and feed you like a baby if you keep resisting."

Drayton smiled. The horses had settled down in the far corner, keeping a wary eye out for predators.

"You'll make a fine gentleman, Bo," Drayton said.

Bo bowed his head. His laughter so punctual it gave the horses a start. "What're you talking about? *Gentleman*? I'm a good ole' boy, Drayton. If you want me out there sipping tea with you in the morning, it ain't going to happen any time soon."

He smacked Drayton on the shoulder, started back for the house laughing as he went. "I'll tell Mama you ain't coming," he called. "You best hide."

1 8

*Y*oung's room was dark except for the blue glow of his computer screen. He was tapping the keys, muttering to himself. Sometimes arguing with himself. He ran his finger down a list of names, mumbling them in supersonic speed. He unfolded a lined sheet of paper and jotted some down. The lead broke. He wheeled the chair around.

Drayton was sitting on his bed.

"Fuck!" He grabbed his chest and heaved. "You going to give me a heart attack. How'd you get in here?"

"You were busy."

Young looked back at the computer. "Yeah, well you win. I can't find you anywhere. You're a man of mystery. I don't have a prize for you, if that's what you came for."

Young went through all the searches he'd done, and they included CIA agents, past and present, and witness protection candidates. He had his doubts how thorough or accurate those databases were but they came up blank anyway.

"I did find a Nassfaurauttu," he said. "It was one name. He came up on a Civil War veteran database. But unless you're a hundred and fifty, I think that was a miss. You don't look a day over a hundred."

Great party, the Civil War.

"The same guy fought for the North and the South. Unless I missed a history lesson, soldiers picked a side and stuck with it." An idea suddenly hit him. "Unless he was a mercenary…"

Young spun around and attacked the keyboard. He compared two lists, side by side. "What am I doing? Who cares, unless he's a relative of yours. Do you think…"

Drayton was looking at the shelf above his bed. Mostly books, a few trophies from Spelling Bees and Academic competitions, a Lego Challenge award and one picture. His mother framed it for him. They were at the beach. Bo had built a huge sand castle for a sand sculpting contest. He got third in his category. In the picture, Bo was lying in the hole in front of the castle. Young was only a few years old. He sat on the castle like a throne. His mother was on his left.

Drayton took the picture down and touched the white space that had been cut out on Young's right. He traced the outline of a man that was once in the picture, now reduced to an empty space.

"What was he like?" Drayton said. "Your father."

"How should I know?" He took the picture from Drayton. "He left."

He wiped the dust from the glass. Drayton heard his pulse bang in his chest. Energy bent the space around him in waves. Young stared at the photo and absently thumped his hand against the armrest of his wheel chair in time to his heartbeat. He moved to thumping his useless leg, beat it with the same steady rhythm.

He left.

Drayton squatted next to the wheelchair. Young stared straight ahead, resolute. Drayton could feel the blue vein just under his skin beat as if it were on the tip of his tongue. He placed his hand over Young's forehead and turned his head, let him look deep into his eyes.

Drayton took Blake Barnes' life. He held his memories in his eyes and Young saw the extent of his father's tortured life. The haunting thoughts. The divided personality. Young saw the insanity that ate his insides and eroded his rationality.

Blake Barnes did not abandon his family, he abandoned life. He did not leave because his son was crippled and broken, he ran because he was frightened. He ran because he lacked courage. He ran because he was lost.

Not because of Young.

A tear rolled down Young's cheek. In those few moments, he absorbed his father's life from Drayton and understood his past. He finally knew what his mother had been telling him all his life. *It's not your fault.*

More than that, the last few words of his father's life absolved much of the pain and heartache Young carried like a string of weights attached to his chair. In two simple words, he gained what he believed he had lost. Drayton delivered the message.

I'm sorry.

Young was still holding the picture. Drayton wasn't there. He was down the long, winding driveway. Young was slumped in his chair, weeping, when he left. Annie came into his room and held him. Drayton heard the wailing. Felt the tenderness of his mother's touch.

19

Drayton stood in the pasture late that night, watching Annie finish in the kitchen. Young was asleep. Bo was watching a Braves game. They thought Drayton was upstairs doing his silent thing. They would come up the next morning to find the door ajar and the bed sheets without wrinkles. They would also find enough money to pay next month's rent.

When Annie next checked her bank account, she would discover she would have enough to cover more than next month's rent. Drayton had accounts all over the world. It only took a few keystrokes on Young's laptop to transfer a sum that would take care of them the rest of their lives.

Annie didn't need money. She only wanted things to be right. Blake Barnes broke her heart, but she'd moved on from that. Her pain and regret were the kids she let get in her husband's path. That would be resolved. And in two years, she would die in peace.

Drayton left the farm.

2 0

al skipped dinner.

He sat on the edge of his bed. The shower ran in the bathroom. Steam flooded from the open door. There was a knock on the bedroom door. "Are you all right?" his wife called.

"I'm fine!" he snapped.

Hal was not fine. A sickness had settled in his stomach. Something foul spread throughout his mid-section. The stench of his insides permeated his senses. He had hovered over the toilet with his finger in his throat, but he couldn't make the ache stop.

He'd had viruses that kept him puking through the night, but never had he felt sickness this deep. A sadness soaked through his stomach and chest. Tears were knotted in his throat. He felt like a pussy.

He retrieved the Pepto-Bismol from the bathroom, fumbled with the lid, dropping it on the floor. He lifted the bottle to his lips, ignored the crusty flakes that slogged down his throat with each chug. But it didn't coat the sickness. Didn't dispel the sadness.

He lifted the bottle again then suddenly dropped it on the bed. The pink liquid glugged over the floral bedspread. Hal clutched his chest. He tried to breathe. He hit the corner of the bed and rolled onto the floor. The world washed past his senses, dark and blurry.

"Hal? Are you all right?" The door knob rattled. "HAL?"

The pain radiated from his heart and engulfed it like an elephant was standing on his chest. Veins bulged along his forehead.

The boy stood at his feet. His skin was as black as the sky outside the window, drawn tightly over his cheeks. He slid his cold fingers over Hal's sternum, making little circles. Hal moved his lips. He knew he invited this monster into his house many years ago, the day he took over all of Blake Barnes' debt. The day he began taking money from his pathetic family. His fate was now massaging his chest.

Hal felt something draining from his chest. It was a smooth flow, like a vaporous stream of wintry air. The boy closed his eyes and tipped his head back. His skin loosened. And as it did, the pressure released Hal's chest. The room started to dim. The last thing he saw was Death's face looking down on him. Suddenly, he felt the urge to confess his sorrow for the thing's he'd done. There were so many of them, but he didn't have the strength. He wanted to cry.

Big sleep fell on Hal. As he parted, he heard the boy's final words and took them with him into the darkness. He left his body as the boy spoke softly, genuinely.

Thank you.

BEARING THE CROSS

BOOK 2

Vengeance is not delivered with a sword.

21

linker on.

Look left. Right.

Two hands on the steering wheel. Eyes on the road.

Andrew Drummond knew the difference between buzzed driving and drunk driving.

He was drunk. Not buzzed. Therefore, he drove like a geezer: hands at ten and two, just under the speed limit. The trick was not to take your eyes off the road. See, most drunks made the mistake of looking in the rearview mirror or down at the speedometer. Problem was, drunk time to sober time was a 10:1 ratio, meaning that if you looked down for one second, ten seconds went by in real time. Unfortunately, for the drunk, you could only drive in real time.

Andrew never looked down.

Highway 61 was not drunk-driver friendly. It was the hills and curves and narrow shoulder. But this late at night, there were few cars. And the trees were dense on each side, creating a tunnel effect on the road. For some reason, that always helped Andrew focus. It was like blinders that funneled his headlights onto the road. This late at night, Andrew drove 61. Always made it home.

His only distraction: a plastic chip swinging from the rearview.

A one-year chip from AA. One year sober. His good-luck charm. *Can't take that down.*

He got that chip six months prior at a Summerville meeting in the United Way. They were sitting on cold metal chairs that numbed your ass no matter how many times you shifted left or right. Carl Fanning, his sponsor, presented it to him. Carl was a good man. Sort of round, always needed to shave. Always full of wisdom.

Carl gave him the chip, saying how proud he was. The meeting applauded with gusto. Some stood, and Carl gave him a bear hug, patting his back like he was trying to kill him. Then the others hugged him, one at a time. Some wept. All the while, Andrew rubbed that plastic poker chip with his thumb like he was shining a coin.

Next day, he fell off the wagon. No, he jumped off. Both feet. Fuck it, if you were going to do it, don't half-ass the motherfucker. Andrew leaped as far off that wagon as he could.

See, those other fuckers at the meeting had their war stories, but you could pile every one of them on top of each other and they still couldn't touch Andrew's shit. He had every right to drink. Honestly, he should be smacked out on every drug known to man, but booze was his way. He'd tried it both ways, sober and stone-ass drunk. Ask him, it was better to get numb than climb those twelve fucking steps. Every. Goddamn. Day.

See, Eric Clapton had it right the first time.

He'd spent half his life on a bender. Then his kid fell from a building. Died. Clapton stayed sober after that. But Clapton didn't lose everything. He just lost a kid. But he didn't lose it all.

He didn't lose it all.

Andrew decided Clapton didn't know shit about losing everything. He came up with his own steps. Step one, numb the pain, the loss and sorrow.

Step two. Repeat.

Wise old Carl said he had to go through the pain, that his life was here and now. That he had a duty to live. It was his motherfucking responsibility. Carl said that things would get better. That behind every gray sky there was light. Whether he could see it or not, it was there. Trust the steps, Andrew. That was what Carl told him. We've all been there. Just trust.

But after a year, Andrew didn't feel better.

After a year, he still lay awake at night. Woke up clenching the sheets if he did sleep. He felt the straps of life's straitjacket, the buckles across his back. He couldn't escape his thoughts. Couldn't escape his life. So fuck Carl and his twelve steps and fuck everyone. Andrew had everything taken from him.

All because of one motherfucker.

One cocksucker.

Took it away.

Find that sonofabitch and maybe he'd give the wagon another ride. Until then, Andrew soothed the ache. Andrew numbed the pain. He rarely went to work. He owned the fucking business and they didn't need him there. They knew what they were doing, fuck it. Andrew didn't care so much anymore.

He drilled a hole in the one-year chip and hung it from the rearview mirror to remind him where he'd been. Until someone gave him a better reason to feel the pain, he was full-speed ahead. Someone needed to pay for this pain. Until he found the one responsible, he'd do it his way—

Antlers.

Two hands on the wheel.

And the world went round and round.

That chip swinging. Round and round.

The end came for Andrew Drummond. Yeah. That sudden. He thought he'd be more relieved.

As the windshield shattered.

2 2

The car, upside down. Wheels spinning.

One headlight beamed crooked across highway 61, spotlighting the deer among the broken windshield scattered like sparkling diamonds. The other headlight, punched out.

Drayton saw it happen a few miles back. He sensed the impending death, knew these things like a shark sensing blood across miles of ocean. He didn't make them happen, he could only see them like Destiny weaving the threads of human lives. Drayton knew where to be when they were finished. His ancient mind sniffed a man named Andrew Drummond. The frayed ends of his life were ending that night.

In a car accident. Alone.

Drayton walked along the empty highway, serenaded by tree frogs and moonlight. Occasionally, a car would drive down the road, but Drayton walked far off the shoulder. Even if their headlights were to catch him, they wouldn't see him. He was the color of the darkness beneath the trees.

Andrew Drummond's car had appeared over the hill, sloshing back and forth between the center line and the edge of the road. The deer blotted out the headlights. Drunk or not, he plowed the buck in the hindquarters before hitting the ditch at fifty-four miles per hour. The Toyota Prius rolled on its side, once then twice, flipped end over end and landed on the hood like a gymnast crashing to the mat.

All hope lost.

Quiet returned to the trees, and the tree frogs filled the silence. Drayton left the shoulder and walked down the middle of the road, toeing the yellow dashes. Eventually, a car would come along and see the disaster. Someone would stop. Call the police. They'd look inside to find Andrew Drummond's lifeless body.

For now, he lived.

Steam was rising from the underside of the car. Something loose was rubbing. Inside the car, Andrew's soul was slipping away. His essence.

There were many words to describe the life that permeated a human's body, how it pumped the heart for decades and escaped upon death. Drayton typically didn't use words to describe it. He could taste it beneath his tongue when he interacted with humans. This essence had many qualities, depending on the person, the emotions, age, and on and on. So many variables shifted the color and taste, but it was especially cool and intense when it was leaking away from the dying body. Where it was going, Drayton didn't know.

But it was that very essence he craved.

Once upon a time, he took it from them whenever he was compelled. Brought them down in the prime of their lives. Even children. He drank their blood and relished the fear that spiked the essence with an intoxicating flavor. Like crack. But that was hundreds of years ago.

The broken windshield crunched like silicone pebbles beneath his boots. The car gave a dying hiss. The deer lay motionless. Its eye, black and glassy. Drayton dragged his fingers down the scuffed bumper, the chrome edges nibbling at his fingertips. Beneath the fumes of gasoline and the smell of burnt rubber was the faint scent of whisky. Scotch. All of that took a backseat to the metallic tang of draining blood. He took a deep breath, then gently squatted down. Andrew was piled upside down.

Eyes open.

"It's about time."

His neck was propped at an odd angle, dark stains streaking his scrunched face. He blinked heavily. It was less of a blink, more like closing his eyes and deciding to open them seconds later. His breathing did the same.

Drayton could feel the man's life essence seeping from his pores like vapor. He would take what was left, absorb it into his own body and satisfy the starvation that gnawed inside him. Always urging. Always gnawing.

But Andrew Drummond was holding onto what was rightfully his. As long as his lungs contracted and expanded, he would cling to his life. But those rises and falls were numbered.

Drayton watched.

The two locked eyes in calm repose, like they were sitting for tea. A stream of blood, dark in the dim light, suddenly raced over his upside-down chin, over his lips and into his nostril like a spigot had been opened somewhere in his chest. It filled his sinus, but Andrew didn't blink. Drayton reached inside the metal carnage and brushed the red rivulet from his lips, redirecting the flow down the side of his face and into his gray hair. The dark blood seemed to absorb into Drayton's fingertips, his skin as dark as charcoal, blackened by centuries of sunlight. Skin without wrinkles. Skin that appeared human.

Andrew thought Drayton was Death. Everyone Drayton visited did the same. Some with panic. Some with calm. He appeared at the moment when death was upon them. He wasn't there to take them to the other side. That was their assumption. One thing was sure, he would be the last thing they saw.

"You." Andrew spit the word. Red flecks puffed off his lips. "Don't let the…"

His throat seized. There would be no more words sliding through it. His voice would no longer be heard. Those were the last words he would ever utter, and they were unfinished. Like his life. If he could move, he would've grabbed Drayton's hand still soaking up blood. He would've made sure Drayton heard the rest. *Don't let the bastard get away with it.*

Somehow, Andrew knew he heard anyway. He was Death, after all. Right? Maybe he imagined it. Maybe his mind tricked him to believe he was Death when, in fact, it was just a young man watching him die. Regardless. He just wanted someone to hear his last will and testament.

Drayton did hear. He could manipulate thoughts like his fingers and toes, could see them and feel them, could make humans believe his thoughts like they were their own. Could make them believe what he wished. Could make them forget. Could erase their pain. Or give it.

He absorbed Andrew's thoughts like they were Braille pressed onto the fabric of his mind. Drayton nodded.

Andrew saw it. He knew he'd been heard. Knew his request would be carried forth because the Angel of Death was required to do such things. Right?

Even though Drayton was required to do nothing of the sort—he didn't know what he was, just not Death—he still accepted last requests. After all, Andrew was giving his gift of life. His essence. Whether he gave it willingly or not, Drayton accepted that sort of thing with gratitude. Who was he to deny the man's dying wish? For it was a just request.

When Andrew Drummond left this world, his eyes were open. He didn't convulse or fight the cold or the stillness of his heart. He only went. He was alone.

Fitting. He'd been alone for years.

Drayton's pitch-black face was the last he saw. The young man's eyes were liquid. Calming. He didn't feel his hand touch his sternum, only saw the flutter of his lips, the muttering of two words. It was the last thing Andrew Drummond experienced before his life concluded.

"Thank you," he heard.

23

He woke to ringing. Inside his head, it was ringing.

The sound a metal pole makes when smacked with a hammer. The reverberations sang numbly inside his skull, trapped and doomed to echo for eternity.

The man slid his hand across silky sheets that were cool and slithery. His fingers crawled across the bed, finding the empty space next to him. He couldn't remember his name, but he wondered where the body was his hand automatically sought. In fact, who was he searching for?

Wife.

The thought emerged from the ringing fog that obscured everything else in his aching head. *Where's my wife?*

The man cracked an eyelid. The crimson sheet was blurry. Even after a couple blinks, nothing made sense. He smacked his gummy lips, rubbing the eye-boogers from his eyes. Rolled on his back. Took a hot breath. Stared at a slow-moving ceiling fan.

Where am I?

Blackouts did that. Not only had the previous night obliterated his whereabouts, it wiped out his name.

He lugged his body upright. His brain splashed like runny oatmeal.

His image stared back. A mirror, anchored on the dresser across the room. A dresser covered with perfumes and pictures and the detritus of life. His hair was black, matted on one side from the pillow and spiked on the other from... whatever. *Parker. My name is Parker Samson.*

It wasn't every day you had to make a conscious effort to remember your name. But whatever it takes, you do what you got to do. A hodgepodge of tattoos littered his chest. His arms. His stomach. Things like knives and skulls and snakes. Macabre scenes. A naked woman with the name Sandy below.

Sandy. Sandy. My wife, Sandy.

Wife. It tasted like a dirty sock. Or was that the ghost of the Marlboro Man in his mouth? Of course, my wife.

He rubbed his face, his lips flapping like rubber. Nights like that were sandstorms, leaving an inch of gritty dust over the memories of his life. He just needed a moment to blow things off, uncover his thoughts and get the day kicking.

First, water.

He went to the bathroom, rinsed his mouth, spit in the sink.

Splashed his face.

He stared in the mirror. His eyes pools of blood. Eyes of the devil.

He moved into the steam shower, where he sat down, letting the hot water draw the poison. The pieces of his life clicked into place. Parker Samson lived in downtown Charleston. He owned a successful security company that specialized in VIP protection and, sometimes, special investigation. Owned was the operative word. He wasn't in the trenches anymore. He was floating on top like cream. And where there was cream, there was the richness of life.

He stepped out of the shower a new man. The ringing had stopped.

"No more." He said it in the mirror. "No more of these for a while."

It wasn't right, spending the morning remembering your life.

He opened the wooden blinds next to the bed. Wentworth Avenue was a story below, partially obscured by a live oak trapped in the small square of land between the street and the buckled sidewalk. A man sat on the stoop across the street, elbows propped on his knees and hands folded.

Parker found a pack of Newports in his jacket. And a lighter.

He blew smoke between the blinds.

He hit the cigarette three times and looked around for an ashtray. He settled for the wastebasket next to the dresser. A picture looked back at him. He punched the butt between his lips and picked up the large frame with both hands. The faces were fuzzy. He looked around for glasses, found none, then held the photo further away to focus.

Sandy. A blonde-haired beauty.

Two girls, too. Both blonde.

And Parker. There he was. Although his face looked fuzzier than the others, there he was with his family. Pride and joy.

He looked over his shoulder at the empty space on the bed.

Now where the hell is she?

He pulled another drag out of the cigarette and the smoke streamed through his nostrils. Another drag. Ashes in the trash can.

A moment later and the dust blew off another memory. Sandy was a public attorney. She was up before dawn and taking on the day before Parker finished dreaming. Parker won the lottery with her. Jesus god, she was chiseled from the face of heaven.

He dropped the butt in the trash.

The girls' room was yellowy mustard beneath Jonas Brothers and Bieber Fever posters that were punching it out for their affection. Bieber was winning. Their beds messed up. The drawers open. Shelly. Yeah, Shelly and… Jessie. He muttered to himself, pushing his hand through his damp shag. This bender damn near erased his memory.

Can that happen? Can you forget everything?

He didn't want to think about that.

He decided to talk to the girls about cleaning up their room when he picked them up after school. He picked them up at… four o'clock.

Might want to call his wife to make sure he had that memory dusted off correctly.

Maybe it was three.

First things first. *Coffee.*

Along the way, he twisted the wedding band on his finger. It felt heavy.

2 4

The man on the stoop didn't see Parker open the blinds. He felt him.

He felt him fumble through the bedroom. Felt him when he sat in the shower, sorting through his thoughts. Finding his way.

Drayton stood.

No one would notice him cross the street. No one would notice him until he desired.

He walked to the market. Where he'd wait, and let Parker sort out the rest. Where he'd greet the morning the way he had for nearly three centuries. Or so.

2 5

<hr>

*P*arker stepped out the front door.

The door was red with a mail slot. He flipped the brass door knocker. The name above it was a bit fuzzy. *Samson.* He took a sip of coffee and shook his head. Crazy morning. Like he'd been pushing his way through cobwebs. Maybe he'd cooked a few too many cells last night. He remembered dinner at Magnolias to celebrate Mickey's birthday. Then drinks on the Rooftop. There was a party in a back room somewhere. After that, he wasn't sure.

Things were good, now. Just took a little java to get the synapses snapping. Five cups.

He wore a pair of gray slacks with a tight black T-shirt and a houndstooth jacket. He smoothed the shirt over his chest and sipped again. Let the coffee fumes steam his face.

Now. Where's the car? He was looking for a… a BMW. Silver one. He sipped the coffee, remembering he'd left it in the downtown parking garage. Not like he needed a car to get to work. At least not until he picked the girls up.

A door clicked.

An old woman stepped out next door.

"Morning." Parker lifted the cup.

The old woman stared. She looked confused as she picked up the paper.

Old age. It's a bitch.

Parker left the cup on the top step.

He walked to work.

2 6

Cynthia Birkenstalk walked outside.

Her neighbor startled her. It wasn't like no one ever said good morning. This was Charleston, friendliest city on the East Coast. It was just, she hadn't seen her neighbor in quite some time. Thought for a while something happened to him.

She retrieved the newspaper and locked the door behind her. She'd say good morning next time. She'd be ready.

*D*owntown Charleston was business as usual. Cars, horses, and tourists filled the streets.

Drayton sat outside a café overlooking the long market, where locals set up tables of perfumes, T-shirts, carvings, pictures and whatever else the tourists would buy. It was why they came to Charleston. To get a taste of old America.

He sat at a small black table that wobbled. In a metal chair that wobbled. Somehow, he made both seem elegant the way he crossed his legs with the saucer and cup resting on his thigh. An unusual posture for a young man dressed in loose pants and boots. A white shirt. An unassuming man that appeared to be proper English. Royalty, if one didn't know better.

He was neither.

Drayton steeped the bag of Earl Grey and squeezed it against the spoon. Let it rest in the saucer. He let the fragrance waft under his nose a moment. Sipped. Not the tastiest tea he'd ever experienced. But it would do. It was how he greeted the morning.

Horses clopped down the road, sandwiched between creeping cars, with hordes of travelers. The carriage stalled in front of the café, and in between witty bits of repartee streaming from the well-rehearsed guide, the horse dropped a steaming load into the sack hanging below his tail. Business as usual.

Drayton sipped.

He had planned to leave the Lowcountry a long time ago. But it felt cozy. Homey. The country and the wetlands. The Southern comfort. He decided to stay a bit longer. And now, of course, there was the business of Andrew Drummond. He'd died in a car accident six months earlier. Drayton had time to consider the request. Time to put things in place.

Now Andrew's business was near at hand.

People walked along the sidewalk in bunches, sometimes in strings. Occasionally, there were gaps to reveal the cracked bluestone. A man wearing a tattered military jacket, too hot for the weather, limped along and asked passing tourists for extra cash to help a veteran in need. He said *God Bless You* whether they gave him money or not. Half the time, they did. The gimpy leg was an act, but not the military jacket. He'd served his country, once upon a time. A marine for almost eight years. But now he served a lower calling of wine, whiskey and, when he could get his hands on it, crack cocaine. Because crack is where it's at.

Following a cluster of tourists was a man in gray slacks and a houndstooth jacket. He gathered strange looks from a family of four that passed him in the other direction because Parker Samson had his hand to his ear. Talking into his palm.

Parker had a dollar bill out to the military vagrant that smiled a gummy smile. But then Parker suddenly palmed the money and backed away from the man like he was swarming with bedbugs. Parker shuffled along, keeping his money. Talking into his hand.

The ex-marine watched him go, a little confused.

"Sir?" A young lady was next to Drayton. "More tea?"

"No, thank you kindly," he said, handing her a one-hundred-dollar bill. "Please keep the remainder."

The girl didn't seem to notice the ridiculous tip pointed at her. She was swimming somewhere in the depths of Drayton's eyes. He looked away and felt her blink off the warm spell and return to the present moment.

Drayton took a moment to enjoy the Earl Grey fragrance before following Parker Samson.

*S*amson's an asshole, *thought a smelly ex-marine.*

Beautiful morning.

Parker couldn't remember the last time he'd felt so peppy. Maybe he needed to get his drunk on more often. It felt like he'd been shot full of B12. Or OxyContin. Or something. I mean, the morning air was crisp and clean like he was sucking life out of the ass-end of Lady Luck. He didn't want to spoil it with a cigarette. When was the last time that happened?

He said good morning to everyone he passed. And they said it back. It was contagious. A smile had stamped his face. He felt like Mary Poppins. *Where's the umbrella? I feel like singing.*

He got to the market some twenty minutes later, suppressing the urge to dance. He had a thought.

He found his phone in the inside pocket of his jacket and scrolled through the contacts, not recognizing half the names. He knew a lot of people. No reason to remember them all. He found Sandy and punched it. Crossed the street with it cradled against his face.

Please enjoy the music... he heard... *while your party is reached.*

Black Eyed Peas sang in his ear. He didn't seem to mind. Not this morning.

He waited for his wife to pick up and spotted a bum up ahead.

What the hell. This morning was as good as any to help out a man down on his luck. Even though the begging gig was a charade, he knew. The limp. The pathetic look. The *God Bless You*. It was a hell of an act if you never saw it before. But Parker didn't mind, not this morning. He'd give the man some cash for a bottle of Mad Dog.

You've reached the voicemail of Sandy Samson. *Please leave a message.*

"Hey, babe. I was just wondering if you wanted to go have lunch at school with the girls today. Just do a quick drop-in, they'd love it. We can take some Chick-fil-A, you know. Why don't you pick me up—"

The bum smiled at Parker. Panic clenched his chest. He wasn't scared of the man. The decrepit bum couldn't push over a wet roll of toilet paper. But there was something… his face appeared a little blurry around the edges. And his toothless grin seemed more than happy to see him.

"Parker, you shitbag. Where you been?"

Parker sidestepped him. His stink was raw sewage.

The bum appeared confused at the reaction. Did he not know he smelled like rotten asshole?

"Um… sorry, babe," Parker said into the phone, moving along. "If you can't make it, I'll go it alone and see you at dinner tonight. Love you."

He glanced back. GI Joe still standing. Still staring.

Bastard's hallucinating.

Parker was still holding the phone and noticed a young man sitting at a café. He was staring, too, sitting a little weird. Legs crossed with a China cup to his lips like he was expecting the Queen of England. He suddenly had the feeling he'd crossed into Wonderland. His name wasn't Alice.

But it was a beautiful day.

He was still holding the phone to his face. Put it down.

He whistled as he walked, tipping an imaginary hat to those that passed. The unofficial ambassador of Charleston.

3 0

———

*D*own East Bay another couple blocks, wedged between an attorney's office and an art dealer, was a frosty glass door. *Samson Protective and Investigative Services.* Yeah, that was Parker Samson. His company. He'd built it up from a one-man operation over twenty years ago. There were a lot of vindictive sonofabitches out there, trying to catch their spouses dorking someone else. Parker spent many o' nights in the back of his Suburban with a camera waiting for the right second for the right picture.

He and Sandy got by living in a one-bedroom house in Monck's Corner. She was making scraps working through law school until Parker got the right client. He busted the man's wife in the changing room at Folly Beach. Apparently, he needed help getting out of his Speedos and she accidentally ended up servicing his tool. That winning photo saved her husband a shitload of money.

He liked Parker after that. He believed in him. And he backed it up by investing in his little operation.

As they say… BOOM.

Fifteen years later, Parker had three investigators and a team of legal thugs to provide protective and investigative services. He hadn't had to spend a single night in the back of the Suburban since. People did it for him.

Parker opened the glass door, then a heavier security door just a few feet inside. The tiny reception area smelled like an evergreen car freshener had been completely vaporized. A plastic fig tree was in the corner. A counter next to that had a nameplate. *Marlene.* Marlene wasn't at her post.

"Be right there," came from somewhere in back.

Parker punched the code onto the number pad next to the door, next to Marlene's station. *2-0-4.* Door buzzed. Parker moved into the inner sanctum.

He went down the short hallway. Marlene was behind the door on the left that was mostly shut. Someone with a deep voice was answering her. That was Butchie, Parker's number one investigator and, in a pinch, one hell of a thug. Butchie was the first guy he hired when the business took off.

The door at the end was Parker's.

Another keypad. You couldn't be too safe.

2-0-4.

For a business that specialized in protective services, using the same number for both doors was stupid. But it was Parker's lucky number. So far, luck was with him. Why tell Lady Luck how to do her job?

The office smelled like the inside of an old shoe. Not the stinky kind, more the old leather and beaten sole sitting at the back of the closet. Out of sight. Forgotten.

He closed the door behind him. Thought maybe he'd talk to the cleaning services that kept things picked up. They were doing one hell of a job cleaning, the office looked like a museum. The desk was spotless. Not a single eraser bit. The books on the shelf to the right were square. On any given day, the smell wouldn't bother him. Today, though, he'd been spoiled with fresh air. And now the office felt like a box.

He pulled the blinds and pushed the window open to a wonderful view of a brick wall.

He opened all the drawers, looking for a wayward air freshener. There were pens and a calculator and staplers. No little green Christmas tree.

He dropped in the chair, propped his feet on the window ledge, and fired up a cigarette, blowing the smoke through the screen. He rolled the Newport between his finger and thumb, studied the burning tip, and listened to it crackle when he pulled a drag. He flicked the ashes in the trash can.

He watched the screen saver tick off pictures. Grand Canyon. Carowinds. Jessie when she turned five. Shelly's sixth birthday party. Vacations. Christmas. Sandy on their wedding day.

He took another cigarette out.

He started to reach for the mouse but couldn't bring himself to wipe out the photos. The second he did meant work. Right now, without his calendar, he didn't know what lay ahead. He was lost without a calendar. He couldn't remember one damn thing on his schedule. He just couldn't get himself to lean over and do it. He just didn't want to be there.

Didn't want to work. Period.

Knock. Knock-knock-knock.

A woman's middle-aged face peeked through the crack of the doorway and said, "Um, what the hell—"

"Marlene, hold my calls, will you? I got to get some air." Parker stubbed the cig out on the inside of the trash can. He carefully pushed the chair back under the desk. "Call me if Butchie can't handle something today. Otherwise, I'm a ghost. All right? All right."

He pushed his way between her and the door. He didn't feel like explaining his absence. There was always something to do and, to be frank, he was the boss, so if he felt like taking the day off, well, then, goddamnit, he shouldn't have to explain himself. Marlene could take that snooty look and stuff it.

She stared at him all the way to the front door. He could feel it.

Outside. Parker inhaled the South Carolina morning. He regretted that cigarette now.

Pulled the pack out. Tossed it in the trash.

"Morning," he said to the kid outside the office.
Tip of an imaginary hat.
Not recognizing him from the café.

utchie loomed over his keyboard. His meaty finger pointed at it.

Marlene was pointing at the monitor.

This was their morning routine. Butchie turning on the computer. Butchie yelling for Marlene. He was good at his job. Computers weren't it.

The front door rarely buzzed this time of the morning. So she called out when it did. She'd be right there. Figured whoever needed help could sit quietly until Butchie was back on track.

She didn't hear the security door open.

Didn't hear the office at the end of the hall, either.

Why would she?

No one was out front when she finished. But then she smelled smoke. Had to be the mystery guest. But the smell, it was so strong. She followed her nose down the hall, past Butchie still hunched and pecking. Past the open bathroom on the right. The office at the end was closed. As usual. But then, the smell.

The doorknob turned. Opened.

And that was when she saw Parker.

There was a moment when her mouth opened and nothing came

out. Then she found the words as he got up and told her, matter-of-factly, he was getting out of the office, hold his calls, and something else. She didn't really hear the rest. Too stunned, really.

She watched him march out.

Butchie met her in the hall. She sort of shuffled next to him.

"Is that who I think it is?" Butchie's finger was still pointed.

Marlene nodded. Sort of.

"How the hell'd he get in here?"

Marlene shook her head. Sort of.

There was a long moment of contemplation. It seemed absurd. Impossible.

Insane.

Butchie went inside his office and made a call to one of his guys.

Marlene wanted a cigarette.

Parker stood on the second floor of a parking garage. Hands on his hips. Parking slot empty.

He looked at his watch like it might tell him where he'd parked the night before. He couldn't remember driving it. Swear to God. But it wasn't there. Suppose it was possible it was stolen. But with so much security on it, it was more likely it grew legs and walked off.

Parker looked around. Checked his watch again.

It was getting close to the kids' lunchtime. Sandy still hadn't called. And her voicemail was still picking up.

He'd been sitting down at the Battery, watching the cargo ships and egrets and the tide come in. His phone didn't ring the entire time. They probably didn't need him at the office. Maybe he should look into selling the business. Retire early. They could find a second home, do some traveling. The kids weren't getting any younger and, like old people were always saying, they'll be grown up and gone before you know it.

He was getting to be an old softy. Maybe a good reason to sell a business that dealt with protective services.

He tried Sandy's phone one more time. No answer.

He took the stairs down to the street and called a taxi service. He'd go it alone.

Tell the girls Mama's busy.

Daddy's here.

33

"I'm here to eat lunch with my daughters."

Parker dropped the bag of Chick-fil-A on the counter to prove his point.

"Last name?"

"Samson."

The secretary turned on her chair and pecked at the keyboard. She pointed an exaggerated fingernail tipped with a fake diamond at the monitor.

"They're not here today, sir."

Parker already had the pen leashed to the counter in his hand. "What's that?"

"They didn't come to school."

"What do you mean?"

"They're counted as absent."

"Where are they?" He sort of laughed.

"I don't know, sir. Their teachers counted them as absent this morning."

"I'm sorry." He dropped the pen. "Are you sure there's not a mistake? Their mother brings them every morning. I'd know if they didn't come to school because they'd be at home, and they weren't

87

home this morning. Can you call the teachers' rooms and double-check?"

She looked to her right. Then back. "I suppose sooo…"

He spit a *thank you* at her. "And why wouldn't you call me if they weren't here?"

"We put a call into your wife this morning abouttttt…" Her glittery fingernail dragged down the screen. "Nine o'clock."

"What'd she say?"

"Who's that?"

"My wife."

"No one answered. We left a message, but it hasn't been returned."

He waved his phone at her. "Could've called me."

"Do we have your number?" Her lips stiffened, getting ready to deal with an asshole parent that thought he owned the school because he paid the ridiculous tuition.

"Well, I don't know, do—"

"Excuse me, sir. Can I help you?"

Another woman, gripping a stack of papers. Her face looked surprised, as opposed to the one sitting in front of him, now pushing a stick of gum in her mouth.

"Yeah, I'm here to eat lunch with my daughters." This time, he shook the bag as proof. "And I didn't get a call that they didn't come to school this morning."

"Ummm… well, give me a second and I can check."

She walked to one of the back offices and muttered something. Meanwhile, the long-nailed one excused herself and left. Parker tapped his foot. He felt pressure in his chest. Panic slid beneath his ribcage, clenching his heart coldly.

No big deal. The girls were sick. Just relax. It was a little odd, but just a mix-up. That was all.

He turned his back and dialed Sandy's number.

Please enjoy the music…

Still, a phone call to me would've been appropriate. Parker and Sandy spent a lot of money for a quality education. A phone call was not out of the question. Right? He had a right to know what was going on—

Voicemail.

"Sandy… darling, what's going on? I'm at school and the people are telling me the girls aren't here." He looked over his shoulder and noticed the secretary with two other people now. They were staring. Everyone was staring today. He pushed the phone tighter to his face and half-whispered, half-growled, "I know you're busy, but you need to call me back and tell me where the girls are if they're not at school. I just…" He took a breath. Tried to loosen the straps across his chest. "I just want to know—"

"Sir?"

Parker waved off the woman's voice. Did she not see him on the phone?

"I know you're busy, darling. Just take a second to call me back. All right? It's no big deal, but—"

"Sir." This time the word was demanding. A little much.

"Damnit! A little manners, PLEASE!"

Cold fear poured down his neck and spread across his back.

His thoughts seemed to crash inside his head with a metallic echo. *I'm losing control. I'm losing control. Why am I losing control?*

Secretary's mouth was a frozen O. She was about to tell him something. To go home, his kids were probably there. His wife had them. And if they weren't there, well, then… I'm sorry, sir. That's not our problem. Now, is it, sir.

"Stay here."

Parker put the phone down.

"Stay right here. I just want to make sure my girls aren't here first. Then I'll go. All right?" He pointed at her. Wanted her to drop the ridiculous look. "All right?"

He turned. Down the hall.

He needed to see them. Just to make sure. Because, sometimes, things happen.

Because it was a dangerous world. Especially Parker's.

There were people that wanted to hurt him. People that knew the best way to do that. Once upon a time, he caught a guy screwing around on his wife. Parker helped her take everything from him. Everything. And the scumbag swore he'd fuck over everyone that helped her. Parker was in court when the guy said it, three rows back. And that sonofabitch swung his eyes right on him. Like it was his fault. Like he made him pound some tattooed tramp on all fours in the same bed he slept with his wife.

Parker never forgot that.

"Shelly!"

Especially in moments like this.

"Jessie!"

He quick-stepped from class to class. Throwing his head inside the open doorways. Racing to the next.

No idea what class they were in.

He'd check them all.

People didn't take responsibility for their lives, that was the problem. That bastard in court was looking for someone else to blame. Parker wasn't like that. He took care of his own. He wasn't going to wait around for someone to call back or explain where his girls were.

"SHELLY!"

They depended on him. He was their protector.

He wasn't going to let them down.

"JESSIE!"

A buzzer filled the hallway. Vibrated off his petrified chest.

Stirred the fear in his belly.

The next classroom door was shut. The teacher was backing away from the door. The kids sat at their desks. Staring.

What is it with staring!

More doors shut. Echoed.

That wasn't going to stop him. No locked door could keep him out. Not if he saw his daughters behind it.

As he made his way down the hall, panic rose in his chest like an ancient creature raised from a watery abyss, spewing foul breath. He clenched his sternum. His breath shallow and quick. Like his footsteps. He tried to push it down. It only spread like an oil slick.

He peeked through another door. Kids were distracted, but the teacher was watching. Parker tried the handle, then looked around. He could see his girls' faces in his mind, their blond hair, round cheeks. None in the room, though.

He started for the next room when a young man appeared.

He wore boots.

His steps fell unusually silent on the waxed linoleum. The same linoleum Parker was now glued to. Watching him approach as fear bloomed like wicked flowers inside his body. He didn't wonder why he was overreacting.

He only wanted to see his family.

"Come." The young man held out his hand. "I will tell you about your children."

"My…" His lips, fat. "What about them? What do you know about my…"

The young man only beckoned.

And the poisoned emotions subsided, enough to release his anchored feet. He started back the way he came. Could feel eyes upon him through each door he passed. A small group waited near the office. They parted. The young man, his hand placed gently on Parker's back, nodded to them. They seemed to understand. No words were spoken.

Parker was guided outside, where the sun was bright. Hot. But Parker's skin cooled from the inside, where his fear began to roil like an approaching thunderstorm.

The worst, ahead.

3 4

*C*arla got up to make copies. Not before buzzing a man into the school. Nobody entered without a buzz.

She was heading back to her desk to check him in when the principal asked her a question. After that, she walked into the mail room. Then she picked up her copies. And that was when she noticed the guy she buzzed. He was at the counter. Talking to nobody.

She thought he was on a Bluetooth, maybe. One of those conversations that appeared to be with an imaginary friend. Last time Carla was standing in line at the grocery store, she almost answered the woman behind her on a Bluetooth. Do they really need to talk with someone *allllll* the time? This time, the man she buzzed was having a Bluetooth conversation like the person was sitting in her empty seat at the computer.

And it looked like his imaginary friend delivered some bad news.

So she asked him, "Can I help you?"

Was there bitterness in her tone? Because he looked like his head would explode. She tried to reason with him. It got worse. She went to one of the back offices and told the principal. She looked back and could see him talking again.

Moments later, he went full-scale bonkers. The principal followed standard procedure. Teachers were called to lock their classrooms. She should've called the police, but, for some reason, they gathered in the hall and watched him come unwound.

Strange.

The guy was marching down the hall, screaming his kids' names. He looked dangerous, like a panicked animal. She couldn't understand why he lost his marbles. He didn't even give her a chance to help. He was about to turn the corner at the end of the hall. They still hadn't called the police.

The front door opened.

A man walked toward them. She didn't buzz him in. He walked past them. He moved like silk. Like melted chocolate.

And the man at the end of the hall, he stopped.

She didn't hear what happened.

She only saw them come back.

The Bluetooth man's face was pasty, like it was turning to wax with cold beads resting above his brows. He was muttering. And the other man, a young man now that she looked at him, nodded at the bunch of them gathered near the main office as he guided him out. Everything was going to be all right. She felt it. They all did. Because when he exited with the Bluetooth man, everything felt normal.

The alarm was called off.

Teachers were updated.

School resumed.

Carla went back to her seat. Before she collated her copies, she looked through the school's database, cross-referencing all the Jessies and all the Shellys.

Two Jessies.

Three Shellys.

None related.

3 5

*S*andino was the driver of the cab that dropped Parker off at the school. He looped the roundabout. Some black kid stood near the exit with his hand up. Sandino rolled the window down.

The kid didn't say anything. Held a bill creased between his fingers and pointed at Sandino. It took a moment before he recognized the two zeroes behind the one. And he snatched it before he heard the request.

"Would you kindly wait near the front doors?" the kid said with an odd accent. Like a prince. "I will be with you momentarily."

Sandino didn't say shit.

He swung around and left the cab running.

A few minutes later, the kid walked up. He didn't go inside. Didn't get in the cab. Didn't talk to Sandino. He walked through the turf, into a courtyard to the left of the front doors. He stopped at the flower garden. A big sign out front, it said *Mrs. Shannon's Butterfly Garden.* The kid, he stood there with his hands behind his back. He wasn't smelling anything, just watching the large black and yellow butterfly flutter around a large spike of purple flowers. He held out his finger. The butterfly landed on it.

Listen. If the kid wanted to give Sandino a hundred dollars to sit in his air-conditioned cab to watch a butterfly fuck his finger, that was his business. The meter ran just the same.

But then, just as casually as he had strolled through the garden, he made his way through the doors. Minutes later, he came out with a white man. He looked like he just had a gun shoved in his mouth, his hair plastered to his forehead, lips bluish.

The kid helped him into the backseat. "I'll tell you more later," he told the man. "Go home. Rest."

Then he came around, gave Sandino a downtown address, and walked off.

Sandino tried not to look in the rearview at his fare. Didn't want to see a dead man in the backseat.

Halfway down the road, he said something. Couldn't help it. "You ahright?"

The man wiped his face with a handkerchief. Folded it. Shook his head.

Sandino didn't ask no more questions. He did his job, drove to Wentworth Avenue and let the man out.

When all was said and done, he was one hundred dollars richer.

3 6

Parker stood on the steps, his house in front of him.

The air seemed impossibly thick. Like he needed to swim from the cab just to be standing there.

The cab. He barely remembered the ride. The viscous air was in there, too.

Before the cab, there was the boy. He introduced himself as Drayton.

He remembered his eyes. Large pupils. Holes that went to the end of the universe.

He told Parker that his family was missing. But they were looking for them.

Parker wondered why he didn't ask questions. Like who *they* were. And why was his family missing. He just nodded his head. His family. Missing. The words fell like comets. His body trembled.

He knew it. He felt it when he went to the school. Something was wrong. Something was off. It wasn't just the weird morning, it was that instinctual feeling from way down. Something was missing.

Drayton put Parker in the cab and told him to go home. To wait until further word.

Why wasn't he involved? His specialty was investigation. It was crime.

Crime.

The word tumbled through him, settling in the pit of his stomach along with Drayton's words. Missing. Looking. Now, crime.

He took a deep breath. His chest popped.

The mid-afternoon sun cast shadows across the street, falling over the parked cars. Further down was a black Suburban. It sat alone and still.

The next-door neighbor opened her door. She stared at Parker. He didn't bother with a good afternoon. Instead, he turned and swam up the steps. The front door clanged behind him like metal bars. He even thought he heard the tumble of a lock.

He was going to wait inside his house. He'd wait until he heard from the kid.

About his family.

37

There were no backseats in the Suburban.

Daryl was sweating, but avoided shifting around to get comfortable. Otherwise, the truck would shake. The target had been standing on the steps damn near twenty minutes. Just staring.

When he finally went inside, Daryl opened his phone.

He heard, "Yeah."

"Butchie, you were right."

"He's at the house?"

"Just walked in."

There was a deep sigh on the other end. Daryl could hear Butchie rubbing his chin. Then, "Stay put. I'm going to find out what's going on."

"10-4."

Daryl checked the camera. Checked his watch.

This was going to be twenty-four-hour surveillance.

Overtime.

38

oments after Parker went inside, Drayton stepped around the corner.

He stopped outside the house, just below the window to the left of the steps. He stood there patiently. And he would stay there. He needed to be close to Parker. In order to carry out Andrew Drummond's request, he needed to remain near him.

The neighbor would not see him.

Nor would surveillance in the black Suburban.

He would convince them not to.

Until he brought the events to a close.

39

$\mathcal{M}$orning slants of sunlight crept across the bed, striping Parker's face.

He rolled over. Reaching out, feeling the cool sheets next to him.

He let his fingers walk up the pillow while he bit into his. There was an indention, like she had laid her head. But the pocket was cool. Maybe he elbowed it in the night.

He sat up. Rubbed his face. Tried not to think.

Tried not to think.

Impossible when thoughts were that heavy. They settled like rocks on the bottom of an aquarium. They came in a steady pour, filling Parker's head.

He reached for cigarettes. The flame quivered.

He finished it with continuous drags. Only got up to throw the burning butt in the trash. Caught sight of the framed photo on the dresser and picked it up. He twisted the wedding ring around his finger, the flesh beneath red and worn. The gold was dense and tight. He wouldn't take it off. He would never take it off.

The bedroom felt so small. He tossed the photo down, sought the space of the front room, and passed the girls' bedroom on the way. He didn't look inside. Instead, he reached back without turning his head and pulled the door shut. He didn't want to look in there, not yet. Not until he heard some good news. But he couldn't help catching sight of the pink bedsheets.

He ignored the coffee machine. Walked past the bottle of scotch on the counter from the night before, the lid sitting next to it. He sank into an oversized chair, the cushions breathing air as they swallowed him down. He stared at the blank high-def TV. That was what he did the night before. He stared at it. It was after midnight when he went to the bathroom. He must've fallen in the bed.

He was going to sit there awhile longer. Wait to hear something.

If he hadn't heard anything by lunch, he'd go get the bottle. The thoughts would be pouring by then. He'd need something to help fight them back.

He lit a cigarette.

Flicked the ashes on the floor.

40

Drayton appeared like a statue. Below the window.

People walked by him without a glance.

The neighbor got her newspaper without a word.

Drayton, the ancient, remained motionless. Sleepless. And vigilant.

Inside the house, he felt the undoing of Parker Samson's mind.

41

*D*ay three.

Three bottles of scotch. Two empty. One halfway there. The liquor store delivered. Along with cigarettes.

Parker was in the chair that morning. He stopped going to the bedroom. Only went through it to relieve himself. It felt so small. The sheets, so cold. The photos were face down on the dresser because on day two he sat with the family photo and shined the glass with his thumb. Something the size of a tennis ball swelled in his throat. He couldn't breathe until he looked away. From his wife. Children. So he turned the photo over.

He nodded off in the chair. But he mostly sat there.

A pile of cigarette ash near his foot.

A car door closed.

Parker hauled himself up, split the blinds with two fingers and spied the street below. Just a neighbor.

He watched her all the way up her steps. Watched her fiddle with her keys. Go inside.

When everything was still, he sat back down. Got up only to fill his glass.

42

*P*athetic.

The skin hung off his cheeks like a hound dog. Whiskers scratched against the back of his hand when he wiped his lips.

A week ago, he was a man.

With a family.

Why didn't he go out and find them? Why was he waiting for someone to tell him what had happened?

He didn't know.

A never-ending movie rolled in his head, displaying every possible scenario of what went wrong. Were his girls raped? Strangled?

Alive?

Whenever his eyes swelled, he took another swallow. Whatever shred of manhood remained, he intended on keeping it. By not crying. He would be strong. He would hold down the fort until they returned.

But the house was getting smaller.

The air, thicker.

43

ay five.

There was a smell. Kind of like bad liver.

Parker was chewing on a block of cheese when the phone rang. He picked it up. His voice spurted through a curtain of phlegm. He cleared his throat and tried again.

"Hello."

The other end of the line hissed.

"Drayton? Is that you?"

Sssssssssssssssss.

A hundred thoughts forced their way into his throat. The sound he made resembled something from a native tribal council. The medicine man in a trance.

He snapped the phone closed and dropped it on his lap.

Not until he reached for the cigarettes did he realize the phone wasn't there. He'd put it on his lap when he was done. But now he couldn't find it.

It would come back.

44

It was night when he heard the voice.

The blinds were closed. Curtains drawn.

He was slumped in the chair, cracker crumbs scattered on his shirt. He was in a pained dream. One where he was being chased. He was running. The ground hurt his feet.

Daddy?

His eyes snapped open. Red and waxy. Sunken.

He looked around.

The radio was off. TV, too.

He remained still for a full minute. When he reached for a cigarette, he heard it again. The lighter trembled from his hand. He let out a moan and covered his mouth to keep from vomiting. He stayed pickled and numb with quarts of liquor, but now he began to burble, frothing noxious fumes poisoning his skin. Swelling in his throat.

He reached for the lighter, his fingers suddenly struck with Parkinson's disease, flicking it further away. Sobriety was dangerously close. The images of his family—Sandy, Jessie, Shelly—were beginning to clarify in the mind fog. He had blotted them out. Not to forget them, but to dull the pain.

He was dangerously close to admitting he couldn't handle it.

He couldn't experience the pain of loss. Couldn't imagine his life without them.

And the thought of their suffering.

Unbearable.

He was a coward. Trying to survive a nightmare.

When he lit the cigarette, the voice came again.

"No." He shook his head. "No, no, no, no, no."

His head went back and forth, the flame dancing.

He tried not to look, through the smoke, at the girls' room.

45

In the house. Day seven.

A shell of a man hunched over a bed, clutching the pink sheets with images of Hannah Montana. His face was buried in a salt-soaked stain spreading out from his eyes. From his nose.

His sobs could be heard next door.

rayton moved. For the first time in seven days.

*E*arly, day eight. A knock at the door.

Parker ignored it.

He had ignored the voices. The phone ringing. He knew his thoughts had escaped his head, were haunting him from the outside. Now they were knocking.

But the thuds on the red door continued to echo.

They ached inside Parker's skull.

He winched himself upright, flinching after another round of knocking.

He bounced off a wall and propped himself on the back side of the door. There was a face in the peephole. He pushed his puffy eye closer and it was still there. Parker opened the door.

There was a man. In uniform.

"Mr. Samson?" His nostrils flared. The stench was rancid. "Parker Samson?"

"Yes."

"I'm Officer Stanley Farnsworth."

An awkward silence.

"Can I come in?"

"Are they dead?"

Officer Farnsworth looked over Parker's shoulder in hopes someone would help. "Could we discuss this in a more appropriate—"

"Did you find them? Why haven't you called?"

Parker's voice tilted up at the end, squeaking out the last syllable. He fisted his lips, afraid he'd puke his emotions in the officer's face.

"I'd really like to sit down and discuss it."

"Just tell me. Please."

"Mr. Samson—"

"No. No, goddamnit. Just tell me. I don't want to discuss the details, just tell me."

"Sir, I'd rather—"

Parker grabbed handfuls of uniform. "Please, tell me they're alive."

"You need to let go, Mr. Samson."

"Please… please." Parker attempted to shake him, but his arms were weak. He managed to barely move him. "Please."

Officer Farnsworth gently took Parker's hands and pulled them off. He didn't resist. He bowed his head. Gloom, as dark as tar, as deep as a mine shaft, pushed through the veil of denial. He dropped on his knees. His chin bounced on his chest.

"I'm sorry for your loss." Officer Farnsworth's hand squeezed Parker's shoulder. "We did everything we could."

Parker wrapped his hands around the officer's arm to keep from falling sideways. He couldn't hold back the weeping.

It took him.

Swallowed him.

Destroyed him.

4 8

Cynthia Birkenstalk stepped out to fetch the newspaper off the front step. Among the sounds of traffic, there was a man wailing. She hadn't seen her new neighbor in quite some time. Not really at all since she saw him the one time. Now she heard someone over there crying. It was none of her business. After all, what went on in other people's lives was their business, even if they were out on their front porch crying. So she bent over and retrieved the newspaper.

But curiosity got the best of her.

She turned towards the sound, as if she were merely turning to go inside, letting her eyes fall in the direction of the sobbing. As if she couldn't help it. What she saw made her stall. Her eyes lingered on the odd sight, from where the sobs were coming. It was her neighbor, all right. He was on his knees. Head bowed. Hands clasping the air in front of him. Not in prayer. But as if he was holding something.

She looked around. There was no one anywhere. Just this pathetic soul bawling on his front steps to an empty street.

When he began talking, as if someone was there, she went inside.

It was none of her business, after all.

4 9

Parker sat in the front pew. Alone.

In the aisle were three coffins. The larger one in the middle, flanked by two smaller ones. Their surfaces shined.

The priest gave a moving eulogy. About family. Closeness. About God's plan. How we all have our crosses to bear. Like our Lord and Savior. And some other bullshit.

Parker imagined the priest was looking at him when he said it. But he remained with head bowed, refusing to acknowledge him. He couldn't risk seeing the coffins. Or the faces of those weeping near him. He barely managed to be there.

His cheeks were the color of used sandpaper, his eyes buried deep in their sockets. Even if he wanted to lift his head, give the priest a nod, he didn't have the strength. He barely remembered getting to the front pew.

The past several days were a wash.

The arrangements for the beautiful ceremony were all made from home. He was on the phone at all hours of the day—the mortician, the church, and cemetery. Some even called at night. The family called to offer condolences, making arrangements to fly or drive to Charleston. To be there when he needed them most.

I just can't believe this is happening, a few of them muttered, breathless, on the phone.

Parker couldn't, either.

Days after Officer Farnsworth delivered the news, the chief of police arrived at the house. They sat at the kitchen table. Parker asked how they died, the words stumbling over his lips. The chief only shook his head. *They didn't suffer* was all he said.

After which, Parker broke down. Again.

Now he sat hunched in the pew, his parched cheeks without a tear. There were none left. A man could only cry so much until they were all gone.

But it did nothing for the emptiness inside.

When the priest ended the ceremony, Parker walked briskly down the aisle. Head bowed. Eyes down. The organ faded behind him as the doors closed. He stood on the front steps, the white steeple soaring over him. He lit a cigarette with a quivering flame. Then hurried for his car before the procession followed him out.

He drove to the cemetery alone.

* * *

PARKER HAD PARKED the rental car far from the burial.

He could see the white tent. The people gathering.

He'd driven by ceremonies dozens of times, the line of cars and the people huddled under the canvas tent, heads bowed. Never thought about who was in there. Not once.

Now it was his turn.

He waited, staring at the clock.

At three o'clock, he got out. Closed the door quietly. Walked softly through the grass, between the headstones, until he neared the tent. He could feel their eyes on him. Could feel the crowd part. He saw the headstones first. The sight of their names etched in the stone hit him in the stomach with a lead pipe.

The holes were dug.

The caskets waiting.

And, when he stopped just outside the tent, still in the sun, the priest delivered the final procession.

The wind blew against his hardened face, carrying the soft whimpers of family. Parker tried not to look up, but he felt the pain around him. The women were clutching tissues, dabbing at their eyes. Men stood erect, an arm around a woman or hands upon a child's shoulders. Some were grieving outwardly. Others stoic. But inside, Parker felt the agony twist like serpents. Their pain seeped from them like sweat, evaporated in the atmosphere and clung to his skin. Weighed on him like a wet suit, absorbing more and more. Heavier. Thicker.

He could barely manage to carry his own suffering. It wasn't fair to take on theirs, too. He didn't have the strength.

He wasn't strong enough.

Parker closed his eyes. Dry sobs shook his chest. He tensed against the others' suffering, but their pain trickled inside him. Filling him. Weighing on him.

Breaking him.

His mouth opened and closed with gummy white strings attached to his lips. Words didn't come out. He opened his eyes.

An old lady was weeping.

A man holding a child. His face tear tracked.

A woman wringing her hands.

All of them, devastated. Bearing the cross of their suffering.

Parker turned. Hesitated. The first step was the hardest. After that, he was running.

Between the headstones.

He couldn't take it.

50

*D*aryl raised the binoculars.

He waited outside the church for Parker and followed him to the cemetery. He parked down a road parallel to the one Parker was on, with live oaks in between. Parker appeared to be reluctant, whatever he was doing. But at three o'clock, he got out of his car and walked across the cemetery. Between headstones and over graves.

Daryl shook his head. *Bad luck, son.*

Three hundred yards later, he stopped at a headstone. Daryl focused the binoculars. He couldn't read the inscription, but recognized the two smaller headstones that flanked it. He'd been to that site before. He'd been to that exact funeral.

He got Butchie on the phone. "You're not going to believe this shit."

He told him.

Butchie told him to continue surveillance. He would make some calls.

So Daryl sat with binoculars, watching his target standing alone. Atop a hill with his head bowed in front of the graves of a woman and her two daughters. The grass around him cleanly cut and manicured.

5 1

Parker fumbled with the keys in his front door.

He just wanted to get inside. He wanted to get away. His chest was about to cave under the weight. He needed to breathe. He needed to forget.

This can't be happening.

The door swung open, crashed into the wall and closed with its own momentum. Parker dropped the keys and started for the kitchen. Licking his lips. Wiping his forehead.

Drayton was at the table. Legs crossed.

"How the hell did you get in here?"

"I have come to tell you what has happened to your life."

Parker looked around, trying to focus. The floor seemed to sway. "What are you doing in my house?"

Drayton remained still. Placid eyes like ink.

Parker licked his lips again. When he was steady, he pulled a chair from the table and sat carefully, afraid to disturb the frail balance of his teetering mind. He poured a drink. The bottle rattled against the rim of the glass like the earth was shaking.

He drank.

When he was done, he poured another.

He had trouble swallowing the second one. His stomach was knotted. He forced it to untangle and take the second drink. So he could pour a third.

He looked around the room, acting oblivious to Drayton. What was more interesting was the sudden strangeness of his house. It didn't feel like his. He had the queer sensation that he was a stranger sitting in someone else's home. Almost like he broke inside. Like he didn't belong here. It wrapped around his guts like a twisting wire.

He was halfway through the third drink when his stomach revolted.

He clamped his lips.

Slapped his hand over them.

Vomit gushed under his tongue, squirted between his teeth.

He ran through the bedroom and emptied his guts until he puked green slime into the toilet. He continued to retch, all the way from his toes, feeling the muscle between his balls clench. He pressed his forehead against the cool floor tiles.

He pulled up on the sink and stumbled into the bedroom.

The family photo on the dresser, it was sitting up. Facing him.

He blinked.

The faces. They were the same. Except his.

Leaned closer. Had to focus to be sure. Be sure what he was seeing. That he was seeing another man in the photo with his family.

His fucking family!

He sat on the bed, rubbing his thumb over the glass. Shook his head. Blinked and blinked. It didn't change. He realized, before, when he looked at it, that his face was blurry. But now, the face in the photo, the one that was not him, it was as clear as the others. Like it belonged.

He also noticed the ring on his finger felt heavy. The skin beneath, chapped.

He stopped in the doorway.

"Did you do this?" He held up the frame.

"Please, have a seat."

Drayton stood, pulled a chair out from the table. Waited.

Parker realized his legs were partially numb. Not from drink, but fear. It was cold and stinging. He touched the wall, the couch, the table on his way to the chair. Drayton sat opposite him. He tried to pour another drink, but his hand was now convulsing. The liquor splashed on the family photo. Parker wiped it.

"His name is Andrew Drummond," Drayton said, his voice soothing. The words like jewels. "He died six months ago in a car accident."

Parker moaned. He thought he was going to be sick again.

"Three years ago, he owned his own business. He had a wife and two young girls." He gestured around the room. "They lived here."

Parker knew where *here* was. He meant this house. They lived here. Parker looked around with the urge to flee.

"Three years ago, Andrew Drummond went away on business. He was out of town for the evening. He spoke to his wife before he lay down for the night. She put the girls on the phone. They told him about school and about a birthday party. They blew kisses when they said goodnight."

Parker shined the photo with his fingers. He had a thought, remembering the door at his office. On the glass facing the street. The name. It wasn't Samson. *Drummond Protective and Investigative Services.*

Drummond.

Not Samson.

He tried to remember how it looked when he was there. Samson, it said. It was there, Samson was on the door. It was fuzzy when the rest of the words were clear. Like the picture.

But now it said Drummond.

"When he returned, he found his family in his house. They were dead."

The family photo clattered on the table.

"Andrew Drummond buried his family on a day with the sun shining. He lived without them for the years that followed. And he suffered greatly."

Parker covered his mouth. His eyes bulged.

"He suffered greatly." Drayton repeated.

Someone knocked.

Parker jerked in his seat. His head shook. Tried to push away from the table. Tried to escape. Thoughts were folding their wings and diving on him. He waited for the room to stop spinning. Waited to see a new reality. But it spun. It spun.

Until he looked into Drayton's eyes.

Open. Deep. And liquid.

He looked. He saw. And he remembered. He remembered.

Parker Samson did not live on Wentworth Avenue.

He owned three tattoo parlors. He lived in the back of the one on King Street, where he moved drugs and other elements of illegal nature. Like crack cocaine to the likes of the military vagrant he saw a few weeks back. The one that knew him. Of course he knew him.

Andrew Drummond was the investigator that helped Parker's wife arrest him. Andrew Drummond helped the police put him in jail. He helped his wife take everything from him.

Parker Samson lost it all.

But he wasn't afraid to go to jail. He wasn't afraid to die.

And he wasn't afraid to kill.

And he was determined to make someone pay. If not his whore wife, then the motherfucker that helped her.

The night he made it happen, he disconnected the alarm system. Snuck into the house and stood in the bedroom. He watched Andrew's wife sleep. A squeak escaped her throat, but nothing else got past the garrote pulled tightly against the cords in her neck. Cutting off the breath. Crushing the larynx. She twitched. Scratched. She became a lump.

Parker felt a rush through his groin surge into his legs. Spinning his guts. It gave him strength. Power. And he liked it.

He took it to the bedroom down the hall. The girls slept soundly. Like little girls do.

"Mr. Samson." The knocking on the front door was louder. "Mr. Samson, could you answer the door. We have a few questions."

Parker looked at the door. It was blurry. He wiped his eyes. Suddenly, he couldn't get enough breath into his lungs. The loss. The emptiness. The agony of losing his wife. His children. *But they're not my wife. Not my girls. NOT MY FAMILY!*

But they were, now. They felt like family. The loss was his, no matter what he tried to tell himself. He felt the raging emptiness. The bottomless pain. The endless gray sky.

Drayton stood. "Now you will carry his burden."

Knocking. The doorknob jiggled.

"Please." Parker tried to stand. His legs could not. "I can't."

Drayton turned. Parker grappled his hands, pulling him back. "Kill me. I don't deserve to live, I deserve to die. I need to die." He closed his eyes, shaking. "Kill me."

Drayton touched Parker's forehead. With that gesture, Parker knew that death would not come to him. His fate was much worse. He didn't want to die because he deserved it. He wanted death because he was afraid. He didn't want to live with the suffering inside him, the suffering he brought to Andrew Drummond. But Drayton's touch told him different. That death he did not deserve. That it would not come. Andrew's suffering, and the suffering of all his family, was his to carry now.

His cross to bear.

Drayton opened the door.

The police came into the house.

They found their man hunched over at a table. Weeping.

5 2

Butchie, Daryl and Marlene were on the sidewalk, the dark Suburban behind them, between police cars. They watched Parker Samson led out of Andrew Drummond's house.

Andrew, their former employer. Their dead friend.

When his family was murdered, Parker was on a list of suspects. But there was never enough evidence. Only suspicion. And as the case grew colder, Andrew became more distant. He was coming in hungover. He began drinking at the office. Then he stopped coming to work. He sobered up, but when he fell off the wagon, he fell hard. They were talking about an intervention when he died.

They closed the door to his office. It hadn't been opened since.

They didn't know why Parker Samson had slipped in there. Or how.

Butchie wanted to kill him right there. On the spot.

Marlene convinced him otherwise.

They followed him. As they did, incriminating evidence just seemed to appear—fingerprints, DNA, a weapon. It happened so fast, like a fairy was planting it. They built a case in weeks.

Now they watched him stumble down the steps in handcuffs, wailing like a broken man.

"What got into his skull?" Daryl mumbled.

Butchie and Marlene didn't have an answer.

The lead officer came over to Butchie. They discussed where they were taking him and how they wanted to collaborate on the case. No one noticed the young man that walked out of the house. The young man that moved with grace down the steps, down the sidewalk.

5 3

"Here you go, sir. Can I get you anything else?"

"No, thank you. That's very kind of you," Drayton said.

"You from around here?"

"No, ma'am."

The Poogan's Porch waitress crossed her arms. "Well, how long you in town?"

"For a while longer, I believe."

The waitress was in her twenties. A college student. She bent over to take the silverware off the table, exposing the low cut of her blouse and the curves of her breasts. Drayton tugged at the string hanging out of his cup, steeping the tea bag. She looked over at him with a smile and made direct contact with his eyes. His lovely black eyes. Her hand slowed.

Drayton looked away.

She moved slowly back inside the yellow house that served as a downtown restaurant. She went to help other customers, forgetting the thrill of Drayton's gaze.

He sat alone at a table for two. The upper porch faced Queen Street.

It was late.

The downtown sounds of nightlife were alive.

Andrew Drummond was not.

Parker Samson was.

Andrew wanted him to pay. He wanted him dead. But Drayton knew the ends of revenge. That the blood of payback was cold, indeed. Drayton knew because he'd spent hundreds of years paying for the suffering he'd inflicted on his victims, back in a time when he was ruthless. When he was an animal. When he was what a novelist would call a vampire. He destroyed lives at will, drank the blood from their arteries rich with essence. And the longer he existed, the heavier the chains became. He owed for his indulgence. His insolence. Ignorance.

Not until he learned to bear his victims' suffering had he been delivered from his own.

And it had taken far longer than a human life.

Drayton might have been an immortal, but he was not a god. He did not know where the dying went, whether there was a heaven or hell or their awareness was merely spread among the cosmic winds like ash. Maybe Andrew was sitting next to him, right there on Poogan's Porch.

His last request, fulfilled.

Drayton removed the teabag, squeezed the contents, and placed it on the saucer. A sip.

A sigh.

A couple walked up the steps to find a table at Poogan's Porch. They were in their fifties. The woman was dainty, walking with short, quick steps. The man appeared reasonably fit. He walked with a limp from a recent accident. He broke an ankle falling off a bike.

Drayton's nostrils flared.

The taste of his essence pulsed beneath Drayton's tongue. It had been six months since Andrew Drummond's passing. Six months since Drayton had fed. His skin was drawing tight.

"How's your tea?" The waitress leaned over.

"Savory."

"Good. I just want to tempt you one last time. We've got the best crabcakes in the area. I could bring you out an appetizer to prove it."

"Very kind, but no, thank you."

She pouted. "Are you sure you're not hungry."

The limping man stopped at the doorway. Sweat was building on his shiny head. Cheeks flushing. The host greeted them brightly and gestured to a table toward the back of the house. The limping man took a deep breath for the trip inside, unaware that a blood clot had formed in his artery. Drayton could feel it on a path for his heart.

"I think I'll have something a bit later."

Perhaps around midnight.

SWIFT IS THE CURRENT

BOOK 3

Some bad seeds are worth saving.

5 4

ondor Current stabbed the smoldering butt into a pile of spent cigarettes and blew smoke into a ceiling fan wilting in the South Carolina humidity. The veranda overlooked a square courtyard contained by three sides of a mansion and overlooked the ocean off Kiawah Island, a chunk of South Carolina that Condor Current did not own, but was in line to inherit. If he was lucky, it would all be his in the next couple hours.

The house staff was dragging plastic bags through the courtyard and picking up plastic cups with extended grabbers. The shrubbery looked raped, but that was the cost of a good party. *A fund-raiser,* he reminded himself. The only difference between a fund-raiser and a depraved good time was the money it raised for a local no-kill animal shelter. Imagine that, a killer party that was responsible for the death of thousands of brain cells also supported a no-kill cause.

Condor dug his thumb into his right temple. *That's a lot of gray matter.*

If Condor's father taught him anything, it was to have a good time. His father, the same guy that drove his Maserati into an oak tree while his girlfriend was plowing him with her mouth. The same guy that

128

gave him the name Condor. *Your grandfather's name,* he said. *Something to be proud of, a name like that.*

Then why don't you take the name, Robert?

Because you're taking one for the family, son.

That little conversation was all in Condor's head. Just thoughts. But he'd been having conversations like this in his own brain for so long he could no longer recall if they actually happened or not. Condor knew they were thoughts, but he believed them and they hurt because Robert Current used to finish every conversation with a devilish chuckle that sucked the soul right out his ears. Robert Current owned people with that laugh.

Condor raised his glass and drained the icy remains. *Here's to you, Robert. You dead fuck.*

He popped out another soldier from the cigarette pack. His phone vibrated on the glass table. He waved away the smoke to focus on the text.

Where r u?

He didn't recognize the number. Then he realized it must be the girl sleeping in the guest room. Well, passed out. Condor slipped something in her drink when the party began to wind down. She was coming onto Condor the second she stepped through the front door, her eyes lighting up on the palatial foyer. A house on the beach made one out of three girls wet, that was a fact in Condor's book. Even Condor—short and fat and black straw hair—could score with a house like that. Money was the world's best aphrodisiac.

Nonetheless, Condor liked them to be asleep when he had fun. He owned a brown bottle of chloroform, but he didn't have the nerve to use something that potent. Not yet. He wanted them to wake up in the morning and not die. But he had it, just in case the roofie wore off.

As long as she was sleeping, she wouldn't have any evidence to convict him of rape. Technically, he didn't touch her, so it wasn't rape, but he doubted a judge would see it that way. It wasn't illegal to put her in different poses. Maybe it was a tiny bit illegal to undress her...

There were times he knocked out two or three girls and stacked them like flapjacks. But he never touched them. Never, ever. Sometimes he wasn't even in the same room; he just arranged them like dolls then hid in his closet and peeked through the slats of the door. Any evidence of foul play went into a tissue and got double-flushed down a toilet. Always double-flush.

"Sir." Stanley the manservant stepped onto the balcony. "A call."

He handed Condor the house phone and turned toward the sliding door. He stopped at the sound of rattling ice. Condor was holding a glass tumbler above his head, crushing an ice cube between his teeth. Stanley the manservant retrieved the glass. Condor waited for the door to slide shut before he said hello.

The call was short. Not more than a minute. Condor didn't say much, just a few uh-huhs and then a sure. He added to his vocabulary when he hung up.

"Fuck."

Stanley the manservant returned to the balcony and passed Condor a fresh Bloody Mary. He took the phone in exchange for the drink.

"Good news?"

"Fantastic," Condor said flatly. "Grandmother is coming home this afternoon."

"You sound ecstatic."

"Hmm."

Stanley paused in case Condor had more to say. A memory suddenly popped into Condor's awareness. It was Christmas and he was expecting a Range Rover to be waiting for him in the morning with a ribbon tied around it. Instead, it was a BMW, used. He remembered the sinking feeling, like something untouchable was slipping between his fingers. He had the same feeling now.

Ruthie Current adjusted the oxygen tube chafing her upper lip. Her other hand scratched at the leather of the backseat like the hand didn't belong to her, like some mutated spider, spotted and wrinkled, trying to escape the end of her arm.

The skin was faded around one of her fingers where her wedding ring used to be, a wedding band that was ten feet below ground in her ex-husband's casket. She stopped wearing it long before he died. She kept it on when she caught him cheating the first time because he said he was sorry. The second time, though, Ruthie took it off for good and divorced him and took everything he had. Everything. Not like she needed it, she was born into money. But who ever said taking someone's money was about the money. When he died, she paid the embalmer a handsome sum to insert the ring six inches up her ex-husband's anus.

Her hand was still scratching, so she put it in her lap.

She was supposed to still be in the hospital. The doctors refused to release her, but Ruthie told them, in no uncertain terms, she was leaving. That was that. She would send for her entire staff to retrieve her if that was what it took. The doctors seemed ready to challenge her, but then her driver showed up and everyone seemed to calm down and saw it her way. People always saw it Ruthie's way, sooner or later.

Her head seemed loosely attached. It swayed with the turns. This far out on Kiawah Island, there were many scenic turns. People paid lots of money for those turns. Ruthie wanted to vomit. She wanted to lean her head out the window and hurl down the waxed side of her car, but that would look rather coarse. When one rode in the back of a luxury automobile, it was one's duty to do it with class. So she sat back, adjusted the oxygen tube, and took a deep breath.

The live oaks swam out of a mist, their branches reaching out like muscled arms. She blinked and realized the fog wasn't outside the car but inside her head. She just couldn't think straight. A fuzzy thought told her to go back to the hospital, but she'd rather be home.

Her driver had not said a word. Her staff had always been instructed to do so. He was a good soldier, but appeared to be wearing a black T-shirt and was without a cap. She would have to have a talk about his uniform. Currents are not casual, certainly not their staff.

The skin on the back of his neck was blacker than the hood of her Bentley. It wasn't that Ruthie wasn't accustomed to African-Americans, she just had not employed one so dark. Perhaps he was Kenyan.

Or perhaps this was a dream.

She recalled the disconnected memories of discomfort of the previous days. Of needles piercing her skin. The beeps of machines. The scent of hospital disinfectant still soaked her white hair. Before that, she couldn't remember much. Only the distinct feeling she wasn't supposed to be here. Not in the car, just here. In the world.

She was supposed to be dead.

The iron gates were swinging open ahead of the car, the grand letter C splitting open to let them in. Her estate was beyond. She was home.

Her driver had brought her home.

5 6

"**W**hy aren't you here?" Condor said into the phone. "You said you'd be here if there were any problems, and guess what? You're not here."

Condor paced across the foyer, his shoes clacking on the shined floor. He pulled the drapes aside and looked out the window.

"You're the one that started this—"

Condor pulled the phone off his ear and winced. His sister's voice came out like a spike. He held the phone to his chest, feeling it vibrate on his sternum. He pulled aside the drapes again. When the phone felt quiet, he spoke into it without putting it against his head.

"Well, when are you going to be here?" The silence was long enough that Condor finally pressed the phone closer. Carrie was back in control, speaking softly. Condor listened without moving away from the window. He answered, "That's too long… you said…"

Carrie spoke some more.

Condor suddenly felt that weakness in his knees, like when he did something wrong. Like when he was in trouble. Grandmother Ruthie had been in the hospital for a week and Condor hadn't gone to visit her. He was busy organizing the fund-raiser, he told himself. Truth was this: He didn't expect her to come home.

133

The doctors only gave her a couple days, said they would keep her comfortable. They didn't know what was wrong, but she was old and sometimes that was all the reason you needed. But then she came out of it. The doctors couldn't explain it, called it a miracle recovery. The idiots didn't even know what was wrong with her, so how would they fix her? Condor knew what was wrong, and he knew she shouldn't have recovered. That was the real miracle.

The gates began to open. The front end of the Bentley eased onto the entry drive. He clutched the drapes. His lips fluttered against the phone, but nothing came out.

"Just hurry," he blurted.

Condor looked in the polished mirror next to the front doors. His skin looked like cream cheese. He wiped his forehead and took a deep breath. His sister's voice buzzed from the phone.

"I can…" He swallowed. *I can't do this.*

He cleared his throat and lifted his chin, like his father taught him. Condor pointed his chin at his reflection and looked down his nose. He puffed his chest out.

"I can do this."

He hung up before Carrie told him to say it again and stared at the reflection. His nostrils flared. He willed the weakness to leave his knees. Told the reflection, out loud, that he was a Current. That was that.

He looked out the window as the car circled around the fountain and stopped in front of the doors. No one got out. Condor cupped his hand in front of his mouth and huffed a couple times. He dug a roll of breath mints out of his pocket and chewed three of them like cereal. He gave his breath another test, peeking out the window. The driver's door cracked open.

Condor threw open the front doors. The trunk was already open. The driver whipped a wheelchair out like it was made of paper and snapped it open before reaching for the back door. Condor assumed it was the driver, but it was no one he knew.

"Grandmother!" Condor met her at the bottom step. "It does my heart good to see you so well. We've all been worried sick."

He bent over and kissed her cheek. It was soft like a spent tissue and smelled damp. Grandmother Ruthie looked straight ahead with her lips tightly clamped. Condor clasped his hands to his chest, feeling the cold weakness rush to his knees.

She knows I didn't visit. She knows.

The driver looked like a boy, his skin dark and smooth. Barely out of high school. He held out his hand. "You must be from the hospital. My name is Condor."

The idiot driver shook his hand but didn't even look at him. Condor looked stunned. The driver spun the wheelchair and moved Grandmother Ruthie up the steps. She didn't jostle in the seat, as if the driver lifted the chair with the eighty-five-pound old woman.

"We need a ramp, Condor," Grandmother Ruthie said. "See to it. Tastefully."

And the front doors closed. Condor was on the steps alone.

5 7

---

arrie Current placed the phone on a small table. She sipped the last of her rejuvenation drink and leaned against the balcony railing. She was still sweating. Her personal trainer worked her to exhaustion, holding various yoga poses while the surf washed around their ankles and predawn temperatures dimpled her bronze skin. Endorphins were still tingling beneath her scalp, but they were losing the battle with the fury burning in her chest.

If she wasn't looking at one of the most scenic beaches on the planet, she would've thrown the phone, the cup, and the table into the trees below. But just that moment, the sun had crested the horizon and lit the ocean with fiery lines. There was nothing between her and the ocean but palms and a pristine beach.

My beach.

This thought calmed her. Having things brought her peace. She didn't believe in borrowing, that was for librarians. If Carrie liked it, she made it hers. Sharing was not a virtue. This piece of paradise was hers, she reminded herself. She needed that thought right at that moment. Because things had suddenly gotten so fucked.

Her family always had the good grace of a timely death. All of them, except dear old grandmother. The old hag clung to life like a barnacle. Death couldn't scrape her off with a shovel. Carrie's plan to assist Death wasn't elaborate, just a trace of toxin slipped into her morning tea that would give the appearance of death by natural causes. But Connie fucked that up, too.

She could still hear her brother's voice whining. He had the spine of an earthworm. She should've spiked his drink first and killed that perverted asshole. She ground her teeth, fighting the urge to fling the phone Frisbee-style.

Carrie refused to call him Condor. It implied strength and aggression. Domination from above. Her shithead father thought he could make his son a man with a powerful name, but it didn't work that way. Dogshit was dogshit, no matter what you called it.

Now she'd have to fly all the way back to Charleston to clean up the mess. She'd give it a few days. If she went back now, if she saw Connie's face too soon, she'd put a knee square in it. And that would do no good. No, she'd cool off before returning. By then, she'd be ready to bend over and kiss Grandmother's eighty-five-year-old lips that felt like two slugs fighting over fake teeth. Carrie swished the last of her drink like mouthwash.

A breeze shook the palms. Carrie closed her eyes and sucked the ocean air through her nostrils. She imagined a beach unbroken by footprints, untainted by tourists. Nothing but smooth sand and rolling surf. A place that was hers.

Her heartbeat slowed.

Another breath and the endorphins oozed down her neck. She counted her breaths until the peaceful feeling was in her toes. Seagulls called distantly. She stayed in the darkness behind her eyelids, resting in the peace of a million-dollar cabana on a tropical island.

Bare feet padded up behind her. She felt the touch of callused fingers, still damp from the shower, stroke her bare back. She moaned slightly. He would stop if she didn't acknowledge his touch. He knew better.

The hands kneaded her shoulders. She dropped her head while the knuckles traced down her trapezius. Over and over, they worked rhythmically through the tension building in her back. Her sweat lubricated the long, slow strokes until the hands slipped below her waist and slid her panties down.

And then he took her from behind with the same firmness, slow and rhythmic.

Carrie's belly filled with another fury, one of desire. She could feel the ridges of his abdomen on her back as he leaned over. He bundled her blonde hair in his hand and pulled it to the side. His breath raised gooseflesh on her neck.

"Don't kiss me," she said. "Just fuck."

She didn't want to think of slugs.

58

When the car stopped in front of her house, the driver sat quietly. Ruthie wondered what he was doing, but she felt such peace she didn't want to spoil it. And then her grandson opened the door with that enormous grin. Tension gripped her forehead.

The driver moved swiftly from behind the steering wheel. She took his outstretched hand. Muscles moved beneath his forearm like thick ropes. His eyes were downcast, shadows hiding them beneath his brows. He was younger than she suspected, but it did not matter. He was certainly capable.

She endured a kiss from Condor that smelled of mint and cigarettes. She deplored the latter. What else had he done? Then he stood there, useless. In her foggy memory of the events before she went to the hospital, she recalled him standing there much the same as the paramedics lifted her into the ambulance. *I don't know what's wrong with her,* he was saying. But his voice rose as he said it, which meant he did know.

The best schools in Charleston ruined him, just like his father. They had the best teachers, but nothing undermined a person like a sense of entitlement.

How did it all go wrong?

Ruthie's father was a model citizen. A man's man. A wonderful human being that made a fortune as an investor and a human rights lawyer. But he had given birth to a litter of squabbling rats. Ruthie never excluded herself from the bunch. She knew what she was, but she conducted herself with dignity. Perhaps that was not enough to tip the scales of karma in her favor for her own deplorable behavior, but it was all she could do. Her son was proof that the worst in her genetics had been passed down. Her son never stood a chance, with a mother like her and a father that fornicated like a dog, fought like a badger and cheated like a thief. Rats, all of them.

Ruthie was guided up the steps by her driver. It occurred to her there was no ramp, regardless of the fact she was gliding toward the door. Condor was at the bottom step, shading his eyes from the sun. She told him to build a ramp. That would give him something to do.

Ruthie entered the cool interior of her home. She was asleep before her driver had wheeled her to her bed.

Drayton snipped another flower from a rosebush. A thorn pierced his finger, but blood did not arise, the wound simply closed. He replaced the pruners on his belt and tucked the stem into a wicker basket with black-eyed Susans and stalks of sea oats. Later, he would arrange them in a vase near the back doors.

It had been a week since he brought Ms. Ruth home from the hospital. In that time, he had gone from chauffeur to gardener without question. The staff was too busy catering to Ms. Ruth to be bothered by the young man manicuring the courtyard, especially since Ms. Ruth valued her garden above all else. If curiosity arose, Drayton simply willed their interest away from him.

Ms. Ruth was wheeled out to the second story veranda every morning of the week, with a blanket over her lap. Her trusted chambermaid would be by her side. They would watch Drayton tend to the weeds, to the careful trimming of the roses and shaping of the boxwoods. She would come out again after lunch, this time with her grandson standing a few steps behind her. He stood there like a good boy and stared, too. His curiosity was greatest of all. Like the others, he did nothing with it.

It was the afternoon, the teeth of the summer sun. Sweat did not break upon Drayton's brow. His shirt did not moisten in the heat. His skin absorbed the sun's rays but never warmed. His muscles could be seen writhing beneath his shirt but never tired. His movements were smooth and fluid, like a gardener moving in a ballet. The sound of the ocean was his orchestra.

Drayton took the basket to a toolshed beneath a mossy grove of oaks and put the flowers in water. When he returned to the courtyard, Ms. Ruth had gone inside for her afternoon nap. Her grandson remained, staring. Drayton collected the spent flowers in a wheelbarrow.

Ms. Ruth was dying in the hospital when Drayton came upon her. He had not come to the hospital for her. He was there for other reasons. He walked quietly unnoticed throughout the floors, sensing the waning lives all around him. He chose his victims carefully. While he did not care to call them victims, it was apt. Drayton absorbed their life essence as they passed from the physical world. It was not murder any more than if he pushed a person that was already falling from a cliff. The fall was inevitable, and in the moments before that person hit the rocks, Drayton drew out their life, their savory essence. It filled him. Fed him.

The measure of a man is what he does with power. Drayton was alive when Socrates made that statement. That was a time when Drayton took essence remorselessly, ruthlessly. Drinking it from their salty blood draining from their necks and down his chin.

That was no longer Drayton's way.

So he had walked the hospital, sniffing the air like a connoisseur, seeking the distinctive essence that would satisfy his current hunger. If there were none to satisfy his taste, he would leave and come back another time. He was not greedy. He would eventually find something suitable. He always did.

Ms. Ruth was close to death when he passed into her room. The attending doctor was consulting a team of nurses, giving them instructions and advising them to notify next of kin. She wasn't going to make it through the evening. The doctor left the room without noticing the young man standing at the end of the bed, wearing ordinary clothes and boots. Smooth skin. Black skin. Both quite the opposite of the withered woman in the bed, mouth indignantly hanging open.

Drayton cocked his head. Her essence tanged the end of his tongue and hung thickly inside his nostrils. He only needed to draw it and there would be no more suffering. But Drayton sensed something beyond his need to take. Ms. Ruth had an unresolved life. Drayton couldn't say what that resolution was; he only felt its urgency. He was not an angel. He had lived as long as humans had existed and still did not know what he was. But he'd learned the subtleties of life and when a wrong needed to be made right.

Drayton filled Ms. Ruth with life. He blew what little essence he contained back into her waning body. The unidentified toxins that were killing her were neutralized. By morning, Ms. Ruth awoke to inform the hospital staff that she would return home. Drayton was waiting with her car.

He assumed a gardener's duties when he arrived at the house. Since there currently was not one on staff, he moved easily into the position. He would continue to care for the estate as Ms. Ruth recovered. He knew not what his duty was to her or how to aid her unresolved life. If his countless years of existence had taught him anything, it was to let life unfold.

Drayton took the bucket filled with dead flowers down a sandy path between the dunes. He stopped on the hard-packed sand, where the foamy waves gently glided landward before receding. Drayton emptied them into the water. The dead petals spread out, carried out to deeper water. Drifting in, then out. The undercurrent beneath the surface was strong and unseen.

Drayton returned to the garden.

60

"Condor." Grandmother Ruthie raised her hand, fingers curled like hooks.

That was Condor's signal to come closer. He stepped away from the balcony door and stooped by her side, his ear turned toward her lips. Grandmother Ruthie made no effort to come closer, not even turning her head. She had the transfixed look on her face, staring ahead, eyes fixed on the gardener. Every day like this, come to the balcony and watch him rake, watch him clip goddamn flowers.

Condor wondered where he went at night. He asked some of the help, but they thought he was nuts. *Gardener?* Even the nurse, the homely Guatemalan lady that was by Grandmother Ruthie's side every day, didn't seem to know what he was talking about. Like she had fucking amnesia.

Didn't matter. Why would Condor give a fuck? He shook the kid's hand when he met him that first day he pulled up in the car, and it was the strangest feeling. It was firm and normal, but cold, like shock waves driving through his arm, and Condor felt something quiver at the back of his head and suddenly there was a howling emptiness inside. He couldn't let go fast enough. Let the crazy asshole sleep in the trees, he couldn't care less.

Condor's back ached while he waited for Grandmother Ruthie to say something, anything. *I'm waiting here, old lady!*

He glanced at the nurse and she was staring back. Condor quickly looked away. A little too quickly. Carrie called a few days back and asked if he could access her food again. Condor hung up on her. She was batshit, saying that out loud and on a phone! Why not just put it on a billboard? *I POISONED MY GRANDMOTHER.*

Dumb bitch called back, but Condor didn't answer. She called again and he turned his phone off. He'd pay for that tomorrow when she got home, but it was worth it. She made all the trouble, she could clean it up. When he told her about the driver/gardener kid, she didn't speak for a whole minute. Condor let the phone lay silent in his hand. She was thinking. He stumped her, for once. She didn't know what to do.

Good. That was how Condor's whole life felt. He just went from one cigarette to the next. One party to another. Sometimes he felt like a child just waiting for the next Christmas. If the unexamined life was a waste, Condor knew he was more useless than a dog tick. But at least he wasn't thinking up the shit Carrie was. She was going to burn in fires a lot hotter than Condor when this was all over with.

"Prepare my bed," Grandmother Ruthie whispered. "Now."

"Yes, ma'am."

She never looked at him. Just dropped her hand like she was done with him.

Condor closed the door behind him and leaned against it, relieved to feel the air-conditioning. The cold rushed over him and into his knees; then he realized that wasn't relief. *Fear.*

He stepped quickly. He'd prepare Grandmother's bed, then smoke half a dozen cigarettes.

"Just who the fuck are you?"

She had been secretly watching Drayton from the house since she'd arrived earlier that morning. He had pulled weeds in the concrete planters that ran the length of the pool. Crabgrass had overrun the flowers, drooping down to the paver deck with nodding seed heads. The longer the weeds became, the more seeds they produced. The planters were a network of scratchy stems.

He was nearly finished with weeding by mid-afternoon when Carrie finally appeared poolside to ask him just who he was. Until then, no one even noticed. If Drayton willed it, Carrie wouldn't have noticed him, either. But she was one of the reasons he had come into their lives.

She anchored her hands on her hips, her sculpted arms tense. Ample breasts bulged in the bikini top. Her glare was as hot as the summer heat. Drayton looked back and smiled briefly, long enough to acknowledge her. As if to say hello and thank you. Then he went back to sweeping soil into a pile.

The tension in Carrie's arms radiated through her neck and across her cheeks, tugging at the corners of her mouth. She bit back the next string of curse words that threatened to spew out. Instead, she squatted next to the pool and cupped water onto her bare arms to cool them. She looked at her reflection. When calm returned, she stood.

Drayton had moved to the ground below the pool that sloped away from the house toward the dunes. Carrie remained on the pool deck, looking down.

"You don't exist," she said. "I ran your picture through a global face-recognition database and you're not there. Now, that might just mean you're a nobody, so I ran your fingerprints, too. So far, you don't exist, my gardening friend. So if you don't mind, I'd like to know what you're doing here."

He paused and looked up. "Drayton. My name is Drayton."

The sun was behind Carrie's head, casting a shadow over him. But he didn't squint in the sunlight. Just a slight smile. His eyes were engorged with blackness. The pupils enlarged. Deep. She had the sudden sensation of falling into them, like water swirling into a drain hole. Her insides swirled, then opened. She felt a chasm beneath. A hole. A mine shaft that bored deep down into her beingness that was bottomless. She felt like clawing her way back to hard ground. She felt like crying.

And then he looked away, back to the bag of weeds.

There were tears on the rims of her eyes. Emptiness still quivered at the bottom of her gut. She refused to wipe her eyes. Instead, she set her jaw. Her stomach hardened, her body taut. And like she'd done many times when the situation needed her to be an arrow, she launched herself at her target.

"Don't fuck with me, *boy*. You get your belongings together and be on the bricks in the next ten minutes. If I look out the window and see you planting pansies when your time is up, I will have your arms twisted off your shoulders and rammed up your black ass."

Drayton placed the last of the pulled weeds into the bag. He looked away from Carrie, out toward the dunes. A breeze washed through the sea oats and over him. He closed his eyes, letting the ocean air pass through him.

"Play stupid. See what that gets you," she said.

When a smile touched his lips again, she felt her emotions pulling her down the steps. She was helpless to indulge the guttural hunger that growled in her chest. She stepped in front of him, but he refused to open his eyes. She hoped he would open them again, a part of her hungry for the fall she experienced only moments before, even though it was frightening, it was terrifying. She wanted it. There was something real inside the hole.

But Drayton did not open his eyes. He only drew air through his nostrils. His skin was precious. Smooth. Only when she felt the coolness of his cheeks did she realize that she had clamped her hand over his jaw. The impossible cold radiated through her palm, tingling in her groin. Her nipples suddenly hardened.

"You fuck." Her lips moistened. She fought the urge to bite his face. Her nails dug into the softness of his cheeks. She wanted to crush him. Tear him. Kiss him. Put him inside her.

She trembled. She was drowning in desire; she couldn't understand it. She needed him to be gone. He was beautiful. And he threatened everything she fought to gain. If he stayed, she would disappear.

"Get..." There was a grinding noise in her ears. "Out."

She pulled his face closer. She could smell her own perspiration. It was animal rage. It was primal lust. It was consuming her.

And when he opened his eyes, her desire turned to a raging fire. There was blankness. There was whiteness. There was nothing but emptiness. There was nothing.

She was nothing.

She was nothing.

You're nothing. She heard her father say. *You're nothing,* he said. He was buckling his belt, looking down at her. She was on the floor. He was looking down at her, buckling his belt. Looking down because she was nothing.

She meant nothing.

She didn't matter.

And she was falling. She was falling.

Falling.

Into nothingness.

And its ache had no end.

"That will be enough, Carrie Suzanne."

Carrie was staring at Drayton's closed eyes, both hands locked onto his face. Her fingernails dented his skin.

"Carrie Suzanne?"

Carrie looked over her shoulder. Grandmother Ruthie was poolside, sitting in her wheelchair. The Guatemalan chambermaid was behind her. Carrie's lips fluttered. An unintelligible sound escaped. Grandmother Ruthie excused her with a nod.

Carrie's legs were weak, but she stepped slowly up the steps toward the house.

Grandmother Ruthie followed.

Carrie rushed to the bathroom and locked the door. She pressed a towel against her face to soak the tears, but she wouldn't let a cry escape. She swallowed that shit down. Forced it back into a dark place. She didn't know what happened. Was she remembering something? Was that a hallucination?

She dropped the towel only when she had control again. The weakness was still there, but she was in control.

She walked down the hall. Her pace was slow and sure, not betraying her agitation. She found Connie in the kitchen. She slammed the refrigerator door on him. He looked up, angry, but quickly softened.

"You're nothing without me, Connie," she said. She jabbed her finger at his face. "*Nothing.*"

She left him standing there. And she felt strong again. She was back. Because you don't fuck with Carrie.

She promptly went to her bedroom and buried a vibrator between her legs.

63

A week passed.

Drayton was escorted to the third floor. He followed the chambermaid down a long hallway that ended with double doors. He waited while she went inside and announced his arrival. Only when she returned to swing the doors open wide did he advance.

"Madam would like to know if you'd prefer something to drink?"

"Tea would be nice," Drayton answered. "Thank you."

"Sweetened?"

"That won't be necessary. Earl Grey, if you have it. Steeped three and a half minutes."

The maid nodded. Drayton thanked her again.

The room was circular with a pitched ceiling that met at a point in the center, just above a round table. The walls were glass, giving an observer a nearly 360-degree view of the ocean and the beach in both directions.

Ms. Ruth was on the far side. She was parked with her back to Drayton, facing the sharp line of the horizon. There was a small window in front of her that looked custom made, large enough to allow the breeze to rustle her hair and the room to smell wide open.

Drayton waited patiently until the chambermaid arrived with a cup of tea. She pulled the chair from the table and gestured for him to sit. Drayton did so and crossed his legs. He lifted the cup and inhaled the astringent aroma of Earl Grey.

"When I was a child," Ms. Ruth said, "I would dream of flying. I would simply raise my arms and I would float off the ground, over the ocean. It was such a blissful experience of freedom, unfettered by our human condition, this heavy body cursed to plod the ground from beginning to end. But I stopped having that dream when I was still very young. I have rarely dreamed since, until recently.

"I dreamed again that I was flying. I was nowhere in particular, but I was experiencing freedom again, soaring through a grayness towards home, I believe. I was unfettered, once again. Until I felt you."

She turned the wheelchair around.

"I suddenly felt too heavy to fly anymore, young man. And I awoke in the hospital, in this fettered body. And you were there."

Ms. Ruth eased up to the table and crossed her hands on her lap. She gestured to Drayton and he sipped from the cup. She smiled. "What is your name?"

"Drayton, ma'am."

"I see," she said, nodding.

The stillness was broken by the staff opening the doors and wheeling in a cart. While they arranged their plates with pasta salad, pickled shrimp and crackers, Ms. Ruth only watched Drayton. He sipped again.

When they left, she took a bite and wiped her mouth, chewing slowly.

"Why are you here, Mr. Drayton?"

Drayton simply nodded, as if she already knew the answer.

"I see," she said mildly. "Are you an angel? A demon? A dream thief?"

"I am none of those. Simply here."

She watched him with her lips slightly agape. Her studied gaze took in his expression, her mind piecing together his posture. His energy. Ms. Ruth was a good people reader. She felt like she simply absorbed subtleties of the whole package, but she was missing entirely on the young man seated properly at her table, holding a saucer in one hand while waving the cup beneath his nose with the other.

"I was raised Catholic, you see." She took another bite and sat back. "We Catholics don't like mysteries. We like to know why we're here and where we're going. Heaven, hell, or whatever is beyond, we like to plan for that journey, you see. Tell me, Drayton, what is beyond our reach? Where do we go after this life?"

An imperceptible shake of his head. "I don't know."

"You're just living in the here and now, is that what you're telling me? How very Zen of you. It doesn't answer the question."

"Perhaps it cannot be answered."

"Perhaps."

Ms. Ruth took a few more bites. Drayton's food remained untouched. Only the clinking sounds of silverware and the rhythmic rush of the ocean were in the room.

"Do you know who I am?" she asked.

Drayton nodded. He knew everything about her. While Ms. Ruth felt like she could learn about a person by absorbing their actions, Drayton actually absorbed a person's mind: their thoughts and emotions, their memories. He knew more about Ms. Ruth than she would ever remember about herself, and he knew it the instant he sensed her in the hospital.

Ms. Ruth suddenly seemed to understand this by observing his expression. She was a good people reader. "I see."

She dropped her napkin on her plate and wheeled back over to her window.

"You know I'm not a good person, Mr. Drayton. I know this, and I know that if there is a hell, then I am surely going there. Perhaps you're the devil and I'm already there."

She didn't look at Drayton when she said this.

"I hope you understand that change—real change—is difficult. Our lives are like undercurrents that we cannot change, we can only drift along if we are to survive. I am no different than every other human being, having lived the tainted hand I've been dealt. And it's clear I've condemned my grandchildren to the same miserable fate. And cursed the world with them, as well."

"Free will, then," Drayton said, "does not exist?"

"Free will?" She chuckled, whimsically plucking at the window. "It's a dream, Mr. Drayton. We're victims of our thoughts, our genes, DNA, the malfunctions given to us by our parents and environment. Free will, Mr. Drayton, is a concept. It does not exist."

"And who is saying that?"

"I am."

"And who are you? Your thoughts?"

She looked over at him. A moment of clarity lightened the tension in her forehead. Perhaps she was something other than her thoughts. Something more substantial. More present. They watched each other for a long time.

"Do you know what a sport is, Mr. Drayton?" Ms. Ruth closed the window. "Come now, if you're going to play the gardener, you must know what a sport is."

"It is a branch on a tree that is genetically different than all the rest."

"Quite correct. If it exhibits good qualities, such as color or texture, it is propagated. But if the sport has exceptionally poor qualities, it will threaten to overcome the rest of the tree. Am I correct?"

Drayton nodded.

"And how to remedy such a situation as a vicious sport?"

Drayton set his cup and saucer on the table and placed his hands on his lap. Thoughtfully, he said, "The sport is pruned from the tree."

Ms. Ruth smiled. "I see."

The room was suddenly stagnant.

"You may continue to act as my gardener as long as you like, Mr. Drayton. On one condition."

The doors opened. The chambermaid was waiting. Ms. Ruth wheeled her chair over to her and turned around to face Drayton.

"Promise you will not save me again."

Drayton nodded. The doors closed.

He enjoyed the remainder of his tea.

6 4

____

*C*ondor had been smoking a lot more than usual. In the month since Grandmother Ruthie came home, he'd gone through three cartons.

That wouldn't be so unusual, but he'd put those cigarettes away without going outside. When Grandmother Ruthie wasn't napping, she was sitting on the veranda, watching Drayton do his thing in the garden. Occasionally, she'd take a meeting with the lawyers in his father's office, the one with the giant oak desk and the fake oil painting of Robert Current watching over it. But other than that it was sleep and watch, sleep and watch. She was obsessed to the point she didn't notice Condor wasn't there anymore.

He couldn't stand the sight of Drayton without shaking. He saw him clear out on the dunes, carrying the dead flowers out to the ocean, and Condor spilled his drink like a goddamn epileptic.

He didn't like the way that felt, so he spent most days in his room. To be more exact, in his closet.

He had stopped going to parties, stopped returning calls and ignored texts. He kept the phone off in case his sister called. Carrie had been gone for weeks, ever since she went out to confront Drayton. She got a little taste of what Condor got, and she didn't like it,

155

either. Maybe she got the shakes, too, so she left, the bitch. All Condor could do was hide in his closet, the safest place on earth.

There, in his closet, he'd wrap himself in a sheet and settle into the darkest corner. He had a little table for an ashtray and smokes. The clothes smelled like burning leaves, so he punched a hole in the door and set up a little fan to get some ventilation. When he got bored, he'd surf porn on his iPad. Sometimes he'd find a good scene, prop it on his bed and peek at it through the hole in the closet door. Then promptly fall asleep.

At night, he'd creep to the kitchen when the staff was away. He'd wander through the house, pretending Grandmother was dead and it was all his. Until he looked out and, by the light of the moon, saw a shadow moving in the garden. He couldn't make out the details, but when the shakes hit him, he knew who it was.

He took all the food he could carry to his closet, vowing not to prowl again.

65

The StairMaster was spotted with sweat dripping from Carrie's nose, chin and elbows. Her stomach pumped in and out, heaving beneath her ribs. Minutes earlier, she forced herself to drink a can of Ensure to keep up calorie intake. She hadn't eaten solid food in days. Not by choice. She just couldn't keep it down. Everything tasted spoiled.

She couldn't stop moving, either.

Had to keep the furnace burning. Had to keep the fires stoked, to incinerate the thoughts, the feelings, the things lingering inside her. She was sure she'd scare the kid in the garden, make him shit himself in fear. He was just a kid. But whatever the fuck happened in those five, ten, twenty minutes, she was trying to forget. It turned her inside out.

You're nothing.

All her life, her personality sat firmly on a foundation forged from a long line of successful Currents. They weren't all millionaires by accident. It took fortitude, will, and strength to be good. It took a foundation of bedrock to get what they wanted. And, goddamnit, Carrie wasn't about to let the cracks in that bedrock get any deeper. She'd power through it. She'd reset. She'd come back burying fists and knocking skulls, if that was what it took. She'd mowed over anything or anybody that ever got in the way. This was no different.

He was just a kid.

Nothing.

She needed a little time. Needed to get back on track. Her real estate deal in Italy was coming together, and she could focus on that for a few weeks. A little victory was what she needed. She would fly out to finish the deal. She'd planned on getting out of the country, forget about things, and return refreshed and renewed. Return the same old Carrie and deal with Grandmother. That was before the family lawyer called that morning: Your grandmother just fired me. Out of the blue, she dismissed his services after thirty years. Now Carrie would have to go back and sort that out before Italy.

Nothing.

She pumped the steps harder. She didn't like the cold swell in her stomach. The tang of acid in her throat. Sweat streamed from her elbows. Hot air streamed from her nose.

She squeezed the spongy handle grips. Dipped her head. Dug in.

Someone tapped her arm. Said something. She pushed harder.

Nothing.

The first convulsion hit her in the gut. A fountain of creamy vomit splattered the machine's panel. Her knees buckled. She hit her head on the way down when the second convulsion hit. She covered her mouth but sprayed more liquid vomit between her fingers.

She lay on the floor, the StairMaster dripping. People gathered.

She stumbled out of the room, jerking away from help. Running from the thought that vibrated through her like a tremor.

Belt buckle.

6 6

Drayton placed the shovel on the shed wall and latched the door. He stood in the shade. The beds had been prepared, the flowers replanted, the roses blooming and the irrigation repaired. Birds had returned to the neglected houses. He remained still, watching the dragonflies hover over the lily pads in the pond, seeking a meal. It had been months since Drayton had fed, as well. He was not pained, but he was beginning to ache.

He had not seen Condor or Carrie since he'd shared lunch with Ms. Ruth. Nor had he spoken with Ms. Ruth. Instead, he tended to the garden, letting life unfold as it needed.

Soon, he would be needed.

The chambermaid exited the house. She wandered through the formal garden, the paths lined with boxwoods, past the fountain and toward the shed.

"Madam is ready for you to join her."

"Thank you, Melanie." Drayton bowed. "You've been very kind."

Melanie the chambermaid could not help but smile.

6 7

Ms. Ruth was waiting on the veranda that overlooked the gardens.

There was a small table and chair next to her. A cup of tea.

Drayton sat and crossed his legs. He took the cup and saucer. Together, they watched an egret soar over the sand dunes. The sun was setting behind them, casting the house's long shadow across the yard and over the pool.

"Tell me about your life, Drayton."

Her hands held each other on her lap, shaking. She looked at them and could not stop them. So she looked back to the garden, the shadows a bit longer.

"The time of my birth is too far back for even my memory," he said thoughtfully.

"Perhaps we were not born."

Drayton had considered this before. He had no memories of growing up, only the vague memories of hunger and strength. Of anger, power, and death. He did not just appear on this planet. No, he felt certain he was born.

"I believe, at one time, I was human. Something happened." Now he looked at his hands. "And now I am this."

160

"What is that?"

He remained silent. Drayton did not know the answer.

"I see." Ms. Ruth wrung her hands.

"My earliest memories are primal. Thirst, satisfaction and pain. I slept in wooded areas, drank from streams and fed on the blood of deer and elk."

He was stronger than all the animals in the forest. He was faster. Smarter. In the beginning, his skin was light and he ran amongst the animals, feeding on the smaller and weaker ones, like rabbit and fox. But as he grew stronger, the animals began to fear him, and he took down larger prey, choking them with his bare hands, tearing out their eyes with his nails, biting open their throats.

Then came the settlers. They cut down trees and built their houses. Their children played in the woods and the men hunted animals and the women stayed at the homes. Drayton felt the pang of curiosity, seeing creatures shaped like him. Their skin was much more fair, since his had darkened with time. He stalked them at night, watched them during the day. He imitated the sounds they made until they became words.

He eventually began to hunt them.

"But you are no longer this beast?"

"I am not."

Ms. Ruth studied the darkening sky. Drayton sipped his tea. She was looking at her twisting hands when she said, "Will I have that opportunity? When I die, will I have the chance to become something more than a beast?"

Drayton did not answer. He had the luxury of hundreds of years to learn compassion. He learned the cycle of suffering that resulted from carnal desires. He understood his being, his mind and heart, understood the interconnected nature of the universe. Perhaps it took such a long life to achieve such a state of ordinary enlightenment. A luxury humans did not have.

"What will become of me when I die?" she asked.

"Who are you?"

She chuckled. Drayton sensed the letting go inside her. The answer to that question was in the question itself. "I see," she said.

They remained quiet until night had completely fallen. There was the song of frogs. The night breeze. The moon illuminated the ground. Drayton's tea was long since cold when Melanie came for Ms. Ruth.

"I will require an escort tomorrow evening," she said. "You will meet me on the sand dunes when the sun has set. After all, that is why you are here. Is it not?"

"It would be an honor." Drayton bowed.

Melanie had no idea what they were talking about.

6 8

---

*C*arrie chased the little pill with water. Her trainer gave her the antidepressants after the gym episode. She always refused pills. She liked control. She didn't want to rely on pharmaceuticals to make her feel herself. But Carrie was a realist. She was not in control. The puke-scented Stairmaster was proof.

Her head was a little buzzy, but she was herself. And she liked that. The pill was helping her get back to who she really was, helping her find herself. She'd put off the lawyer fiasco long enough, but now she was ready. Besides, she was leaving for Italy in a few days and she needed to get a handle on the family finances. She had a friend that knew how to wrestle control from older family members when it came to important decisions concerning the estate. Especially ones that would affect her.

She got in the car, ignoring the fear swirling in her belly, clamping her chest.

That's just the pill. Not me.

Condor didn't hear Carrie's car stop in front of the house. He didn't see the headlights flash across the windows or hear the door slam. He was buried deep in his closet, wrapped tightly in a sheet beneath the glow of an iPad.

"Mmmmmmmmmmmmommmm," he hummed to himself. "Mmmmmmy…"

70

Drayton waited atop the sand dune, the sea oats brushing against his legs.

He was breathing, his mind empty. His breath empty.

There was the water. The sand.

Night had come.

And then there were the soft sounds of footsteps behind him. Ms. Ruth was holding her white dress bunched in her hands, her bare feet pushing through the sand. The wind blew the sheer fabric of her dress against her naked body beneath.

Drayton offered his hand and she took it.

"Thank you," she said.

And they journeyed to the beach, where the waves slid over their feet.

"What'd you mean she went for a walk?" Carrie's lips pulled over her teeth. "Do you know what time it is?"

"Madam insisted," Melanie said, shrinking.

"So you just let an eighty-five-year-old woman wander off on her own?"

"No, ma'am. She went with Mr. Drayton."

"You did what? ARE YOU FUCKING INSANE?"

Melanie stepped back. Carrie was grateful the chambermaid was out of reach. She needed to strangle something. She wanted the old woman to disappear, but on her terms. No telling what the gardener would do with her.

"Where's my dipshit brother?"

"His room." Melanie held her hands to her chest and sort of pointed in the direction of Condor's room.

"Jesus Christ." Carrie's footsteps thundered down the hall.

7 2

They walked about three hundred yards. Ms. Ruth stopped, her breath labored.

She was looking at a ship on the horizon, its lights flickering against a backdrop of night sky. Her mouth hung open, then smiled.

"My grandfather was a fisherman," she whispered. "He started with one boat, then had two. He eventually owned half a dozen. But he worked those boats to the day he died. If the sun was up, my grand-daddy was working."

She stepped toward the surf and let go of her dress. The water wicked up the fabric. Drayton walked with her, holding her hand. She squeezed back.

She looked down, reached into the water and pulled up a handful of sand, letting it slip between her fingers. "My daddy bought this land before it was a resort. He provided the best for us, Drayton. He wanted only the best for the world, you understand. He was an opti-mist. He believed in mankind, that we were better than animals."

The sand plopped into the water.

"We let him down, Drayton." Her eyes were wet.

They watched the ship disappear over the horizon. Ms. Ruth clung tightly to Drayton's hand. Her fingers were quivering.

"Grandmother!" Carrie threw open the back door and ran through the garden.

She stood on the sand dune and cupped her hands over her mouth.

"GRANDMOTHER!"

Clouds had moved over the moon. The water was as dark as the sky. Carrie couldn't see anything that resembled an old lady.

She ran back to the house, cursing along the way. She didn't bother brushing the sand from her feet as she stormed through the kitchen and down the hall. "Goddamnit, Connie!" she screamed. "GODDAMNIT!"

She ignored the ugly lump growing in her stomach, the sour taste in her throat. The haunted feel of the house. She ignored all that because she kept her sights trained on her pathetic, sniveling shit-turd brother. This was his fault. Why couldn't he be anything like a Current? Was the asshole adopted from a pot of retards, or did her parents win him at the circus?

"Connie." His door was locked. She knocked. "Connie, open the door. Open the door, Connie. I want to talk to you. Did you know your grandmother went out for a midnight stroll? Huh? Did you know she's been talking to lawyers ABOUT THE FUCKING WILL, YOU BRAINLESS FUCKHOLE!"

She jerked at the doorknob. She pounded on the door, but nothing. She went down to Daddy's office and pulled an ivory bookend off the shelf. It took three swings to knock the doorknob off and a layer of skin from her knuckles.

She kicked the door open. The radio played softly, but the room was empty. Clothes were strewn over the bed and heaped in piles. "Shit!" She chucked the bookend at the radio. She started to leave, but stopped when she heard the murmuring. A fan was blowing inside the closet.

"Connie?"

That was when she noticed the hole in the closet door and the blue glow inside. She stopped on the other side of the door and listened. There was a rhythmic chant. She stepped closer, the door slightly ajar. The stench of smoke made her jerk back. She looked again. An iPad screen illuminated the back corner. Connie was snuggled up, humming.

"Mmmmmmommmmmmommma..."

Carrie threw the door open, light spilling inside. Connie's eyes went wide, but he didn't have a chance to defend himself. Carrie grabbed a handful of hair and dragged him from the closet. His pants were around his knees. The iPad fell off its pedestal and was kicked onto the bedroom floor, the erotic scenes in full detail. Carrie hardly noticed. She dropped a fist into Connie's nose and felt the crack of cartilage beneath her skinned knuckles. She brought her knee into his groin and heard him choke. And each time she swung, his belt buckle jingled around his knees.

You're nothing.

She punched his chest when he covered his face.

Jingle.

She cracked his left orbital when he covered his chest.

"Fuck you, you son of a bitch. Fuck you. FUCK YOU!"

It kept going. And going.

Until she heard Connie's sobs. He was crying through bloody fingers.

Nothing.

She stood up, looking at the blood on her hands. Blood on the floor. She didn't see her brother.

She started down the hall for the office.

74

The sand wrapped around Ruth's ankles as the undercurrent washed toward the ocean, gently pulling her with it. The waves gently lapped against her stomach now. The water was warm. She was cold inside.

Drayton held her hand. He did not move, only supported her efforts.

Ruth knew she had died long before this day. Long before Drayton pulled her from the hospital. She was never quite interested in the living. All her life, she was always getting and having this and that, maybe it was property or power, or the delicious emotion of victory or the touch of a stranger. She had the money to satisfy every desire.

But it meant nothing. Worse, she had a gnawing sensation inside ever since Drayton brought her back. It was the emptiness of a wasted life. She would leave this world no better than she entered it. She hurt people, she took from them. Worst of all, she gave the world her grandchildren that would continue sucking on the world's tit.

The end was near. And nothing in the world could stop it.

She drew closer and put her arms around Drayton's neck. In one sweeping motion, he cradled her so that she was floating on the water. He began to walk deeper. She closed her eyes.

Condor was unconscious on his bedroom floor.

The iPad continued the erotic streaming, flashing against his cheeks, illuminating the sheen of sweat and blood. His eyes were partly open, but he didn't see the action. He had escaped to a dreamy world that was numb and sweet. Far away from the ache of his life. Not the physical pain, so much. More the sinking weight that seemed to fill his chest, the block of emotional ice, a frozen chunk of self-hate and loathing and fear.

In the dream world, he was a baby. His mother had him cradled in her arms, her breast exposed. Condor fumbled the nipple into his mouth and felt the warmth of his mother's love gush down his throat. Fill his belly.

He belonged in this world with the nipple. That was where he wanted to be. He wanted to stay in that baby world. He didn't want to grow up. Didn't want to be an adult. He wanted someone to take care of him, change his diapers and make the bad feelings go away.

But all dreams end, even when you've been knocked unconscious. He awoke to screaming pain knifing through his groin. Fiery throbs in his nose. He tried not to move, but the pain was not going to leave.

It would be like this the rest of his life. He would never get to be a baby again.

With great agony, he rolled on his side, paused to catch his breath, then got to his knees. He crawled to the nightstand by the bed, opened the bottom drawer, and retrieved a brown bottle.

*C*arrie bent at the knees, lifting her father's oak desk. The drawers slid open and all the shit fell on the floor. She dumped it with a crash, then began pulling all the books off all the shelves, ripping out pages and throwing trophies and pictures at the wall, through the window.

The fuck. Her father, the fuck.

Belt buckle.

She craved to put her hands around his neck. To put an elbow into his jaw. To open his veins, to suck out his life. She wanted that fuck dead, dead, dead. She wanted to be the one to do it. And every knick-knack that had been carefully in place in his office, the space he did his business, preserved since the day he died so they could all pretend the fuck was still alive, everything she destroyed. She broke, crushed, flung until she was exhausted.

Heaving, she dropped to her knees.

Around, utter chaos.

And when she realized the weight of her father pressing down on her, the jingle of his belt buckle, the crushing words he spit, his curly chest hair in her face, the smell of sweat and musk and hate and power and… and… and…

Helpless.

When she still felt that, she dropped to the floor and buried her head beneath her arms. She would never escape the current.

The water had reached Drayton's chest when he let go of Ms. Ruth.

She floated for a moment, bobbing on the gentle waves. She was not smiling. She was not happy or pleased. The end was near. She accepted it with regret and sorrow.

Her breath leaked out.

Drayton watched her go beneath the waves, arms crossed over her chest.

As the undercurrent took her to her final resting place, Drayton felt her silky essence seep from her body and cool his tongue. Fill his body. What was once the heartbeat of Ms. Ruth Current was absorbed into Drayton.

He remained in the water, chest deep, until the clouds revealed the moon.

Thank you.

Condor took easy steps.

One of his testicles had ruptured. The right one was the size of a tangerine and rubbed against his leg. He stopped outside his father's office and braced himself. The pain was pulling at his stomach. He wiped his forehead with a handkerchief, staining it with sweat and blood.

He unscrewed a brown bottle, his hands shaking too violently to keep the lid from bouncing on the floor. The sobs from inside the office masked the noise. He doused the rag with the potent contents, feeling his head lighten as the fumes penetrated his sinuses. He put it behind his back, dragging his right leg behind him as he walked through the open door.

Books littered the floor, pages ripped from the bindings. Everything was tipped over, the window broken. His father's portrait was looking over the upturned desk, where Carrie was curled up with her head buried in her arms, her body convulsing with sobs.

Condor wasn't stealthy. He didn't need to be. He only needed to be quick. Only needed to be strong enough for just a few moments. And then it would all be over.

He fell on his sister, jabbing the soaked cloth over her mouth and nose.

Her sudden movement blinded him with pain.

He felt his hand fall, but she quickly slowed.

It took several minutes for him to regain enough strength to stand. Carrie was on her back, mouth open. Unconscious.

Condor scrambled through the wreckage and pulled the lamp from the rubble by the long, brown cord. He lay on his back, staring at the ceiling fan with two broken blades, and wrapped the cord around the knuckles of each hand.

6:00 a.m.

Melanie let herself in the front doors. She went to the kitchen and prepared Ms. Ruth's breakfast. Her thoughts were concerned with her late walk, hoping that she returned safely. She sliced the grapefruit and arranged the cup of black coffee with a small pitcher of cream. Her steps were short and swift as she carried the sterling silver tray down the middle of the hall, elbows out, back straight.

She had nearly passed the office of the late Mr. Current when she dropped everything. The cup shattered. The grapefruit rolled away. She held her hands to her mouth and screamed. That moment she would remember in great detail for the rest of her life.

The books. The overturned desk. The thin curtains waving over the hole in the window. And the bodies.

Ms. Carrie was on the floor, her skin pale. Eyes staring at the fan wobbling on the ceiling. The other was Mr. Condor dangling from a lamp cord tied from a hook on the wall. His face was blue and bloated. His tongue jutted between his rubbery lips like it had been squeezed out.

Melanie ran away and called the police. She stayed in the kitchen until they arrived.

Later, investigators would find a cryptic message scribbled moments before Condor unwrapped the cord from his sister's neck and fastened it around his own. It said: "We were camels that tried to pass through the eye."

No one bothered to make sense of it.

They later found his closet and assumed the note was simply the ramblings of a boy that lost his way.

The funeral was quiet.

Few people were present. Mainly business associates, some of the staff and some distant relatives.

Three coffins were lowered into the ground. One was empty, the body lost at sea.

Few words were said. Most faces were void of emotion, empty expressions of sadness. On a bright, sunny day, the graves were filled with soil while the preacher found good things to say about people he never met. The mourners left and would never come back to see the site again. One person remained, watching the workers disassemble the tent and finish filling the holes. Drayton remained, unnoticed. He read the inscription above the grave that contained the empty casket.

Ruth Current
1926 – 2011
All good things come to an end.
Other things must be cut out.

8 1

month passed when the last will and testament of Ruth Current was delivered.

The office was permanently closed, so the lawyers had convened in the dining room. They spread their papers out, then opened a laptop. The staff was present, as were distant family members. They trembled with excitement.

The lead lawyer explained the legality of Ruth Current's state of mind and the documents she prepared before she was murdered by the gardener, allegedly. Some of those present hoped to use some of the estate's funds to privately investigate the whereabouts of the gardener.

Soon, they were watching a lucid old woman speaking on the laptop. Ruth Current explained the reasons for why she was changing her last will and testament, confirming her sound frame of mind with testimony from a local psychologist. Much of her estate would be dedicated to aiding various charities that specialized in rehabilitation and mental health. A year's salary was given to each of her staff. The only variation was the bonus provided to Melanie for her exceptional dedication to a bitter old woman. She had earned it.

Anyone related to Ruth Current, through blood or marriage, received nothing.

When the meeting was finished, when hands were shook and papers signed and everyone dismissed, Melanie was left to clean up the remains. There were half-filled water bottles and empty Coke cans.

On her way out, sitting on a small table in the corner of the room, was an empty teacup.

*D*ecember was unusually warm.

So much so that Private Investigator Andy Warren was sweating. He stood on the sand dune, watching dolphins dip in and out of the water about a hundred yards off the coast. It wasn't often he got this far out to Kiawah Island. Most of his clients needed him to sit in a car for twenty-some hours outside a hotel. Investigating the murder of an old millionaire was like a vacation.

He knew his luck would run out, so he wasn't surprised when his partner, Peter Simmons, gave him the news.

"Case closed." Peter snapped the phone shut to illustrate his point.

"But we didn't get any evidence."

"Doesn't matter," Peter said. "The estate shut off funding for the investigation. Apparently, they're satisfied with natural cases or missing person or whatever happened to the old lady."

"Huh." Andy ran his palm over his slick forehead. His pits felt sticky. "They still think the kid did it?"

"The grandkid? That sick fuck?" Peter rammed his hands in his pockets. "He strangled his sister, so they pretty much think he offed the old lady, too."

"Someone said something about a gardener."

"Gardener?" Peter said. "There was no gardener, the chambermaid is still reeling. No one else ever heard of the gardener. Naw, it was the boy. He flipped."

"Yeah," Andy said. "Too bad."

"What, about the sister? She was as batshit as the rest of them. You see the testimonies? People were lined up around the corner to sue the estate on her account. You ask me, they're wasting their money on an investigation, it's clear. God did it."

Andy smirked. "God?"

"Yeah, God. Don't laugh. You saw what the kid wrote before he hung himself, that passage about camels going through the eye of a needle. He thought they were cursed with money."

"Well, curse me for a while. Please." Andy looked down the empty beach. "I wouldn't mind this a bit."

"The kid didn't believe the rich would go to heaven."

"So, he sent them all to hell, is that it?"

"Yeah, that's it. They were wasting their money on us, if you ask me. But, hey, money is money. I got kids to feed, too."

Andy took a bottle of water out of his pocket. He suddenly felt parched. It was the wind and sand and the afternoon heat. He needed a nap. Maybe he'd clock out early. There was nothing to do anyway.

The wind whistled into the side of his face, pelting him with sand. He didn't hear the footsteps from behind him. He was startled when a kid came walking around him. A black kid wearing a dark T-shirt and jeans and heavy boots.

"Gentlemen," the kid said.

"How are you?" Andy replied. A moment later, he said, "Kid, this is private property. What're you doing here?"

He turned around, his arm filled with dead roses. "I'm just cleaning up."

"No one lives here."

"I was Ms. Current's gardener."

The investigators looked at each other. "The old lady never had no gardener."

"Today is my last day." The kid looked at each of them. "I'll be on my way when I'm finished."

Beyond the kid, the garden appeared to be overgrown. Andy didn't think much about the kid claiming to be a gardener. He suddenly didn't care and laughed. "You don't sweat much for a gardener, kid."

Drayton looked up at the sun. "I've become accustomed to the heat."

The investigators believed him. And they didn't care. So they wished him well and watched him deposit the spent flowers in the water. The kid stood there until the tide took them out before walking along the beach.

Time seemed to drift. It was cooler, the shadows longer when Peter looked at his watch. "I could've sworn it was only two o'clock."

"What time is it?"

"Dinner, man. Let's hit the bricks."

Andy saw a dead rose on the path and turned around. The beach was empty. He couldn't quite remember why they were there.

YELLOW

BOOK 4

Forgiveness is a difficult journey.

8 3

ather Gordon was a master of sleeping in a chair.

His posture was naturally hunched, whether he was walking up steps or hovered over a plate of pancakes. And the distant look that fogged his eyes, like he was solving the theory of relativity, was ever present. He could even sleep with his eyes open.

Master.

He wasn't sleeping this time. He'd made it through the morning mass on the fumes of strong coffee, but he rarely made it through eleven o'clock mass. The chair was too comfortable and the air so stuffy. The good Lord made late Sunday morning mass for sleeping.

But not this Sunday.

This Sunday, heat pricked his skin like tiny red needles.

Father Gordon raised his eyelids like rusty hinges. The congregation was a blurry mob organized in horizontal lines. He blinked once, twice and they came into focus, wearing their Sunday best. Father Walker was still at the pulpit, his words mushing together like a recording running at the wrong speed.

Father Gordon plumped out his lower lip and hummed. It was a short little affirmation, kind of his own little mantra to bring himself back online. It focused his attention on the present moment. It woke him up.

Hmmmm.

"Corinthians," Father Walker said, "states we should not give for the sake of entering the gates of heaven, but give for the sake of caring for our brothers and sisters. Give, for the sake of God."

Yes, give till it hurts, my children. Give until the basket is brimming with stuffed envelopes and then give some more. Daddy needs a new annex.

Father Gordon suppressed a chuckle. It was no secret they needed to raise some cash to expand the holy facilities. They were in need of restoring the recreational facilities and adding onto day care. Times were tough. The nondenominational churches—the Christian get-togethers, as Father Gordon liked to call them—were luring their sheep away from the Catholic Church with their casual Sunday blue jeans and flip-flops and speaking in tongues.

Father Gordon wasn't about to sit around and watch his flock diminish. They were the Catholic Church. They were the Vatican. They were a superhighway—no, not *a* but THE superhighway through the pearly gates—and he was goddamned if he was going to let souls wander away from his watchful eye.

He raised his left hand, heavy with sleep, and wiped his scalp. He had what the older parishioners called a "Friar Tuck" hairdo. His palm came back wet.

Shit.

He was going to soak through every layer of his holy robes. He didn't see any stains on the pits, that was good. He was naked beneath the robes (the nuns said he needed to confess for such a transgression, but he didn't listen to those cackling hens; he was saving souls, goddamnit). The sweat pooled where his fat thighs rubbed together.

Chance and Suzy Miller, sitting in the third row on the right, were laughing. They saw him check for pit stains and thought it was funny. Father Gordon winked and smirked. He could do that, smile without moving his lips. It was in the eyes and cheeks. He was so unlike Father Walker. That stiff smiled with his mouth, showing his capped teeth without an ounce of mirth. He was a joyless fuck that no one liked.

The guy shined at the pulpit, though. He could deliver a homily like a dagger, save a soul from a thousand miles away, swindle money from the congregation like a class A beggar. But, Christ Almighty, he was a social turd. Father Walker carried a wooden paddle up his ass.

Farther Gordon was thirty years his senior. He was well into his seventies and he was still laying down the word of the Lord. He tried to counsel the young priest, tell him he needed to loosen up, mix it up with the youth, get to know them. Get them to like you, for heaven's sake. This was the twenty-first century. I mean, the days of fire and brimstone, of scaring these lost sheep through the pearly gates, were long gone. Now it was all techno-gadget bullshit and they needed to relate. Learn to text, get on Facebook, send an Instagram. It used to be you had to lug a Bible in the crook of your arm if you needed the scripture. Now you just google a phrase and it was WHABAM!

Instant salvation.

Still, the square sonofabitch sat like a stiff and smiled like a hollow pumpkin. Father Gordon gave up on molding him. They still made a great team. Father Walker could give the homilies and Father Gordon handled the social interactions.

He was good at that.

"I was reminded the other day of giving when Father Gordon and I were in the garden." Father Walker stepped away from the pulpit and stood on the top step. "We were pulling weeds with one of the youths—"

One of the youths? *Holy shit.*

Father Gordon looked at one of the *youths.* She was serving as an altar server like she did every Sunday. She sat dutifully in her chair, hands on her lap, watching the back of Father Walker's head. She was a Mexican cutie with a yellow ribbon in her hair.

Amarillo. That was her God-given name. Her parents were gone, so Father Gordon called her Yellow. As reliable as the sun rising.

Her foster mother was in the front pew. She was white, but, through the eyes of God, she saw no color, no race or creed. She only saw God's children.

She rarely took her eye off the girl, always making sure she did what she was told. Father Gordon liked that woman. She minded her man. She was Old Testament material; she didn't spare the rod. Yellow didn't question adults. She did what she was told.

Father Gordon rather liked that.

He reached into his right sleeve and rubbed the nub at his elbow where his arm ended. He lost that arm at about eight years old, about the same age as Yellow. Farming accident. He fell off a tractor, damn lucky the back wheel didn't squash his head like a melon. He remembered it, though. He remembered hitting the ground, looking up at the blue sky as the back wheel went over his arm. He heard the snapping of bones like dry kindling. He remembered it hanging from his elbow like a dishrag.

After all these years, he still felt like the arm was there. Phantom pain, they called it. As he rubbed the bald nub—slick with perspiration—it wasn't ghost itching but ghost tingling, shooting through his shoulder and out his ghost fingertips.

Because it was so hot.

Hot as hell.

Father Gordon winked at Yellow. She twitched and returned to listening to Father Stick-up-his-ass. She couldn't let her mother see her smile or wink back. That would get her ten licks with a ruler. That woman should've been a nun.

He let his eyelids droop. Despite the sweat tracking down his cheeks and the shooting pain, he found sweet relief in slumber. Father Walker's voice carried him off like a metronome, one that inspired sleep and giving money to the basket. Money that would frame a new building and fill it with children that needed guidance and a firm hand. Father Gordon would have his own little office in the back, one where he could prop a small stereo system on the shelves, show the teens he was hip. He rather liked that Adele singer. She wasn't gospel but, then again, everything didn't have to be about Jesus. Sometimes it could just be good plain fun. Something that made you feel good.

Didn't God want all his children to feel loved?

Father Gordon could even hear the hammer tapping on the new

walls, driving finish nails where he could hang pictures. It was rhythmic. The hammer went *tap-tap-tap…* and it got louder… *tap-tap-tap.*

He pried his eyes open.

The front doors—heavy oak with brass circlet handles—were wide open. A young man was on the threshold; his boots clicked on the historic marble that was purchased from a renovated home in the Charleston historic district.

Father Gordon sat up.

No one seemed to notice the young man, his skin as black as a plantation slave's, dip his fingers in the holy font and cross himself before walking right down the middle of the church. No one paid him any attention as he came all the way to the front—

Tap. Tap. TAP.

—right in front of Father Walker, not more than an arm's reach, and genuflect.

Even stranger, each step that youngster took turned an imaginary vise that squeezed Father Gordon's chest. Tighter.

Tighter.

He sat in the front pew a mere five feet from Yellow's foster mother.

Father Walker's homily didn't skip a beat.

No one turned an eye.

They didn't see this… this kid… sit in front… staring.

Father Gordon's breath was shallow. Sweat stung his eyes.

And his chest was very, very tight.

8 4

*J*t was Sunday.

Time for Father Walker to shine.

Some priests raced through service to get the sheep home in time for kickoff, to appease the fidgeting and the yawning and the sleeping. But not Father Walker. He came to priesthood to lead humanity to heaven through the only begotten Son.

Father Walker prepared his homily by walking dutifully through the church gardens with his hands folded and his mind open to God. He would walk carefully, mindfully, eyes on the ground, letting the Lord's grace rain down on him. His drops of wisdom formed words that linked into sentences that fell into the chalice of Father Walker's heart so that he may deliver them to the sheep.

Father Walker was not going to rush through Sundays. Not when he was shining with God's grace. The children weren't hearing what he was saying, but the words would take root. That was what he told parents that cared not to bring their children to mass because they were too disruptive and not really understanding what he was saying.

But the Lord's Word is like a mustard seed that may lay dormant for many years, awaiting water and sunlight to germinate in the soul.

So Father Walker spread the Lord's seed unselfishly, that all may bathe in its glory. That all may experience the wonder that Father Walker had to offer. On that particular Sunday, they would understand the importance of giving.

"Let us pray."

Father Walker raised his arms until they ached. He held them not so much above his head but out to the sides like his savior that hung on a cross attached to the ceiling above him, watching over the congregation. Sometimes Father Walker liked to imagine spikes driven through his palms. Sometimes, he wished he were given the opportunity to die for his Father, so that he may offer salvation to all of humanity.

He recited the Prayer of the Faithful, pausing for the congregation to respond *Lord, hear our prayer.* He put an extra beat into the pause to really let his prayers sink in.

Take root.

Father Walker began preparing for the Liturgy of the Eucharist by receiving gifts of bread and wine to be placed on the altar while the organ played from the balcony. Sometimes he closed his eyes to let the pipes vibrate inside him.

Father Gordon's hand was shaking.

His complexion resembled wet clay.

"Father Gordon," he said, hardly moving his lips, "are you well?"

"Hmm."

"Would you like to sit during the Eucharist?"

"I'm fine."

Father Walker did not want to alarm anyone. Father Gordon was a stubborn man. He did not listen to Father Walker. Would not. A scene would be most inappropriate at this most holy of moments. Father Walker cupped the chalice with both hands and bowed his head.

Father Gordon wiped his forehead.

"Yellow." Father Walker spoke without turning to the altar server. "Would you please help Father Gordon to his chair?"

Yellow looked at Father Gordon.

He hissed without expression. *"Hacer tal cosa, niña." Do no such thing, girl.*

She dutifully stood at her post, awaiting the Prayer over the Gifts. Father Walker paused an extra beat and then continued. What else could he do?

Father Gordon was a very stubborn man.

8 5

Father Gordon felt sweat racing down his legs.

He felt that black kid in the front pew staring at him while he assisted in the preparation of the Gifts. He felt naked, like somehow he was exposed, standing on the altar for everyone to see him for what he was, secrets and all.

He trembled.

But he stayed his post. That was what he was called to do, stay the post and serve up the body of Christ. Father Walker wanted him to sit. It was an empty gesture, but if he could see how Father Gordon's knees quaked beneath the robes, if he felt the icy shivers drain the strength from his legs, he might have stopped mass and insisted.

Yellow stood next to him, hands dutifully folded in front of her chest. She stared, dead-eyed, at the boy in the front pew. She must've felt the strangeness, too. Father Gordon broke protocol and stroked the ponytail her ribbon held in place.

"Usted preocuparse demasiado." You worry too much.

Her expression didn't change.

Father Walker piously paused for the final incantation.

Father Gordon pressed his hand over his chest in lieu of a prayer

196

pose. The silence hung far too long. A weight pressed against his chest.

"This is the Lamb of God," Father Walker called.

Pain shooting down arm.

"Who takes away the sins of the world."

Heat prickling between shoulders.

Father Gordon kept his gaze down and forward, focusing on breathing while Father Walker continued to break the bread and prepare the vessel. Father Gordon would typically assist, but he felt it necessary to conserve his strength. Mass was almost over and he could get out of these dreadful robes. He could do this. In forty years, he had never abandoned his post. He had done what God had called him to do, regardless of how he felt.

"Happy are those who are called to his supper."

"Lord, I am not worthy to receive you," Father Gordon muttered along with the congregation, "but only say the word and I shall be healed."

He swallowed back the pain, blinking away the salty sting. Father Walker offered him the Body of Christ. He held the white wafer in front of him, pausing long and hard. Father Gordon closed his eyes.

"Amen," Father Gordon muttered.

The wafer stuck to the roof of his mouth. Father Walker offered the chalice of Christ's Blood, and Father Gordon washed it down with three healthy gulps, relieving some of the discomfort. He could've downed the whole thing.

Father Gordon took his share of the Eucharist. He held the wafers up, one by one, and placed them in the congregation's cupped hands. He felt sweat trace his fingers and soak into the dry white wafers. Still, he offered it.

"The Body of Christ."

"Amen."

He avoided wiping his face. He kept his knees locked. But his hand was not steady. It quivered more with each parishioner. Each came with hands cupped, some with tongue out, some with eyes closed, giving themselves to his ability to funnel Jesus Christ to the roof of their mouth.

The church was getting dark. His nub was numb.

Then the boy stepped up.

A dark shirt. Jeans and worn boots.

His hair was cut near the scalp. His skin was smooth and ebony, as if dipped in the blackest of ink.

Father Gordon's teeth began to chatter. He looked into the boy's eyes. His teenage eyes so limpid, so placid.

Wise.

He felt so exposed. As if the boy could see who he was, what he had done all these years.

The clattering of knee rests began to fade. A dark tunnel tightened around his vision until it was just the boy.

Just the boy looking at him.

The boy, seeing him.

Father Gordon held up the wafer. It fluttered to the floor.

Words dribbled from his lips. "Forgive me."

God reached inside his chest and squeezed his heart like a lemon. Pain radiated sparks. His knees broke.

Father Gordon dropped like a dishrag.

*Y*ellow could smell Father Gordon through his robes. She knew he wore nothing when it was hot, that his skin was oily and got moldy beneath the folds of his belly. She could smell that.

It was *podrido.*

He was seventy years old. His body was not ready for weather extremes, he would say. When it was cold, his joints would ache. He would bring coconut oil and have her massage his nub. The weather made it itch where he couldn't scratch. He would close his eyes and let Yellow rub the oil into the bald knob on his arm. When it was hot, he would need his chest powdered. Sometimes he would run two fingers beneath a fat-fold and the smell would waft up like sun-dried cottage cheese.

Repugnante.

She didn't want to look at him. She didn't want to make eye contact, not during mass. She could feel him staring, but if she looked back, he might make it worse. Once he interrupted mass to tell the congregation that she had gotten straight As at school. Father Walker was giving a homily on doing God's work without expectation of reward and Father Gordon brought her to the front of the altar.

She wanted to die.

She never wanted him to do that again. So she didn't look at him, even when he whispered in Spanish. She wasn't supposed to use her native tongue. *You're in America,* chica, her foster mother would say. *You're going to speak English, twenty-four seven. If God wanted you to talk Mexican, you would be in Mexico.*

But Father Gordon didn't listen.

She liked that he spoke Spanish. It reminded her of home, someplace she would never have again. At first he hid it from the foster mom. *Our little secret,* he said. But then he did it right out in the open, like he was teaching her who was boss. Still, Yellow didn't like to participate in front of her. Father Gordon didn't have to go home with her. He didn't know what it was like to kneel on pencils.

But now something was different about him. He was *rojo. Caliente.*

He swayed when he gave her communion, holding the wafer out to place on her tongue. (She didn't cup her hands; Father Gordon said that was *sucias. Impuro.*) His fingers waved beneath her nose and she closed her eyes. She didn't open them until the smell was gone.

The boy that walked in late was still in the front row. He was all by himself, wearing regular clothes. He sat so calmly. She tried not to stare. Father Gordon would scold her for that, it was *descortés* to stare at individuals in the congregation. They were there to hear the word of the Lord, not to be gawked at by a misplaced *chica.* But she couldn't help herself. He was just so... so...

Bonito.

He felt so perfect.

When she looked at him, she felt so *limpia.*

Clean.

She forced herself to look away. Once communion had begun, Father Gordon was occupied and could no longer see Yellow watching the boy sit so gracefully. She watched him stand in line with his hands folded in prayer. He stepped up to Father Gordon and cupped his hands to receive the Body of Christ.

Father Gordon shook.

He said something in English.

Then he crumpled.

He was a pile of sleeves and scarves on the bottom step of the altar and people were shouting 911 and a crowd was huddled over him. Two people came rushing up the aisle—one man, one woman—both shouting for them to step aside because they were doctors. They gave the pile of holy clothes room to breathe. Father Walker was the only one allowed to kneel next to him.

"Get a cold, wet cloth!"

Yellow didn't move. Father Walker turned and looked right at her. His big wire glasses had slid down his nose.

She backed up the steps and moved to the exit at the rear of the altar. Yellow went to the bathroom and pulled paper towels out of the dispenser, running them under the cold tap and squeezing the excess into the sink. She walked back through the anteroom with rows and rows of prayer candles flickering in the draft.

Yellow draped the damp towels over a handrail.

She looked at the unlit candles, each one awaiting a match for someone in need. She knelt in front of the Virgin Mary, her hands out and welcoming, and bowed her head.

She didn't pray for Father Gordon.

She just listened to the calls for help.

8 7

The siren's warning had faded.

The church, empty.

Father Walker shook Dr. Foreman's hand with two hands. He held on a bit longer than a normal handshake, hoping it would convey gratitude for her expertise in this emergency.

"I should've known," he said. "He was not himself. I offered him a chair, but he wouldn't take it. He's from the old school of suffering and penance, you know."

"I doubt that would've stopped it, Father Walker."

"Yes, but he wouldn't have fallen so hard."

"Did he complain of symptoms earlier in the week? This morning, perhaps?"

Father Walker shook his head. "Father Gordon never complains."

"When was the last time he saw a doctor?"

Father Walker started walking down the center aisle. Certainly, Dr. Foreman didn't have time to spare talking about this. She had done more than he could've asked and he was certainly grateful. He hoped that was clear to her. She didn't need to stay any longer.

"Father?" Dr. Foreman asked.

"Yes, um, I was thinking. I don't think Father Gordon has been to the doctor." He rubbed his chin. "Ever."

The doctor frowned.

Father Walker smiled, showing all his teeth. "He's too stubborn to get sick, you see."

Dr. Foreman didn't grin. She was nodding. Thinking.

Father Walker noticed the church was not empty, after all. There, in the back pew, was a young man. He had not seen him in mass before. He sat near the aisle, hands neatly folded on his lap. He watched Father Walker and the doctor approach.

Yellow was sitting next to him.

"Father?" Dr. Foreman said it sternly this time.

"Yes, mm-mmm. I'm sorry, Doctor. I'm a little… distracted. A lot has happened this morning."

"I understand. Do you know if he was on any medication?"

"I, uh, don't know that."

"Can we check his room? They're going to need that information at the hospital—"

"Father Gordon is a very private man. I don't think he'd appreciate us going through his things."

"Father Gordon just suffered a serious heart attack. I think he'll forgive the trespass, Father."

Father Walker was lost in thought, but, if you asked at that moment what he was thinking, he wouldn't be able to answer. He just didn't want anyone going into Father Gordon's room. That was made clear when Father Walker first arrived at St. Michael's.

"Yellow?" he said. "Do you know if Father Gordon takes any medicine?"

The young girl, still dressed in appropriate server attire, only stared.

"*Medicina?*" The doctor pretended to feed herself pills.

"She can speak English, Doctor." Father Walker tried to soften his tone with a cheerless smile. "Yellow, do you know?"

Again, silence.

"Look, Doctor, I'll look in his bathroom and call if I find anything."

There was a little more chat. Dr. Foreman wrote a number to call on the back of a business card. There was no handshake before she left. Father Walker watched her leave before turning to the young man and flashing a mechanical smile.

"Hello," he said, offering his hand. "I'm Father Walker. I don't believe we've met."

"Drayton."

The young man took his hand without standing. He didn't shake Father Walker's hand, merely held it. A cold shiver traveled through his palm and up his wrist. Father Walker had the mild sensation of being transported in an elevator. Up or down, he couldn't say. Only the queer drop in his belly.

Perhaps it was imagined. Like having an x-ray taken, one imagines feeling exposed, but really there's only a short click.

"Drayton, huh?" Father Walker dropped his hand, resisting the urge to wipe it on his sleeve. "You are from around here?"

"Recently, yes."

"I see. Well." Father Walker spread his arms. "Welcome to St. Michael's. You have arrived on a very peculiar day. Father Gordon has taken ill. I suppose it's a miracle that he is still alive."

Father Walker crossed himself.

"Quite lucky that members of your congregation are competent physicians."

"Perhaps. But God made sure they were at the eleven o'clock mass."

Father Walker raised a finger to correct the young man. He frequently tightened up when someone doubted the all-knowing grace of God. And the power of prayer.

"He works in mysterious ways," Drayton said.

"We're mere mortals. Who are we to question his intent?"

"Quite."

It was an odd inflection this young man spoke. Father Walker wasn't a racist, but he expected a little more slang, to see him driving a flashy car with booming speakers, not sitting in repose at the back of a church saying things like *quite.*

"We have many activities here at St. Michael's. There's a pancake breakfast next Saturday to raise funds for our annex and several prayer groups that meet throughout the week." Father Walker looked around. "Were your parents here?"

"They were not."

"I see. An adventurous young man, huh? Well, there is a young person's group that meets on Friday nights for games and movies. Perhaps you'd like to come by and get to know some of the teens?"

Drayton nodded.

"Or you could volunteer in the garden. We have quite an extensive botanical garden, you may have seen on your way in. Several of our parishioners are Master Gardeners and have developed quite a beautiful landscape. I must brag, it would compete with Clemson's, I'm told." His chuckle was rushed and mirthless, as if right on cue. "Yellow could tell you about it."

She didn't.

An uncomfortable silence ensued.

"Well, then. It's nice to make your acquaintance." Father Walker decided not to shake his hand. "Perhaps next time we'll see each other under better circumstances. Come along, Yellow."

No movement. Not even an acknowledgement he'd addressed her.

"Yellow." Father Walker's lips stretched over his white teeth. "*Vamos.*"

She slid out of the pew.

Father Walker patted her shoulder like his hand was wood.

"Father? May I stay in the church?" Drayton asked.

"Why certainly. The chapel is open to the public until nine. There are prayer candles in the back if you choose to light one for Father Gordon."

Father Walker felt better the farther away he got from the youngster. It was nice that he was going to stay and pray for Father Gordon. If he was honest, he would prefer he do it somewhere else.

8 8

Despite the method of grueling punishment the cross was meant to deliver—until death—the image of Jesus was one of serenity. His arms out wide, not nailed to the wood, and a slight smile on his lips. It was comforting and loving. Not excruciating.

Drayton had seen many crucifixions in his life, where criminals were left to bake in the sun and die, their bodies left to warn others what would happen if they behaved as such. People were creative when it came to killing each other.

Drayton had never met Jesus of Nazareth. He was somewhere in the Orient when the man was said to be alive. Those were Drayton's *dark years*. When he savagely stalked his prey, sometimes tore their throats open with his bare hands, and drank the blood as it spilled. During Jesus' short life, Drayton was touring the countryside, walking as he usually did, encountering farmers and having fun. Many called him a demon, and why not. No matter how many times they stabbed or shot him, he just kept coming.

In the dark days, he got stabbed a lot.

He could recall hearing of Jesus many years after his death as his apostles began to carry forth his word. Drayton even served in the church during the twelfth century. You want to talk about power. He started out as a priest and had become a bishop before getting bored. He was a roamer.

Drayton had lingered in the South Carolina Lowcountry for quite some time. He enjoyed the wetlands and the coast, being close to the water. The Charleston area was rich with history. Not like Europe, but for America it was.

No matter where he went, there was never a shortage of death.

He had no intention of stopping at the church. He was merely walking through the country and came near a small town north of Charleston. He intended on going north, perhaps visit the Piedmont. (When you've lived for thousands of years, you're never in a hurry.)

But then he caught a scent.

It was a familiar one. The metal tang of blood clotting. The whine of a heart straining. Drayton could sense an impending heart attack from miles away. When the priest's heart seized and his eyes rolled back, Drayton was there to absorb the waning life force, the silky essence, as it seeped from the body. No more tearing of throats and drinking blood. Drayton simply took the essence of life when a human was done with it.

Much more sophisticated, indeed.

But it wasn't the opportunity to feed that drew him to St. Michael's. The ache wasn't upon him, not yet. This seemed to be something more... *unique.* More interesting. Drayton was always looking for opportunities that piqued his curiosity. Some might say he enjoyed delivering swift justice. Some might even call him an angel.

Angel. This thought always brought a smile. If they only knew the savagery with which he'd slaughtered during the dark years, no one would think him an angel.

This time there was an impending death falling upon a dark soul, and Drayton was there to witness it. He could see the ugliness that clouded the heart and mind of Jon Gordon. Drayton sat in the front pew and watched the man called Father Gordon go about his priestly duties until Death reached into his chest.

Father Gordon, at that moment, knew that his secrets were exposed.

He felt the strange sensation of Drayton looking directly into his mind and sweeping through the dark corners. He knew, at some level, that Drayton didn't need to be told one's secrets. Drayton knew a person's thoughts. He looked into their souls.

He knew.

Father Gordon asked for forgiveness. Drayton had every intention of letting him pass from the world, but perhaps that last request changed his mind. As Drayton inhaled Father Gordon's silky essence as it wafted from his body, he blew it back.

Father Gordon was meant to die, but Drayton gave him life. If he asked for forgiveness, then he would have the opportunity to receive it. Forgiveness, though, is not an easy hill to climb. Asking is the first step of many.

Perhaps that's what intrigued Drayton. If he was honest, he rather enjoyed providing these opportunities. He didn't experience emotions as people did (he wasn't human; he didn't know what he was), but there was something that brought him… joy.

Father Walker was nothing like Father Gordon. He was a rigid man that adhered to the church's doctrine like a mighty soldier. He smiled like a ventriloquist was pulling a string on his back and shook hands like a puppet. He was a good man, but he was not without sin.

Drayton would allow him the opportunity to repent, as well.

Sun beamed yellow, red and green through the stained glass, slicing dusty beams across the church. Under the watchful eye of Jesus, Drayton dipped his fingers on the sponge of holy water. He wondered, as he made the sign of the cross, if anyone prayed for Yellow.

The sign out front of Paradise Estates was chipped and faded. One of the posts had rotted at the base and broke away, causing the sign to lean to the left. Paradise Estates was written in pretty cursive. Palm trees were used instead of the letter t. Music danced from somewhere deep in the rows of mobile homes, where someone argued and something broke and a door slammed.

Drayton stood outside the fifth one from the entrance, on the right. It was white with green trim. The wooden steps were lined with houseplants and a chain-link fence that boxed a black dog sleeping in one of many holes. It didn't bark or stir when Drayton approached. It was dark and only a few streetlights were working.

He looked inside the bay window, where Yellow was washing dishes. Past the kitchen was a darkly paneled room with a giant man laid back in a reclining chair. His face fluttered electric blue, white and pink as he switched through channels. Nothing moved but his eyes and his thumb.

Theresa, Yellow's foster mother, was on the couch playing a game of solitaire in a cloud of smoke. The ashtray—holding down a black Bible with well-studied corners—was smothered in a pile of lipsticked butts. It was reasonably clean.

Reasonably home.

Yellow washed and cleaned pots and dishes, bowls and cups. She dried them and put them away.

"Brush your teeth." Theresa played a card. "I'll be back in a second."

Yellow did that.

When she got to her room, Theresa was kneeling at her bedside with a rosary binding her hands. Her eyes were squeezed shut. Yellow took her place next to her. When her hands were folded, Theresa began to pray out loud while Yellow's lips silently moved. When the prayers were finished, they recited the Holy Rosary.

"In the name of the Father, and of the Son, and of the Holy Spirit. Amen."

They crossed themselves in unison.

"I believe in God, the Father Almighty, Creator of Heaven and earth. And in Jesus Christ, His only Son, our Lord, who was conceived by the Holy Spirit, born of the Virgin Mary..."

They said the words out loud, as if rehearsed a thousand times, touching a bead and reciting each memorized prayer. When they were finished, Theresa pulled back the cover and tucked Yellow into her bed. Without a word, she turned off the light and closed the door.

Yellow lay on her back, arms at her sides.

Somewhere, a bass-driven song rattled her windows.

She remained still for several minutes and then, quietly and carefully, pulled the cover off and padded across the floor. She took a brush off her desk and, in the dark, brushed her hair in the mirror. The yellow ribbon was tied on the post of the old mirror. A ribbon she found a year ago when it fluttered off the antennae of a passing Escalade when she was walking home from St. Michael's. Yellow picked it up and watched the vehicle go down the road. Far, far away.

Drayton watched until she returned to bed and fell asleep. He stayed outside the window that night and the next. On the third night, he walked to a hospital.

90

The music never bothered Yellow.

She stared at the ceiling, warm and cozy in her bed. She remembered what it was like to fall asleep in alleys or park benches or on the floor of a stranger's house, where her mother—her birth mother—did weird things with scary people. She remembered how cold it could get at night.

This is a bed.

Theresa prayed every night and every morning. Sometimes after lunch. That night, Theresa prayed for Father Gordon. "Dear God our Lord and Savior, please watch over the health and well-being of our beloved Father Gordon that has given his life so freely and so unselfishly that he may lead us in your grace. Please, Lord, save him from the ill health that afflicts him now and see that he mends painlessly and quickly, that he may return to the church where he belongs."

Yellow didn't pray for Father Gordon. She moved her lips, but she didn't pray for him.

Gracias a Dios por sentirse bien, para sentirse limpio.

Yellow still felt good and clean ever since she saw the new boy. That feeling was still with her and she thanked God for that. Maybe he had answered her prayers, after all. Theresa made her recite the Holy Rosary out loud, but not her personal prayers. Yellow prayed for an angel.

Perhaps he came to church today.

Gracias a Dios.

9 1

The beat was steady.

Father Gordon didn't realize he was listening to anything; there was just *boom-boom, boom-boom.* There was nothing but the sound. No eyes, no mouth. No flesh.

Just *boom-boom.*

He wasn't sure when the next sound joined the *boom-boom.* It was long and breezy. It went in, then out. A rise and fall. Like the wind blew through a window and back out again.

And then he felt it.

It was the rise and fall of his chest. He was breathing. His heart was beating.

And he felt the floor beneath him.

He opened his eyes to… darkness.

He was on his back, staring into a starless night like he was beneath a lone streetlight. But there was no streetlight above him, no source of light of any kind. Just Father Gordon and the hard, blank floor.

He rolled onto his side, throwing his stump across his body to get up on his elbow. The sleeve of his priestly robe flapped. He sat up and groaned, rubbing his face. He was so foggy. Too much wine, perhaps.

He'd been known to sample the Eucharist outside of mass so he could sleep soundly. This might've been one of those mornings where his memory would come back on its own schedule.

But he always woke in his own bed.

Where the hell am I?

He got to his feet after a series of grunts. His head was stuffed with cotton and his joints ached like winter had arrived.

"Hello?" His voice didn't echo. It just died in the dark.

His wingtips clapped against the floor. No matter what direction he went, the light followed him into more emptiness.

"What's going on here?" he shouted.

More nothing.

Just the clacking of his dress shoes and limitless dark.

He shouted and shouted. He stopped to rest. It was difficult to get up. He wished for a chair. Nothing, nothing, nothing.

Until something on the edge of the dark.

"Hello?"

He took a tentative step. The figure took shape.

It was a young man.

"*You.*" Father Gordon covered his chest.

"Jon Gordon," Drayton said.

"You may address me as Father Gordon."

Drayton stepped into the light.

Father Gordon rubbed his nub. "Where am I?"

Drayton turned his head. Something swirled in the dark. There were shapes out there. Flashes of color.

And then he remembered.

He saw this boy in the eleven o'clock mass. Father Gordon's arms were shooting with numbness and sweat dripped in his eyes.

The darkness whirled like he was standing in the center of a carnival ride. He clutched his chest, staggered a step left and right until the ride slowly stopped and he was standing on a carpet with a pulpit to his left and rows and rows of pews in front of him.

Jesus looked down on him from the cross.

"What the hell is happening?"

"Jon Gordon," Drayton said calmly, "you asked for forgiveness. I guarantee you nothing; I can only offer you the opportunity."

"I have nothing to be forgiven." He straightened up, still holding onto his chest. "I have served God my whole life, he heard my confession. He has forgiven me. Now, get me the hell out of here."

The scenery changed.

The pulpit shifted and pews faded. He was in his bedroom.

Jesus was still above him.

"STOP IT!" Father Gordon threw up his hand and closed his eyes. "The Lord gives me absolution, I don't need your approval! You... you... DEMON!"

He cracked open his eyes and the scenery had changed. This time he was in the confession cubicle. There was an altar girl with him, this time.

And Jesus still looked down.

He covered his face.

"Demon, demon, demon..."

"Jesus may have died for your sins," Drayton said, "but he did not relieve you of your responsibility."

Father Gordon peeked through his fingers. The images were gone. Drayton stood on the edge of darkness.

"Burn in hell," he uttered.

"YOU WERE THEIR SHEPHERD!"

Drayton swelled in size, charging the priest that cowered on his knees. He towered over him, his black eyes deep and fiery. Father Gordon tried to cover his face, protect himself from the blows.

But there were none.

Drayton could destroy a man without raising a finger. Father Gordon only wished for such a release. But death would be an injustice to the universe.

The tables were full.

It was such a success that Father Walker requested ten more tables for the pancake breakfast event, and they were occupied, too. There wasn't even room for them under the blue awning. People ate griddle-fried pancakes with maple syrup in the sun. He had a feeling attendance was going to be booming. It had been almost a week (six days, exactly) since Father Gordon dropped. Word got around.

He hated to admit it, but Father Gordon had done more for their fund-raising efforts with a near-fatal heart attack than anything he'd ever done. God worked in mysterious ways.

Still, he would've liked to have had Father Gordon mixing it up with the crowd. Father Gordon knew how to work an event. Father Walker watched how he would go from table to table, never seeming to be in a hurry but somehow always talking to everyone. At every stop, people would laugh. He didn't really have jokes, he just knew how to point out the humorous.

Now it was just Father Walker and boxes of gallons and gallons of pancake batter.

"How's everyone doing?" Father Walker expounded as he walked between the tables, patting folks on the shoulders and waving and smiling. "There's plenty here, so eat up and get more when you're ready. Eat up. Eat up."

He couldn't suppress a smile—a real, honest-to-goodness smile—until he noticed the near-empty table at the far corner. The young man was sitting there. He wasn't eating the pancakes or sausage, just sitting there with his legs crossed. Sipping coffee.

"Father Walker," someone said.

"Yes?" He watched Drayton.

"How's Father Gordon?"

"I'm sorry?"

"I said how is Father Gordon?" Jack Johnston said.

The Johnston family—boasting nine children—were just getting seated. Cheryl Johnston was cutting up Sandi's pancake and dipping it in a puddle of syrup.

Father Walker plied a grin on his face.

"You know what we used to call those when I was growing up?" Father Walker squatted next to Cheryl and placed his hand on Sandi's shoulder. "*Flapjacks.*"

Sandi had a look of silent terror before crying, reaching for her mama.

"She's a little tired, Father Walker." Cheryl lifted her onto her lap. Sandi stuck her hand in her mouth and nestled into Cheryl's bosom, eyeballing the priest.

"Yes." He patted the little girl on the back. "Flapjacks are funny."

He couldn't think of anything else to say. It clearly wasn't funny.

"How is Father Gordon?" Jack Johnston asked again.

"Well, he's stable. There have been some complications, but the doctors say it's a miracle that he survived."

"We heard he's in a coma."

"He's resting comfortably. You folks enjoy your flapjacks."

Father Walker tried to rustle the youngster's hair and she whined. He needed to keep moving. There were others eating pancakes, not just the Johnstons. Certainly, there were rumors about Father Gordon. And, most likely, there was talk that it had been a week and

Father Walker still had not been to see him. It only took one person to know a fact and it would spread like a common cold.

It was true. He had not gone to see him.

There were things to do in the church. There was the pancake event and the day-to-day business and homilies to prepare. Besides, Father Gordon was in a coma. Father Walker didn't need to be there. He could get updates about him from the church's secretary.

It wasn't like he wasn't doing anything to help. He had gone into Father Gordon's room like Dr. Foreman had asked. The heavy curtains were drawn, sinking the room into dank darkness. Piles of clothes looked like mounds of refuse. He threw open the window to let it air out, avoiding the cluttered desk. He would look through that stuff if there was nothing in the bathroom, he told himself. But he found a few bottles of pills in the medicine cabinet and, proudly, called Dr. Foreman.

"Anything else?" the doctor asked.

"Like what?"

"Psychotropics or antidepressents?"

"No."

An unusual pause.

"What's the matter?" Father Walker shifted the phone to the other ear.

"He's exhibiting some unusual symptoms."

"I know that a heart-induced coma is very unusual, but that doesn't seem alarming."

"That's not it," the doctor said. "The nurses have had to bind his wrists to keep him from pulling out his IV and knocking things over."

"That's a good sign, right? I mean, he's moving around, doesn't that mean he'll be coming out of the coma soon?"

"Not necessarily. The fits pass and he falls right back into the coma. A neurologist will be looking at him tomorrow. We'll need you to come down and fill out some paperwork."

"Yes, of course."

Father Walker would have to go to the hospital.

"Can you finish this for me?" a kid said.

"Huh?" Father Walker realized he was standing in front of a table, not in Father Gordon's room. The folks sitting there were smiling. Little Grady Philmore was holding up his plate with a half-eaten pancake.

"Can you finish this for me, Father?"

He paused. "Yes. I can."

He sat down and ate the pancake. Then got up and left.

9 3

Father Walker walked across the Medical University of South Carolina's campus. He'd been there many times to administer communion to the sick or comfort someone undergoing surgery. However, he rarely went without Father Gordon.

In fact, he'd never gone without him.

He crossed the green courtyard beneath the live oaks and past the colorful flowerbeds towards Ashley River Tower. He took the steps to the third floor. He always took the steps, giving him a chance to reflect on his mission. And exercise.

He took the steps one at a time, slow and thoughtful. He was slightly winded when he reached the door with a number three. He fought the urge to turn around. He pushed the door open, his senses assaulted with antiseptic. He passed nurses working at mobile computer stations in the brightly lit hallway until he found the correct door.

GOR was on the tag.

He pushed the heavy door open. The single bed was surrounded by doctors and medical students. He stood inside the room, listening to the discussion.

"Father Walker." Dr. Foreman stepped out of the crowd. "Please, come in."

She put her arm around his waist and stiffly guided him to the foot of the bed.

Father Gordon's hair tufted out from the sides. A clear tube ran under his nose, just above his gaping mouth. White pads were attached to his scalp and chest, with wires running to various beeping machines.

The Adam's apple bobbed in Father Walker's throat.

Dr. Foreman made introductions. The doctors shook hands curtly and without expression.

"And this is Drs. Marc and Eva Espada," Dr. Foreman said. "They are neurologists from the Department of Psychiatry."

"Hello." Father Walker reached out and grasped his hand first, then the woman's. Both were warm. "You have the same name?"

"Husband and wife," he said, flashing a brief smile.

"Neurologists. That should make marriage easy," Father Walker said dryly.

He was surprised to get a laugh from the room. First time he had done so and he wasn't even trying.

"Yes, yes," Dr. Marc said. "Always analyzing each other. You know, we met you once, very briefly."

"Oh?"

"Yes, we've been working with Catholic Charities and met with Father Gordon on a few occasions. We had even planned to attend mass when we heard of his condition."

"We're very sorry," Dr. Eva said. "It must be difficult for you and your members."

"It hasn't been easy," Father Walker said distantly.

Father Gordon's wrists were bound to the bed rails by flexible bands. He looked like a mental case.

"Are those really necessary?"

"That's why Drs. Espada are here," Dr. Foreman said. "Physically, Father Gordon is very stable. He'll likely need a stent, but if he changes his diet and follows our recommendations, he should make a full recovery."

"Then why the binders?"

The doctors exchanged glances. The students remained still. A few scribbled on notepads or tapped on iPads as Dr. Marc explained.

"Father Gordon appears to be experiencing night terrors."

There was discussion between the doctors as they analyzed some of the readings. The students took notes. There was mention of the unusual nature of this coma, how the patient seemed conscious at times but unresponsive to external stimuli. They spoke like Father Walker wasn't in the room.

Father Walker sat next to the window and looked outside. He couldn't look at Father Gordon. It had been some time since he'd seen him without the clerical collar. He looked so ordinary.

So human.

He watched the clouds drift by.

He thought about how long he should stay.

Father Gordon wouldn't know if he left. Once the paperwork was in order, he could return to the parish, where he belonged. He could begin working on—

The beeps moved closer together.

Father Gordon moaned.

His head pivoted back and forth. Another moan.

And then the screams.

His hands thrashed against the plastic bed rails. The mattress bounced as he slammed his head against the pillow.

The door flew open and nurses rushed in.

They all spoke in doctor language. Father Walker pressed against the wall and watched them do everything they could, but nothing helped.

He thrashed and cried like he was burning in the fires of Hell.

Perhaps he should.

Father Walker extinguished that thought.

He excused himself without anyone noticing.

9 4

The Medical University of South Carolina had many seating areas, depending on which building and what procedure a loved one was undergoing. Drayton sat in a chair near revolving doors on the first floor. It wasn't exactly a waiting room, just a few seats amongst tropical planters.

He sat quietly, calmly. He sat listening and watching the sorrow and grief.

He remained that way until a priest emerged from the stairwell. Father Walker bumped into a large orderly and moved around him with an apology. He was pale and the knob in his throat pumped up and down.

Father Walker pulled up short of the revolving doors in order to time his exit.

He made his way across the lawn with long strides.

Drayton stayed seated.

9 5

Sunday morning.

The children were screaming. Samuel Barrett pulled himself up the wooden ladder into the playground fort and beat his chest. Three adults sat on plastic benches, watching the toddlers get it out of their system before Sunday school.

Yellow was around the corner, deep into the butterfly garden. She couldn't see the rambunctious little ones, but their laughter carried for miles. She typically worked in the gardens on Saturdays, but it had rained the day before. Theresa said it was their duty to keep their commitment to the butterfly section.

Yellow didn't mind so much. She enjoyed getting lost in lantana and coreopsis and butterfly weed. Sometimes she'd crouch so low that people would wander the gravel path that meandered through the vegetable sections and hummingbird plots and annual flowers without seeing her. She rather liked that.

Theresa was at the end of the path, next to a sign that indicated the direction of the orchard. She was working on her third cigarette, gossiping with Ms. Granderson about how strange Father Walker had become.

"Well, it took him a week just to go visit Father Gordon," Ms.

224

Granderson said. "You'd think he would be up there every day since he's a man of God. You know, bless his heart, but Father Walker just doesn't have a backbone, if you ask me."

"Perhaps he's just grieving," Theresa said.

Yellow plucked a wily clump of crabgrass and shook the soil from the white roots. She placed it in a neat pile while Ms. Granderson looked in three directions before half-whispering about a sexual affair she'd heard. She didn't spare the details.

Theresa fired up her fourth cigarette.

Drayton stood in the gravel path ten feet from Yellow. He was conspicuous, hands at his sides, staring at the girl making piles of weeds, but Theresa and Ms. Granderson didn't seem to notice.

Yellow rooted up the betony tubers and piled them like white rattles. She picked the dead flowers off the coreopsis.

"*Usted puede ayudar*," she said. *You can help.*

She didn't look up when she said it. She'd just finished making a pile of dead flowers. She crawled to the back of the garden beneath the butterfly bush growing against the building and attacked a mat of doveweed. Drayton's boots pressed into the soft mulch on the other side of the butterfly bush. He knelt down and reached for a clump of nutsedge.

Yellow handed him a pair of brown gloves.

He took them. "*Gracias.*"

"*¿Habla español?*"

"*Si.*"

Yellow pushed her weeds between them and watched Drayton yank out the nutsedge. He laid it on top of her pile.

"*Que necesita para obtener los tubérculos o la maleza volverá.*" *You need to get the tubers or the weeds will come back.*

The corner of Drayton's mouth turned up. "*Si.*"

Yellow giggled.

If he wanted to weed, he needed to do it right.

They worked in silence, cleaning up the ground around the butterfly bush before moving over to the coneflowers and a runaway patch of Bermuda grass. Theresa and Ms. Granderson had moved down the path to sit on a bench. She was on her fifth cigarette. That meant the gossip was good.

"*¿Quién es usted?*" *Who are you?*

Drayton knocked the dirt from his hands. "A friend."

She looked into his eyes—deep, dark, and endless—and felt her stomach begin to melt. She thought she would cry and didn't know why.

"*¿Es usted un ángel?*" *Are you an angel?*

Drayton chuckled.

"*Algunas personas creen que soy un demonio.*" *Some believe I'm a demon.*

Yellow didn't think a demon would make her feel this way. He wouldn't make her feel clean. Feel right.

"What people think does not define you," she said. "My mother used to say that."

"Your mother was a wise woman."

Yellow found more nutsedge. "She died of an overdose."

Drayton knew Yellow's past. He absorbed her thoughts like they were vapor. Her father returned to Mexico. Her mother was troubled. She was found in an abandoned trailer. Yellow was born in the United States and became a ward of the state of South Carolina.

Perhaps she was better off.

Perhaps not.

"What did you do to Father Gordon?" she asked.

"He had a heart attack."

"I know." She moved closer to him. It was like orbiting the sun. "But what did *you* do to him?"

Drayton paused with his fingers in the mulch.

"I offered him redemption."

"Are you Jesus?"

"I am not. I showed him what he'd become."

"So you're a mirror."

"Perhaps."

They worked quietly again. They crawled around the bee balm and unearthed another invasion of betony. The gravel path was lined with neat piles of unwanted weeds, and the mulch was smoothed around the plants. A swallowtail landed on a black-eyed Susan, slowly fanning its wings. Drayton and Yellow stopped working and watched. The church bells rang.

And the swallowtail took flight.

"You will leave," she said.

"Not yet."

Yellow removed her gloves, eyes downcast. "*Gracias.*"

She bathed in the wonderful feeling, knowing it would be gone when he left. She felt sadness for not wanting that feeling to go away.

"Yellow." Theresa crushed a butt in a weed pile. "Come on, child. Mass is about to start. You need to change or Father Walker will have a fit. You can finish when mass is over, come along."

Yellow got up and brushed off. Theresa put her arm over her shoulder and hustled her along the way. The gravel crunched underfoot. Yellow did not look back.

Drayton finished the weeding.

9 6

Father Walker fumbled with the plastic container, almost dropping it.

He read the lid again, trying to figure out if there were arrows to line up or some other method to get past the childproofing. He palmed the lid, pushed and turned, and felt it unbuckle.

He tapped a baby blue pill out.

Zoloft.

He wasn't sure about this. Ms. Sidling—she worked in the front office on a part-time basis—offered him the medicine. *She said medicine, not pills.* Father Walker always preached against using emotional aids exactly like this. He advocated praying for God's grace to lead one through difficult times. But after his last homily, he decided maybe he would take Ms. Sidling up on her previous offer.

He had prepared a nice talk regarding selflessness in the eyes of the Lord. What did it really mean to be compassionate? What did it really mean to be a true friend? What did it mean to truly help our brothers and sisters?

Father Walker never used cards for his homily. He did that the first couple of years, but he considered himself an old pro. He preferred to walk freely and expound the truth. But then the words were getting slippery and he found himself pacing in silence before he could recall his next passage. He hid his hands in his sleeves.

They were shaking.

He was going to tie the homily into giving money for the annex. Their fund-raising efforts were moving along nicely. Father Gordon's continued coma actually boosted the giving. But then a child cried in the back of the church.

A child cried.

And then he forgot the rest.

His hands never stopped shaking.

Father Walker finished mass and even stood out front to greet the congregation as they left. Some looked at him with concern. Others waited until they were out of earshot before talking. He decided his next homily should be on gossip.

"Hello, Father." Dr. Marc Espada gripped Father Walker's hand. "I'm Marc Espada and this is my wife, Eva."

Father Walker shook both their hands with the hollow smile he reserved for faking recognition.

"We met you at MUSC," Eva said. "In Father Gordon's room."

"Oh, yes. Of course."

"We're very sorry for his condition."

"Thank you." Father Walker flicked a glance back into the church, hoping they would realize how many people he still had to greet. "Have there been any changes?"

"I'm afraid not," Marc said. "He's still physically stable but suffering from periodic terrors."

"Hmm." Father Walker narrowed his eyes. *Perfect. Nailed it. Concern with a touch of strength.*

There was a long pause. Drs. Espada smiled and thanked him for the mass. They would be back, they said.

God's grace got him through that day. By the end of it, his hands had stopped shaking. He even had conversations concerning Father Gordon—something that seemed to get the hands going—with minimal agitation.

Now he stared at the blue pill, thinking maybe he was weak for doing this. Did he really need to drug himself to get through this suffering? Lord Jesus Christ carried his cross without the aid of psychotropics, perhaps he should follow in his Savior's footsteps and do the same.

But that was a different era.

Father Walker popped the pill onto his tongue. He chased it with water.

It was such a fine line between God and man. If God gave man the intelligence to create medicine to help with difficult times, perhaps he should use it. He would be of better service to his flock; he would be an effective shepherd if he had his wits in order.

He just needed a little help. Just to get through this ordeal.

At least until there was closure with Father Gordon.

One way or the other.

97

A walk through the park and a stellar homily the following week and Father Walker was back. He could feel it, too. The congregation was rapt with attention as he delivered a scathing sermon on the vicious nature of gossip. Many of them nodded their heads; others wouldn't look him in the eye when he shook hands after mass.

Confidence pills.

That was what Ms. Sidling called them.

It was illegal what he was doing, taking prescription pills without a prescription. But it was temporary. And if he needed more of them, well, he wasn't beyond going to a doctor to get his own prescription. Anyone could understand the stress he was under, and the confidence that was in his stride proved that the little pills were a benefit in spreading God's word.

Father Walker had the church in order. The donations were coming in strong and steady. He had even planned a trip to see Father Gordon very soon. He felt that he could face his withering body now that he had his stride back.

Yes. God's grace is good.

It was Saturday.

Father Walker stepped into the confessional. He particularly liked confessions. It wasn't so much hearing the mundane sins that his flock had committed (sometime quite egregious), it was the moments in between confessions he cherished. He sat in his cubicle and meditated on God's word. He felt it was his duty to be open to the Lord so that he may hear the confessions and offer absolution to his children.

Father Walker was a conduit. And, he had to admit, it felt good to be special.

That Saturday was no different than most. Although there was a screen that separated him from the confessor, he knew their voices. He knew who had stolen from their neighbor, who had impure thoughts of a friend, and who had taken the Lord's name in vain. Father Walker listened, inquired as to how they could repair the damage they had inflicted on family and friends, and then provided a list of penance to earn the Lord's forgiveness. Hail Mary's, the Lord's Prayer, and such.

Late in the afternoon, Father Walker was feeling sleepy. The confessional was stuffy that time of day. He closed his eyes and leaned his head back. He would remain another twenty minutes before closing confession.

He felt good. He was doing God's work. In that manner, he earned his own forgiveness. That was his penance.

The door opened.

Someone sat.

Father Walker sat up and cleared his throat, smoothing out the wrinkles on his lap. The silence stretched out. He tried not to look through the screen, feeling that privacy was due to the confessor. But he couldn't help himself, not when a minute had gone by without a word. However, he couldn't see who was there.

Perhaps the person was new to confession.

"Forgive me, Father, for I have sinned," Father Walker said. "You begin with that when you enter confession."

Silence.

Strangely, a cold shiver ran down Father Walker's back. He folded his hands on his lap, feeling the quiver in his palms.

"You shake," the confessor said. "Do you know why?"

Father Walker swallowed, but his throat was dry.

"Do you know why you fear?" the confessor continued.

"Son, this is a confessional. You need to confess *your* sins so that I may offer you God's absolution in return."

Silence filled the confessional.

Father Walker's insides turned icy.

His mouth worked silently. His tongue was gummy. The medicine had that effect on him, but now his tongue was stuck to the roof of his mouth like a communion wafer.

"Who do you confess to, Father?"

"The Lord hears my confessions."

"Does anyone else?"

"Listen, son, you need to—"

"Does anyone know the secrets you keep?"

The anger that attempted to burn away the cold shivers was snuffed by a paralyzing grip of fear. *He knows. Oh, dear Lord, he knows. He knows.*

"The Lord is my shepherd," Father Walker muttered. "Yea, though I walk through the valley of the shadow of death—"

"What about your flock? Are you not their shepherd?"

"The Lord hears my prayers. He guides my hand and words. He forgives. He sent his only begotten Son to die for the sins of the world. Only he has the power to forgive."

Father Walker squeezed his hands like one was trying to strangle the other.

"You have no right to come into my Father's house and cast judgment."

He took a deep breath.

Pressed his face to the screen.

"You have no right."

Father Walker stood up, his knees weak.

"YOU HAVE NO RIGHT TO JUDGE ME IN THE PRESENCE OF THE LORD!"

Father Walker jumped out and reached for the confessor's door.

He had no right to expose a confessor, but this was no ordinary confessor. This was not one of his flock. This was an intruder imitating the word of God, casting stones in his house. It was Father Walker's duty to clean the Lord's house.

To purge it.

He threw open the confessional.

Empty.

His breath laboring, he stepped in and looked around the tiny room no bigger than a closet. There was no way, no way, no way, *no way, no way, NO WAY, NO WAY...*

"Father?"

Ms. Sidling was standing outside the confessional, her purse over her shoulder and her eyebrows knitted with concern.

Father Walker left the church. He wasn't running. He wasn't exactly walking. He just needed out. He needed a breath. He needed to clear his mind.

And he could use a pill.

9 8

Father Walker believed in structure.

He didn't feel like walking in the park, but it was Wednesday. He needed to walk; he needed to prepare his homily. It wasn't like he could call off mass.

But you can call in sick.

I'm not sick.

Yes. You are.

Not like that—

He shook his head. Ever since he started with the Zoloft, he started having conversations with himself. They were just thoughts, but they felt real. Too real.

Fresh air.

Father Walker parked his car at the entrance and started his typical route around the baseball diamonds and toward the lake. He walked slowly, hands folded over his stomach, and focused on one foot and then the other. Usually, the sounds of squabbling ducks and the smell of cut grass cleared his mind and his homily unfolded. In cases like today, he reached for a notebook with scriptures that would inspire him.

He opened it at random.

Proverbs 28:13. Whoso confesseth and forsaketh them shall have mercy.

The book clapped shut.

Father Walker put it in his pocket. His pace quickened.

He didn't want to think of confession. He'd confessed his sins already. He had been forgiven. He didn't need approval of his fellow man, only the Lord.

Only Jesus.

Father Walker finished his walk.

He got in his car and headed back to the rectory without a word prepared for his homily. Nothing came to him.

99

The hospital room was softly lit over the head of the bed.

Father Gordon was breathing softly. The tube was beneath his nose, the wires still in place on his head and chest. His wrists still bound to the bed.

Father Walker let the door close behind him.

It had been a month. Father Gordon's complexion was ashen, his cheeks sagging. A line of saliva glistened from the corner of his mouth.

Father Walker remained standing.

He didn't want to sit.

He didn't want to stay.

He just wanted to see the man. Guilt gnawed at the thoughts he was entertaining. Thoughts of ripping the cords from his head, yanking away the oxygen tube; thoughts of wrapping his hands around his throat and hurting him.

Hurting him badly.

Something Father Walker couldn't do when the old man was alive and well. Father Gordon was just too cantankerous. Just too mean.

Now he was withering in a hospital bed and, somehow, he still weighed on Father Walker. Still a burden. He always thought when he was dead and gone, that he would pay for his sins when he faced the Lord, and Father Walker would be free of his burden so that he could be a true shepherd to his flock.

But he wouldn't die.

He just wouldn't die.

"Why must I suffer for you?" Father Walker muttered.

You choose to suffer, he answered himself.

Father Walker stood at the door, hand on the knob, afraid to get any closer to the old man, afraid he would do something he would regret. He stayed until a nurse came into the room to record his vital signs.

Father Walker rushed to the steps.

Who takes your confession?

Shut up.

Who hears your sins?

He sprinted down the steps.

Sprinted to his car.

100

Yellow pulled the last bag of mulch off the wheelbarrow.

She wiped the sweat from her forehead. The flowerbed was clean of weeds. The entire thing. She was sure there was so much more to do, but someone was keeping the weeds out of the ground.

And she knew who.

He's still here.

She slept well at night. She slept deep and clean. She never saw him outside the trailer or when she walked to the church or even in the garden, but he was around.

Theresa sat on the bench and blew smoke at the sky. She'd strained a muscle loading one of the bags of mulch into the truck and had to rest. She moved the bench back under the shade of the crape myrtle and resumed a relaxed position.

Yellow tore open a bag of cedar and took a moment to inhale the fragrance. Of all the chores, this was her favorite. It used to be that the smell of earth and wood brought her closer to feeling special—closer to God. She enjoyed the warm feeling of the shredded chips in her hands and the way it looked when it was spread evenly among the plants.

Bag after bag, she emptied it into the garden and spread it on hands and knees. Theresa even got up after a while to pick up the empty plastic bags. Yellow continued mulching. Theresa tapped her on the shoulder and held out a bottle. Yellow took a swig of water and wiped her face.

She went back to work.

Until a shadow fell over her.

She looked up at a man.

A very grave man.

1 0 1

Father Walker paced inside his study.

It was Saturday. Mass was at 5:15 p.m. He was not finished with the homily. In fact, he had not written a single word. Instead, he paced back and forth, occasionally looking out the window. At some level, he knew what the homily was going to be. But first, he just needed to do something. Maybe if he did this something, he could go back to a homily that was safe and helpful to his congregation.

Safe.

I just want to feel safe.

Lord, forgive us our trespasses.

A car door slammed.

Father Walker peeked out the window. Theresa was getting out of her red truck. She opened the tailgate while Yellow came around the other side with the wheelbarrow.

Father Walker turned away.

He paced again. He thumped his hand against his legs, thinking and thinking. Fear spread throughout his stomach like ice crystals. He splashed water on his face. He just needed to do this. He was acting ridiculous.

Like a child.

He was a leader of men. He was a chosen voice of God and he was hiding from the truth. It was just words. It was what he needed to do.

Forgive us our trespasses, as we forgive those who trespass against us.

Father Walker forced his door open. He forced his way outside.

The sun was fierce.

He covered his eyes with sunglasses.

Children were squealing at the playground. The Johnstons and Gladstones were having a picnic. There were several other cars in the parking lot. Someone was getting out of a red Mustang and waved at Father Walker. It was that doctor. Dr. Espada.

He ducked around the building.

His wingtips crunched in the gravel.

Theresa was standing at the end of the path, holding plastic bags. She was watching the black ponytail bob above the bed of coleus. The yellow ribbon flipped back and forth as Yellow spread mulch. The ribbon was bright, like the sun. The ribbon fluttered and shined against the blackness of her hair.

Lead us not into temptation.

Father Walker forced his feet to continue forward.

He forced each one, cold with fear, to aim for the bouncing ribbon.

His thighs were numb.

His chest, cold and tingly.

He stopped over the young girl with her hands buried in the fresh mulch.

"Hello, Father Walker," Theresa said.

Father Walker stood there.

Yellow looked up.

Their eyes met.

He was remembering things he'd seen like it was yesterday. Things that happened. He imagined all the things that happened that he didn't see. He knew the things that had happened and Father Walker said nothing, said nothing, said nothing.

NOTHING.

But deliver us from evil.

"I'm sorry, Amarillo," he said.

"Father Walker?" Theresa said. "Are you all right?"

Yellow stood on her knees.

She couldn't see his eyes behind the dark lens. She couldn't see the redness and the wetness.

She looked behind Father Walker.

"Father Walker, hello." A young woman—blond hair and black leather satchel—came down the path. "We have an appointment at two."

The blond woman smiled at Yellow, saying hello to her. She said hello to Theresa. She held out her hand to Father Walker.

"I'm Amanda Spaulding from Catholic Charities."

Father Walker just stared.

Just stared.

Just stared.

"I'm sorry, am I interrupting…"

Father Walker walked off.

Amanda's smile faltered. She followed him down the path, where a dark-skinned couple waited. They were looking at Yellow. They greeted Father Walker.

"What was that all about?" Theresa said.

Yellow shook her head.

They watched Father Walker and the three people look back before going around the corner.

Theresa lit a cigarette. "What was he saying sorry for?" she asked.

Yellow grabbed another bag. She went back to work.

Her hands were shaking.

The organ pipes vibrated the walls.

Father Walker stood in front of the mirror, adjusting his sleeves and collar. He combed his hair, his eyes never leaving the reflection. He took the large wireframe glasses off, put them on the shelf, and noticed the dark rings beneath his eyes, how deeply they appeared to be set in his gaunt face.

He'd become a ghost.

An empty man.

"Father?" Jimmy Farris cracked open the door. He was holding the golden cross. "Shouldn't we be going?"

The organist had started the procession hymn over.

5:25.

Yes. Yes, we must go.

Father Walker left his glasses.

He joined the two altar boys waiting at the doors. The ushers stood next to them, nodding to Father Walker. He assumed a holy pose and followed the boys down the red-carpeted aisle that divided the church in half.

Father Walker felt naked.

He felt the eyes of the congregation. They watched him walk to the altar. Watched him walk the three steps to take his place and raise his hands.

He felt Jesus on the cross, hanging above the altar, watching him begin mass. Jesus with the spikes through his palms, through his feet. Jesus with the crown of thorns and wounds in his sides.

Jesus, who died for their sins.

Jesus, who cleansed the world.

Sin is still in the world.

Sin is among us.

We are born into it.

Father Walker operated like a machine, reciting the opening prayers and procedures, something he'd done thousands of times. He kept his eyes cast down as he took his seat and allowed the lectors to read passages from the Bible. He sat numbly.

He sat coldly.

The stained-glass windows cast colored light on the parishioners. The windows depicted the Stations of the Cross. The windows illustrated Jesus dragging his cross to Golgotha while Roman soldiers stood by and watched. Jesus bled in the streets while people watched.

He was crucified while we watched.

While we did nothing.

Jesus was crucified.

A long silence hung in the church. Some folks began to murmur. Jimmy leaned over.

"Father?"

Father Walker stood up. He paused long enough for sensation to return to his legs. He did not want to fall, but he could not feel much besides the quiver of fear.

He took his place at the podium.

Eyes upon him.

Jesus watching.

He stood there. There were no note cards. There was no homily.

Father Walker stood there, alone.

He looked out.

The congregation looked back. Heads tipped toward one another and whispers fluttered off the walls. The silence continued until the doors opened.

A boy stepped into the church.

Drayton dipped his fingers in the holy font and crossed himself. He remained in the back.

Father Walker stood quite still. He saw his people. He saw their children.

I am the Roman soldier.

"Father Gordon," he said.

I stood by.

His voice quivered. It was loud enough to get the attention of everyone. It was pained enough to hold their curiosity.

I watched.

"Father Gordon… molested…"

I did nothing.

"Your children."

A collective breath. Confused expressions.

Father Walker held onto the podium. His knees knocked into the lower portion, but he held on to keep from falling. He held on to finish what he needed to do.

He was so cold. So scared.

"And I knew this," Father Walker continued, his voice cracking. "I have known what he has been doing for ten years."

Several people stood up.

Families in the back rushed out the doors, hands over the children's ears.

Someone shouted.

"I'm sorry," he whispered. "I'm so sorry."

And Father Walker began to weep.

He let go of the podium. He fell into a heap and cried into his hands, feeling the hot flush of tears pooling in his palms. Heard angry shouts. Heard the shuffle of a crowd. Some people came to him.

Some left.

Most remained, confused.

Drayton left Father Walker to his confession. His opportunity at redemption.

1 0 3

*Y*ellow pulled the brush through her hair still wet from the shower.

The ribbon was draped over the mirror while she ran the knots from her hair. When she finished with the left side, she started on the right. She put the brush down, pulled her hair back with both hands with an elastic band between her lips, and tied it off.

Someone knocked on the front door.

There were strange voices. The volume on the television was turned down. She didn't recognize who it was. She was relieved. She didn't want Father Walker coming over to the house. She didn't want anyone from the church coming over. Theresa asked her, again, why Father Walker would apologize. Someone had called after 5:15 mass that night and said Father Walker made some weird confession on the altar. Theresa said it was hogwash, that Father Walker was under stress and sometimes people say things they don't mean. Still, she wanted to know why he apologized.

Yellow considered lying, perhaps telling Theresa that he broke one of Yellow's favorite toys in the back room, but that didn't seem right.

So she just said, again and again, she didn't know.

That was a lie, too.

Theresa was going to ask Father Walker when she saw him.

That was why Yellow should've lied.

"Yellow!" Theresa called from the front. "Come out here!"

Yellow knew why Father Walker apologized.

He knew what was happening.

He knew what Father Gordon made her do. He knew how Father Gordon made her feel so little, so insignificant.

So empty.

And now he was sorry.

Now he was sorry.

"Yellow." Theresa opened the door. "Young lady, I told you to come up front. Let's go, honey. Front and center."

Yellow pulled the ribbon around her ponytail and tied it off.

She followed Theresa through the narrow hallway to the front room, where her foster dad filled the recliner. There were three people behind him. One of them was Ms. Amanda from earlier that day. The others were the olive-skinned couple she'd seen earlier that day, too. They were waiting at the end of the path for Father Walker after he apologized.

They were smiling.

They were all smiling, except for her foster dad and Theresa.

"Mi nombre es Eva Espada."

The man stood next to her, smiling. *"¿Cómo le gustaría venir con nosotros?"* he said.

How would you like to come home with us?

The woman put her hands on her knees and leveled her face with Yellow's. Her smile was bright and warm. Her smile was yellow.

The woman said, *"Amarillo."*

Yellow burst into tears.

She covered her face and cried.

And Eva and Marc wrapped their arms around her. They let her cry.

They let Amarillo cry.

104

The garden was weeded.

It was mulched.

It was clean.

Drayton walked along the path that ground beneath his boots while car doors slammed and left in a hurry. Voices could be heard from the church. Some angry.

Some weeping.

Drayton followed the path out of the garden and through the orchard, where gardenias filled the air with fragrance.

St. Michaels forever behind him.

father Gordon woke up. It seemed like he'd been trying to wake up for quite some time. Even now, he lay there trying to open his eyes while he listened to birds chirp at the rising sun. He could smell cut grass, too.

He opened his eyes, blinking back the light until his eyes adjusted. He couldn't remember where he'd been, but he woke up sitting on a bench in a small room. An organ was vibrating items on a small shelf next to him. He was holding a long, golden rod with a cross on top.

It all seemed so strange.

His eyes wanted to shut again. His head was so stuffy and sort of numb. He rubbed his eyes, yawning. He was supposed to be someone else, he was sure of it. He was supposed to be somewhere else, too. But he couldn't quite remember who or where.

He couldn't even remember his name.

He rubbed his *eyes.*

He rubbed both eyes. *With both hands.*

There was a pile of clothes on the floor. Across the room, looking back from a full-length mirror, was a shirtless young man sitting on the edge of a bench. He was holding a bunched-up robe on his lap as if he'd just began to get undressed after church service. He had a full head of sandy locks and a slight hunch in the shoulders. Father Gordon waved and the reflection waved back.

Vertigo whirled through him.

"Knock-knock." Someone tapped on the door and peered through the crack. "You in here, Jon?"

Father Gordon stared at a man opening the door. He looked for a shirt.

"That's all right, I won't stay long."

The man quietly closed the door behind him. Father Gordon heard the faint snick of a door lock fall in place.

The man looked around the room and frowned. "You'll need to do a better job of cleaning up after yourself, Jon. Cleanliness is close to godliness, and you, my son, are darn near the gates of Hell."

He smiled with all his teeth.

"Listen, you did a great job in mass today. It was your first time as a server and you did everything perfectly."

The man held up his fingers in a circle. *Okeydokey.*

"I spoke with your parents to let you stay around and clean up. I'll take you home when we're done. How's that sound?"

Father Gordon nodded absently. His voice was not there. He opened his mouth and words did not come out.

He couldn't say no.

Even if he wanted to.

"I want to talk with you about today's homily, Jon. *Hablar de culpabilidad.*" *About guilt.*

Why did he just speak Spanish?

The man sat on the bench and put his hand on Father Gordon's bare shoulder. He was the size of a grizzly. Curly hair tufted from his collar. He smelled like a long day's work.

The man's leg pressed against Father Gordon's.

Something ugly and rotten broke open in Father Gordon's stomach, spilling foul emotions into his chest and throat.

The man's hand was soft and lotioned.

Fear blossomed in Father Gordon's stomach like an acid stain. He wanted to move, to jump off the bed, to scream… but he was just so… scared.

"You're far from perfect, Jon."

The man gestured to the mess on the floor.

"I can help you find God's grace. But first, you must promise me something."

The man traced a small circle on Father Gordon's shoulder. His finger went round and round.

Round and round.

"Este es nuestro secreto."

Tickling his skin.

Our secret.

106

"**N**URSE!"

The nurse's aide tried to hold Father Gordon's feet on the bed. The old man thrashed with surprising strength, knocking the pitcher of water on the floor.

The nurse hustled into the room and helped her subdue the other leg. Father Gordon's hands slammed against the side bars. The bands dug into his skin. He went stiff as a plank, grinding his teeth. And then let loose a shriek that could be heard at the other end of the hall.

There were four nurses in the room when he fell limp. They held him tightly for another couple minutes, until they were sure it was over.

"That was the worse seizure yet." The nurse took a breath.

The nurse's aide picked up the pitcher and mopped up the spill. The others helped straighten up and check that all the monitors were still attached. The on-duty nurse made a note that leg restraints were required.

"When was the last seizure?" the nurse asked.

The aide checked the computer station she had rolled into the room just before all hell broke loose. "Yesterday, about this time."

"Okay, well, record this one."

The on-duty nurse and aide remained for another ten minutes until Father Gordon's breathing returned to normal. He began to softly whimper, like a child. A tear pooled against the bridge of his nose.

"Have you ever seen anything like this?" the aide asked.

"No." The nurse shook her head. "Never."

Neither one of them noticed the boy sitting in the corner of the room.

107

Drayton sat quietly in Father Gordon's room. Even after the nurses left and there was just the soft glow of the instruments and the old man's rattling breath, he stayed seated. He would remain at Father Gordon's side for many months to come. Absolution would not be easy.

And if the hunger were to fall upon Drayton, well, it was a hospital.

NUMBERS

BOOK 5

If you knew, would you tell?

108

_L_AST DAY

The world is bleeding watercolor.

My eyes are open. I think. I feel the dry sting, the impact of each droplet, but there's nothing to see. Just a watery grave. A spinning carnival ride.

The ground slurps up the rain; drops spatter my ears. A continuous patter of harmless bullets drill the earth. Smack. Smack. Smack.

I'm sinking. I think. The ground swallows me, its embrace warm and fluid. Rain taps between my eyes—my burning, stinging eyes—flowing through my head like a cracked egg, spilling a steady ooze, washing away the aches and pains.

Killing me from inside out.

I don't feel it, though.

I don't feel much of anything. Just the sky falling. Just the earth melting.

I turn my head, I don't know how. Mud squishes in my right ear,

258

rain gurgles into my left as it funnels into the canal and pools over the drum, drawing a liquid veil over the world.

Forms emerge from the gray wash. A pineapple. A pier.

There's a scent of pluff mud.

I know where I am. I grew up here. I live here.

Die here.

He was right.

It's so hard to draw a breath. My chest is so heavy. I rest between each inhale/exhale, conserve my energy to draw one more—just one more—while the warmth bleeds out of my head and into my groin, into my legs, filling my toes.

Someone shouts. Its sounds more like damaged audio, syllables smeared across a warped record. Filled with urgency. Fear. I don't have the strength to turn my head. Not anymore.

And I don't want to. I just want Mother Earth. *Dust to dust. Mud to mud.*

Sounds become large and smudgy. The rain dances louder but stops falling. I blink away the rain, taste salt.

The world darkens. An umbrella hovers over me. Someone looks down. Don't know him. Or her. Do I?

More people come. Maybe I know them, too. It doesn't matter. Out there among the fuzzy pier and splashing pineapple fountain, a dark figure approaches. His steps, slow and steady. Always slow and steady. I know him.

He told me this was coming.

He counted the days.

Now he comes for my last moments.

109

DAY 5

DAY FIVE IS A FRIDAY.

The day starts like they all do.

I take my bike up King Street to grab coffee at Starbucks. The streets are clean, the puddles slick with rainbows. The horses are already out, hauling early rising tourists eager to hear about the ghost of General Sherman still committing war crimes in Charleston. That's something you don't read about in textbooks, kids. I get off King, turn onto Wentworth, hopping curbs to avoid traffic.

My office is a small house off the street, hidden behind palms and an extremely large loquat tree. Seems silly to use it as an office when I could rent the thing for a small treasure. Fortunately, my ancestors bought several Charleston houses hundreds of years ago, paid what a hotdog costs today. That's no shit.

There's a tarnished plate next to the front door. *Dr. Gallagher.*

That's all. No letters at the end of the name, no titles. Hell, I wouldn't even put doctor, but folks need to know I have some training. You don't open your soul to just any guy that rides his bike to work.

A bell rings when I open the door. Old-fashioned, sure, but it goes with the house. Reminds some of my clients of five and dimes. The front room serves as the waiting room. It's spacious, comfy, magazines, that sort of thing. Not that it gets used much. I schedule folks with plenty of space in between. The back door rarely gets used.

The hallway door was installed to separate the front room from the rest of the house. I lean the bike against the wall and flip a switch on the Zen waterfall. Water trickles down a rough-hewn slab, disappearing into a rock basin. It's tranquil, white noise. The whole setup reminds me of a Zen center where I once practiced. The teacher was in a back room, meeting with attendees one at a time. We would sit zazen until we heard a tiny bell tinkle. And then the line would move up one until the next bell.

I've got a tiny bell, but I'm no Zen center.

I help people with their problems, but I'm only checking in three days a week. I don't need the money, really. I rent most of the ancient Gallagher houses; they pay for everything. I keep up the therapy, quite frankly, because that Zen teacher—the one with the tinkling bell— once said, "If you think the purpose of life is to pursue pleasure, then your practice is misguided."

So I do this to serve Life, as she would say.

And then I serve drinks.

I'm kidding. Actually, I'm not.

The bike goes in one of the closed rooms. I go into the back room. The office. Where the magic happens. Furnished entirely at Morris Sokol on King. Each chair puts your ass in total comfort. Why? Because when clarifying problems of the mind, it helps to forget the problems of the body. And my clients have both. Plus money.

The drapes are heavy. I wrap them back, letting daylight inside. The bird feeders are empty. I check my phone. No appointments until eleven o'clock. That gives me a few hours to finish my dark roast and sit meditation. But first, the birds are hungry.

* * *

THE BELL RINGS.

I look up from the *Post and Courier*, look at the small clock mounted on the mahogany bookshelf. It's 9:55. I check my phone again, and this time see a name for a 10:00 that wasn't there an hour ago and I don't remember scheduling. And a name I don't remember. I place the phone and newspaper on the small table and pause. I don't have a weapon in the house. And, honestly, I don't know why I just thought that.

Why the hell would I need a weapon?

I open the hallway door.

A young man is there. He's standing in the middle of the room, very still. Plainly dressed. Very dark skin.

"I'm sorry," I say. "I don't remember scheduling you."

"You didn't."

Okay. All right. Now I'm thinking about that weapon again. It's just me and this stranger in a small house. He's odd. Not threatening. Just standing there in the dimly lit room.

The Zen fountain bubbling.

"Then how'd you get one?"

He tilts his head slightly. That's it.

Suppose that would freak me out. It should. It doesn't, though, and I don't know why. But as my Zen teacher would say, Life calls. Practice always answers. I don't normally take on new clients like this. In fact, I never do. But then it's only ten o'clock. I got time.

And I'm curious. *Let's have a look.*

"All right, then." I step aside. "Come on back."

He takes a moment before starting forward, his heavy boots clopping on the wood floor. I feel foolish for thinking about a weapon. Is it because he's black? I don't consider myself racist, but would I feel threatened if he was white?

But I felt scared before seeing him.

The young man wanders into the office and looks out the window.

"I'm Dr. Gallagher, but you can call me Jimmy, if you like."

I don't always make that offer. In fact, I never do. Don't know why I did. And that's two things I never do in less than two minutes. Three, if you count my lack of freaking.

"Drayton." He's staring at the clock on the bookshelf.

"You'll need to fill out some paperwork before we get started." I find a blank form in the filing cabinet. "It just goes over fees and release statements, personal information. That sort of thing."

Drayton picks up the wooden Buddha next to the clock. He turns it over, rubbing the belly with his thumb.

"Flea market, ninety-nine cents," I say. "You meditate?"

He carefully puts it back, his motion so mindful and fluid. It's clear he does. There's a certain presence that fills a room, a light beaming from someone accomplished in meditation. Joriki, it's called, I think. Star Wars geeks call it The Force.

And that's when he says something.

I remember staring at the clock, the numbers 10:02. You remember something like this when you hear it. You remember every detail. Every smell, every sensation. A snapshot that defines the rest of your life.

He turns slowly and says, "You will die in five days."

Fuck. I need a weapon.

Icy water drains into my legs. I'm moved by the sudden urge to urinate a Starbucks grande down my pant leg. The phone is on the nightstand and I'm in the corner, next to the filing cabinet, stupid fucking forms in my hands. The back door and hallway door are too far away.

"Are you threatening me?" I try to sound unperturbed. At the very least, not like I'm twelve. I'm not sure I pull it off.

Drayton eases into the Habersham chair, across from my usual seat, crossing his legs like he's ready to begin his session.

"You will suffer an aneurysmal subarachnoid hemorrhage," he says lightly. "Bleeding between the first two layers of tissue that protect the brain. I'm afraid you won't survive."

"Uh-huh. And how the hell could you know that?"

Drayton's nostrils flare.

I don't trust my legs, but if I don't sit down I just might crumble. The surreal moment is causing vertigo. I grasp the filing cabinet, reach for the back of my chair and collapse. I look into the eyes of my possible killer. The pupils are large, circled with dark brown irises. His face so smooth, so relaxed. I fall into his gaze, the room darkening.

Disappearing.

An ancient hand falls on my soul, an immovable presence that removes the fearful sensations clenching my legs, hardened in my stomach.

He blinks.

I'm back, seated in my chair. No longer concerned about wetting myself.

I remember him. I saw this kid the other day, downtown, when Tommy walked by. This kid saw me pinching my nose, laying back on the bench with a migraine. This little shit is in on some sick joke. I got clients that blame me for their problems, maybe one of them put him up to this. Or maybe Tommy's busting my balls, the sonofabitch. I should've made this creep pay up front, my fees getting the last laugh.

"This is not a joke," he says.

And the icy legs return. "You can leave now. No charge."

"You know this is true."

"Look, get the hell out of here before I call the cops." Big-boy voice activated. "And tell whoever the fuck sent you to knock it off or I'll have them arrested."

Not sure what I was going to do if he just sat there. Suppose I was going to pick up the phone. But then he stands up, looking around the office. He doesn't nod or even acknowledge me. Come to think of it, he never even looked threatening. He just came in, said I was going to die, and then he walked out like some goddamn bike messenger.

The hallway door closes, his boots echo through the front room. The bell rings.

And I can't move.

Just fucking weird, man. I've had threats before, but nothing like this. I rub my forehead. It feels just fine. And five days? Whoever paid this kid got their money's worth.

It's ten thirty by the time I get up.

* * *

MY WIFE and I stand outside Grill 225. Not my favorite place on a Friday night. The streets smell sour and the sidewalks are crowded with college students and tourists and vendors. I stare through the large plate glass. My reflection is gaunt. I chalk it up to the dark window, not lingering thoughts. I keep my arms folded, avoiding the temptation to rub my forehead, where a foretold vein (or is it an artery?) is ready to burst, hosing my brain down like a bloody—

Stop.

Runaway thoughts, all day long. I sat in the therapist's chair, riding out three more appointments after Drayton left. The fact that I still remember his name upsets me. I've got to give props to whoever dreamed that goof up. Kid was convincing. It wasn't what he said, just the way he filled the room when he walked in, delivered the message, deadpan. Next time I see Tommy, I'll shake his hand and smack him in the balls.

Good one, Tommy. Got me good.

"Honey." Brenda grabs my arm. "You're staring."

The couple at the table nearest the window snicker at me. I look like a mindless zombie watching them eat. I turn away, one last glimpse of the shadows across my reflection.

"Hannah said they'd be here at seven," Brenda says. "What time is it?"

The case isn't on my belt. "Left my phone at the office."

"Oh, there they are." Brenda waves.

Pete and Hannah Edwards cross through the market. Brenda greets them at the corner. I put my hands in my pockets—slightly annoyed they're late for everything—and find something. At first, I think maybe it's my phone, maybe I didn't forget it. It's a stack of hundred-dollar bills, crisp and neatly folded with a crease. Ten of them.

I don't remember packing cash. In fact, I almost never carry cash, and certainly not in my pocket—

A white card flutters out.

It falls on the cracked bluestone, a black-ink number facing up.

I'm afraid to bend over, afraid I'll fall over if I do. Afraid to touch the card, that'll make it real. That'll mean today is day number five, if I pick it up. Instead, I just look away, pretending this joke is going too far.

"Hey, killer. You paying tonight?" Pete shakes my empty hand, his Clemson class ring grinding into my finger.

"Honey, what are you doing with all that money?" Brenda asks.

I'm speechless, really. I'd drop the bills right on top of the card, covering that number, if it wouldn't make a scene. Instead, I put them back in my pocket and feel them dirty my palm when I let go, like I just accepted the Devil's terms.

I leave the 5 on the pavement.

We go in the restaurant. We eat the finest steak in town.

I don't taste a single bite.

110

DAY 4

DAY FOUR IS SATURDAY.

No clients today. No problems to solve. Just me and the truck and a handful of projects at the rental houses. I could sub the repairs out, but I like to clean out fountains and fix irrigation. I like pruning shrubs and planting flowers because they don't talk back.

My travel mug of coffee is near empty, but all that caffeine isn't helping. I slept very little the night before, lying in bed and watching the cobwebs waver near the vents. The mind has a tremendous ability to make sense out of illogical events.

I'm no different.

How did the card get in my pocket? And the money? If it's a goof, it's a goddamn good one. I'm genuinely freaking out. But I've seen Criss Angel pop a basketball and pull out a card with someone's number on it. That sort of shit can be done. I don't know how, but it's not magic.

And someone is pulling a Criss Angel on me.

I had an explanation before I fell asleep somewhere in the three o'clock hour. Tommy had to be in on it, but that goon doesn't have the brains for something like this. Phil does, though. We used to goof on that asshole all through high school. How many times did we leave his ass in the woods? I would've called him at 4:00 a.m. if I had my phone.

The cash sits on my dash. *But if you're going to goof, you don't give some stooge one thousand dollars.*

My fragile house of rationalization begins to crumble.

It completely falls when I pull up to the office. There's a boy at the front door. A claw clenches my chest and doesn't let go.

I turn the truck off.

We stare.

He stands with hands behind his back, tilting his head as if questioning what I'm doing. The engine ticks beneath the hood. And my pulse thuds behind my eardrums. I reach into the glove box and grab the pepper spray.

I open the door and drop one foot on the ground. "What are you doing?"

"I paid for five sessions."

"The hell you talking about?"

I didn't even make him pay for the first—*one thousand dollars.* At two hundred a pop, that's five sessions.

"Phil put you up to this? Tommy? Tell those bastards this isn't funny."

"I'd simply like to talk."

"I'm closed. You come back on Monday." I reach inside the truck and fling the money. Green bills flutter to the ground. "In fact, don't come back Monday. Here's your refund. Tell whoever put you up to this I'm done."

"That's your money, James. I paid for five sessions, you accepted."

"That supposed to scare me?"

"I only want my hour. I'll be on my way."

He's wearing the same clothes as yesterday. But he's not filthy, doubt he slept in a homeless shelter. Doesn't look like he has a thousand dollars for counseling. He's calm, though. So calm.

And peace trickles through me, warm and soft. Washing away the tension, the cold fear. And it's me and him. With nowhere else to be.

* * *

THE COFFEE MACHINE pops and kicks on the kitchen counter. "You want some?" I ask.

"Tea, if you have it."

I just so happen to have tea in the cabinet. What good Southerner would not? I pour a cup of coffee and he walks into the kitchen, spooking me.

"I'll get it," he says, taking the box of tea from the counter.

My phone is in the office, right where I left it. I put it in my pocket so I won't have to return again. He may have paid for five sessions, but he'll get them on my time. Not his. The fountain bubbles in the front room. He must've turned it on. I take small sips, listening to his boots rap the kitchen floor, the microwave *bing*, and notice the bird feeders are full.

And I forgot to fill them yesterday.

He walks into the back office, surprisingly light-footed with heavy boots. He sits on the duvet, carefully balancing a fine china teacup and saucer that must have been in the back of the cabinet. A funny look, really. This very dark-skinned young man sitting with his legs elegantly crossed, a dainty cup beneath his nose. He inhales the steam, eyes closed.

We sit in silence, not really looking at each other. I usually let the client begin the session. I don't know what the fuck this kid wants, though. What do I say to a jerkoff that's counting down my life?

The silence stretches.

I lace my hands over my lap and glance at the clock. Minutes tick away and Drayton sips the tea, occasionally inhaling the steam. I close my eyes, too, listening to the birds quibble at the feeders, the old bones of the house settle. Feel the confines of the walls, the easy pull of my breath.

"I was born sometime before Christ." He says it softly. Matter-a-factly. Like maybe he just asked if I thought it would rain tomorrow.

The absurd statement hangs between us. It goes along with the rest of this ridiculous show. When he doesn't follow it, I say, "So you're two thousand years old?"

"Much older."

"How much?"

"I recall invading Greece as an Achaean."

"Greece?" I raise my eyebrows, stifling a reaction. "That would make you four thousand years old, if I remember ancient history. And anyway, I would've guessed you were from Africa, not Greece."

He strokes the back of his hand, the skin smooth and unblemished. "I was much fairer during the Bronze Age. Thousands of years in the sun has altered my appearance."

"Bronze Age? So now you're talking seven or eight thousand years old."

"Perhaps older."

"You don't remember?"

"I do not." He sips again, pinky out, and places the cup on the table in front of him. "The early days are quite obscure."

He seems content with the exchange. We sit in another prolonged silence. Perhaps it would've stayed that way, but now I'm entertained.

"Do you have a mother and father?"

"I don't know that. Quite honestly, James, I don't know how I came to be."

"You just appeared?"

"Do you remember sliding from the birth canal? Can you recall your first years of existence?"

"I grew up with parents, that much I know."

"I had no such luxury." He closes his eyes, folding his hands on his lap. "The early years were very difficult. It took quite some time to learn who I am."

Something tugs the corner of his mouth. Perhaps a memory.

"This is fascinating, Drayton. I mean, it's your money or someone's money, so you can spend it however you want, but if you want to tell me stories, I'll be honest, I'm not interested. There are plenty of people that need help, far more interested in real growth than you. You're eighteen years old and you tell me you're eight thousand. You tell me I'm going to die of a stroke. You need help, son, but the help you need is beyond my ability. You need to check yourself into MUSC's psych ward. I'll drive you there, if you don't have a ride—"

"Let me explain."

I stop from rising out of the chair. Perhaps it's the urgency in his tone or the chill I feel on the back of my neck. I sit. Drayton stands. I reach into my pocket, grasping the pepper spray, but he walks over to the window, where the birds are busy. Squirrels are nosing around the ground, grabbing scraps.

"I remember hunger," he says.

He seems to recall something in history, perhaps triggered by the desperate scavenging squirrels.

"It was deep and consuming. A blinding hunger." His voice is even and calm, but an edge commands me to stay. To listen. "It was a hunger that no breast would satisfy, nothing plucked from the earth or gathered from stems could satiate. It was all-consuming, James."

He taps the glass, his pink nail framed in black flesh. The squirrels scatter.

"A predator, I was. A very good predator." He looks back, pupils engorged.

Vertigo twirls in my groin. I press my feet against the floor. When he looks out the window, the fear of falling dissipates. "Humans don't live thousands of years," I mutter.

"As I've said, I know not what I am. Or why."

"That doesn't make sense."

He smudges the glass with his fingertips. I wonder if he'll leave fingerprints behind. I don't know why I care.

The squirrels creep back.

"Humans are warm-blooded," he says. "They contain red blood cells. They age. They die."

"And you don't?"

"A human is nearly twenty-five percent red blood cells. They depend on these erythrocytes to bind oxygen, to circulate through the body at ninety-seven point nine degrees. Red blood cells are the life of an animal. Would you agree?"

"I see," I say because I see where he's going. He's thousands of years old and he drinks blood. Everyone wants to be a fucking vampire. *Twilight* ruined these delusional kids. Whatever fear that shivered through me quickly sloughs away.

He thinks he's one of them. He's a vampire.

"I don't think that, James. I don't know what I am."

What?

"I can only tell you that I hunted the animals in the forest. At first it was the smaller ones, the weaker prey. I relied on my senses and cunning, setting traps and running them until they were exhausted. I tore the meat from the bone like a jackal, but mostly I savored the iron-rich hemoglobin. The salty tang satiated the ache that howled in the back of my throat, the richness fulfilling the emptiness of my being. I lived like that for centuries."

His hand slides off the window.

Fear returns like a ghostly hand trembling over my skin, raising gooseflesh in its wake. Goddamn, this kid is killing me. I check the clock. Only twenty minutes left and I'll clock him out, call Dr. Franklin at MUSC for a possible admittance. He doesn't feel threatening, but the delusion is frightening.

But the last twenty minutes of the session change everything.

Drayton comes back to the couch and sits across from me. Crosses his legs.

"You still doubt," he says. "I understand."

I try to look away, but his eyes are so deep and black and bottomless, holding me with the gravity of a black hole. I'm catatonic, imprisoned in my own body.

"It was Greece." His voice is silk, sliding into my ears, entering my brain. "I first tasted a human."

And I see.

I am in the streets of Ancient Greece, the cobbled stones slick with rain. The moon illuminates puddles and distant dogs whine. I see her ahead, lurking in the doorway. *No, I smell her.* Beneath the cloud of perfume and sour alcohol, I sense the rich flow of her blood pulsing through the carotid artery.

She steps into the street. Her fingers curl like dancers, beckoning me forth. She knows I lust but not for what. The flesh holds no power over my groin. It's the red blood that grips my throat, pulls me into its embrace. She cackles with laughter, stumbling into my arms. Her neck—sticky with saliva and wine—is exposed. I drag the tip of my tongue across it, tasting the sweat. Feel the pulse. It vibrates in my own throat.

She moans.

Limp in my embrace, she gives herself to me. Her neck breaks easily. Her head flops over, stretching the skin. The artery thumps like a temptress. And I resist no more.

I tear the flesh like rice paper, my jaws strengthened on the hide of animals, the incisors long and eviscerating. Blood spills over my chin and I dig into the open meat, searching with my tongue until I find the severed artery, pulling it between my lips.

I suck the blood from it. So much lighter than an animal's, the blood infused with something… different. Intoxicating.

Essential.

I empty her of life.

And it fills me. I am whole. Present.

Alive.

The sensation follows me back to the chair. I find myself in my office, cold and stiff. Unblinking, tears stream from my burning eyes. I snatch a deep breath and lunge forward, onto my feet.

It takes time to recognize my surroundings. The windows and the birds. The empty couch. Drayton's gone.

The salty tang of iron lingers.

* * *

IT's the third time I've washed my body, scrubbing with a bar soap,

273

suds pooling around my feet. Still, I can't rid the sense of dread that's thick and heavy, coating me like an oily film.

I step out, wrap a towel around my waist, and stand in front of the mirror. My hair is thick, but it's gray and slapped against my forehead. I push it back, water beading on my shoulders. How many times have I stood in front of the mirror, never really paying attention to who looks back?

I lean closer, pulling down the bottom eyelids. The irises blue, but the whites are red. The pupils shrink down to tiny holes as I near the lights. The mirror fogs with my breath, slowly obscuring my face. My finger squeaks across the glass and I stand back, observing the number four freshly etched in the cloudy mirror.

I rub my head, imagining an artery bursting open, my brain drowning in blood.

Four days.

I pull the knot loose; the towel gathers around my ankles. I step back, looking at what fifty years has done to my body. The slight pooch above my waist, the sag beneath my breasts. The sag elsewhere. My ass dimpled with cottage-cheese texture. I never thought I'd look like this. Youth is forever hopeful, eternally blind. And here I am, watching the number four fade from the mirror, wondering how this kid got ass-deep inside my fucking head.

"Honey?"

"Whoa!" I jerk at the sound of the voice.

Brenda doesn't hide her smile. "Caught you looking, huh?"

"Just assessing the damage."

"Jamie and I are about to start a movie. You coming?"

"No. Go ahead."

"All right." She starts away. I pull open the drawer and push around tubes of toothpaste and combs, trying to look normal. Trying to look like I'm not staring at the number four.

"You okay?" she asks. "You've been a little quiet today."

I consider lying. That never works. That's what happens when psychiatrists marry.

"Yeah. Just... there's this new client that got to me today."

"Since when did you take on new clients?"

"Long story."

"You want to talk about it?"

"No big deal." I run a comb through my hair. "I'm working through it, you go on. I'll be down in a second."

Brenda watches me slick my hair back, looking through me with x-ray vision. She finally gives up. I'll talk if it's still bothering me, she knows that.

I keep combing, staring at the four still streaked on the mirror.

1 1 1

AY 3

Good day for a jog. Good day to run.

Right now, I feel like running away, maybe California or the North Pole. I settle for a brisk jog along the Battery.

I run until my lungs burn. Endorphins wash out the confusion, leaving my mind fresh and clean, like a morning after a heavy rain, the trash swept out of the gutters. I rationalize everything that's happened, minimize it with the precision of a mental surgeon.

People don't live thousands of years. They don't drink blood or sparkle in the sunlight.

But how'd he make me see it?

I run out of steam somewhere on Logan Street, just north of Broad. Dark edges creep around my vision. No matter how fast or how far, I can't outrun that question—the reality—that I experienced some sort of horrific hallucination. I stalked a prostitute and tore her open with the viciousness of a starving predator. No hatred, no anger.

Just pure lust.

Even the incisors were lengthened, like a lion.

Or vampire.

I begin the rudimentary technique of thought-labeling, something I learned early on in Zen practice. It goes something like *Having a thought, he's insane. Having a thought, this is illogical. Having a thought, this can't happen. Having a thought, vampires don't exist.*

Because they don't. Vampires don't exist and this is all a goof and someone's got me on the run and I'm not fucking dying, for Christ's sake. I'm as healthy as a newborn and that little fuck should be arrested—

I stop labeling and indulge in them. Entertain them. The best drama in the world is inside the mind, running nonstop, twenty-four hours a day.

My legs are weak. That's how it feels when I run this hard. And when I'm terrified. I can barely feel them.

I start up again. Left, right. Left, right.

A better pace this time. I let my breath take control, guiding me through the backstreets. As the thoughts fall away, autopilot takes the wheel. I don't see the trees or the cars, the houses or pedestrians. I step over tree roots, leap from curb to curb.

Mindless.

Buzzing.

I stop for traffic, running in place. Maybe I'll turn right, but then I recognize the house behind me. Notice the street sign. *Wentworth.*

And two houses to the right, across the street, there's a small white house sandwiched between two larger ones. Palms out front. I plant my hands on my hips, head down.

Shit.

I'm two houses away from my office.

How many miles did I run before ending up here? I can't remember. It's all a fog. I wasn't paying attention. I could turn around, run straight home. Never look back. I shouldn't look.

But I have to.

I walk down the sidewalk, hands on my hips, wiping the sweat from my cheeks with the bottom of my T-shirt. Slowly, the corner of my office house comes into view. The palm. The front door. And someone leaning against the wall.

Plain clothes. Black skin.

And we stare at each other from across the street. Sweat stings my eyes, blurring my vision. But I feel his gaze. He's waiting for his appointment. I could walk away, but I'm compelled to cross the street. Call it curiosity.

Call it insanity.

"How'd you do that?" I announce.

"I have more to tell."

"No, first tell me. How'd you make me see that?"

He straightens and looks off. He's not going to say anything. He wants to go inside.

"What if I say no?" I say. "What if I say no more appointments? What're you going to do?"

"Never say no."

A teacher once said that. Say yes to experience, she said. Good or bad, yes. Be curious because the sun will rise with or without you. Perhaps he knows that memory is inside my head; he says it to freak me out. To get deeper. Or maybe he says those things and it's just a coincidence.

Fuck.

I go inside.

* * *

MY PHONE VIBRATES. WHY? my wife texts back.

I text *Explain later.* I can't tell her I'll be home late because a vampire has insisted on an unscheduled appointment. And I consented because I want a rational explanation so I can sleep tonight. I want this goof to end so I won't be dead in three days.

My heart is thumping. Sweat soaks into the chair. Drayton comes into the back office, stirring a cup of tea.

"How'd you do it?" I ask.

He sits down carefully and sips. A gentle smacking of his lips evaluates the flavor. He closes his eyes, inhaling the aroma before putting the cup down.

"I have developed certain *abilities*."

"You're a telepath?"

"The mind has tremendous potential."

"And your teeth?" I expose my teeth, rubbing the left incisor. "You want me to believe you have fangs?"

"Once I did. No longer."

He doesn't show me, but I know he doesn't have fangs. That's something I would've noticed on day five. *Goddamnit, I'm thinking like there's a countdown!*

"Your teeth shrank?"

"I don't need them. Not anymore."

"You don't eat people?"

He lifts the teacup again and goes through the same motions, savoring the full experience. He places it back on the table and sits back with legs crossed.

"I never did."

"Then explain what I saw."

"Animal instincts. I began life with animal instincts, my life driven by emotions and lust and carnal desire. You felt the tug of satisfaction in the belly when the blood spilled—"

"The blood?" I sit forward, flush with anger. "That's not human, Drayton! We don't lust to spill another person's blood, savor the warmth on our chins and fullness in our throats…"

A tiny smile. "I don't believe I'm human."

"You're a vampire."

"As I've said, James, I don't know what I am."

"You prey on humans, drink their blood, pretend to be human. That's the definition."

"Movies can't define me. Nor you."

"That would explain how you walk in daylight in the Holy City. Can you see your reflection?"

"Myths begin with a germ of truth, I suppose. Stories of my life have been passed down through the centuries, but I assure you I don't sleep in a coffin or hiss in the presence of a crucifix. And a stake through the heart would kill you much sooner than me."

He starts the tea ceremony again. I bolt out of the chair and pace the office. I can't believe I'm buying this bullshit. Just because I can't explain how he's doing it doesn't mean I have to believe.

The birdfeeders are empty. I hear the teacup return to the table, the gentle repositioning of legs.

"Why are you here?" I stare out the window.

"To escort you through your final days."

I chuckle. "I never knew Death was so gracious."

"I am not Death."

"I know. You don't know what you are. Instead, you stalk your victims, show them cards with the exact number of days they have left."

"You are not a victim. Death is inevitable. It comes to all."

"Except you."

He sits quietly. I lean against the window, sit on the sill, arms crossed. The glass is cold on my damp T-shirt. He doesn't turn to face me but sits there staring forward.

"Why the numbers?" I ask.

"Do you appreciate each moment?"

"I don't appreciate it enough, I need the help of a vampire—the undead—to make the most of my life, is that it? This is for my benefit?"

I tap my foot, tensing my arms, suddenly overwhelmed with the urge to grab the antique vase from the rolltop desk and shatter it over his right ear.

"If that's the case," I say through stiff lips, "then our arrangement is over. Your appointments are officially concluded with my analysis: you're insane. Delusional. I'm not dying, as you want me to believe. Maybe you've made some fast cash pulling off the con of the century. I recommend you take your act to Hollywood or New York City or someplace where your talents are appreciated, because they're being wasted on me. You're good. Sick, but good. Now, if you'll excuse me—"

I see him lift his hand.

I hear the teacup clatter.

Hear laughter.

I'm in a tavern, of sorts. Candles flicker on wooden tables and lanterns beam. A man with a bushy mustache is behind a bar, staring at me. I hear laughter again. Realize it's coming from me.

I'm in a corner. The square table deeply gouged.

There are men. They are unwashed, weighted with heavy clothing, their beards and long hair matted with filth. They watch me with large cups of mead in their fists. They're waiting for someone to arrive. Their thoughts buzz like fuzzy words, tuning in and out of frequency. They're not moving until *he* arrives.

I smell them. Not the filth. *The fear.* Each of them emits the emotion like a pungent fragrance that stings my nostrils. A tang is at the back of my throat. I inhale their fear like sampling fine wine. *What one of them will be the appetizer? The main course?*

This is why I laugh.

The barmaid is a heavyset woman, her breasts bulging from the ill-fitting corset. A missing tooth. She ignores me, dropping a drink on one of the tables. Her mind squabbles with random thoughts, unconcerned with the brewing violence. There's always something. She just wants it to be over. All of it.

Perhaps she'll be dessert.

The front door slams open, not so much from the beast of a man that fills the doorway but the vicious wind breathing inside. He throws the lock on the door. He brushes sleet from the pelts piled on his shoulders and shakes the snow from his thick mane.

His eyes are set deeply. He mutters something in Gaelic. *Lock the doors.*

The men stand. One goes to the door on the opposite side of the room.

The bartender rounds the bar with a club and I'm relaxed.

No tension. No fear.

I watch these murderers with curiosity, tracking the change in emotions. The barmaid steps behind the bar, sits down and lights a pipe, hoping there isn't too much to mop up when this is finished.

I laugh again. There will be much.

But she needn't worry about cleaning.

The barbarians pull the tables across the floor, clearing a space. My apparent insanity keeps them restrained. The big man approaches. He takes the furs off, laying them on a chair. His hands are like hammers, the knuckles hardened like stones. He stamps them on the table in front of me and leans over; bits of meat glisten in his curly whiskers.

I like the way he smells. The anger. The hatred. The distillation of testosterone that's channeled into fury, his will of domination. It wafts among the others' fear. I let it linger in my senses, titillating my sinuses until there's a stir in my groin, a primal urge to satisfy my desires.

Tension builds in the man-beast.

He grabs the edge of the table—

Caisg.

I plant that thought in his mind. He stops. His body responds. He's frozen like winter soil, the meaty knuckles clutching the table. I pull the chair out and slowly step around him. His men shuffle away, confused. Their eyes follow me to the bar, where the barmaid sucks the stick-end of a pipe, smoke streaming from her nostrils. I will her mind to empty, the thoughts to evaporate. She can't look away, her eyes locked on me. I project thoughts at her. She accepts them, unable to deny them.

Mindlessly, she steps around the bar.

Mindlessly, I bend her over.

The men watch as I heedlessly violate her. I feel no sexual satisfaction despite performing the act. It's her helpless horror that shoots through my groin, rising to my throat. Saliva fills my mouth, my teeth shimmer. When the fear peaks, I snap her neck and tear into her throat. Her body is slack. I let it fall to the ground. I slake my thirst on the exposed arteries, eyes fluttering, feeding on my hands and knees like an animal tearing at a carcass.

I climax as I watch the men quiver, a climax much different than I'm accustomed to. An orgasm that is deep and twisted, all-consuming and limitless. I fall on my back, releasing my grip on the men, and let them have their bodies. Let their fear flow. Let the anger and rage mix.

"*Mì-naomha,*" one of them mutters. *Unholy.*

All the emotions twirl like an intoxicating brew. I close my eyes, drink it through my pores—

A sword slides between my ribs, gouging my liver, exiting my back. Its tip *thunks* into the floor below me. The bearded barbarian is at the other end of the long sword, eyes buried in ruddy flesh. A smile erupts from the dark whiskers, discolored teeth crooked and cracked.

I bellow with laughter, pushing off the floor, the sword sliding through me. I feel nothing but thrilling horror ooze from him. His smile vanishes. The men bolt for the exits. I project a thought and their muscles lock. They fall to the floor like carvings made of wood. I snatch the oversized warrior's beard and pull him near. I lick my lips. *Now, the main course.*

His eyes wide, he experiences something he rarely feels.

Terror.

The night is young. So much fun.

So much unadulterated, unstoppable fun.

I'm on my back, my shirt soaked in sweat. Not blood. My office floor below me. Pleasure lingers in my belly.

Carnal satisfaction.

AY 2

THERE'S a jar of cotton balls on the table next to a well-read *Sports Illustrated*. I count my steps in the well-lit room. Count my breaths—one, two, three—but the tension just winds and winds and winds… I'm about to punch a hole through the door when it opens.

"Hi there." A humorless man in a white coat walks in, hand extended. "I'm Dr. Sheffield. You're Mr. Gallagher?"

"*Doctor* Gallagher."

"What can I do for you?" He looks at his chart, unimpressed.

"I explained everything to the nurse."

"Yes. It says you believe you're going to have a stroke in two days."

"I don't think I said two days."

Dr. Sheffield looks at his folder and says, "Have you experienced any numbness on one side of the face?"

"No."

He checks the folder with a pencil. "Any numbness in the arm or leg?"

"No."

"Have you had any difficulty speaking?"

"No."

"Severe headaches?"

"Yes." I point at the folder. *Got one.*

"How often?"

"It comes and goes. I've had them all my life."

"Has there been an increase in frequency?"

"No."

The doctor scribbles a few notes and says while writing, "Have you experienced sudden confusion or difficulty with vision?"

"Do hallucinations count?"

The pencil stops. Dr. Sheffield looks up like he's peering over invisible glasses. "Are you having hallucinations?"

I shake my head, looking away. Not ready to let that one out. Can't tell him I'm talking to an honest-to-god vampire that's given me two days to live. I mean, psychosis is my specialty, not his.

"No," I finally say. "Just clarifying. No, I'm not having confusion or, uh, difficulty seeing."

The doctor gives me a few moments to come clean before flipping through his notes. I cross my arms. The silence make me feel dumber. I stop myself from leaving.

"Dr. Gallagher, your blood pressure is normal and I see nothing that indicates an impending stroke—"

"Aneurysmal subarachnoid hemorrhage."

He closes the folder. "Have you been on WebMD?"

"No, no. Just something someone told me."

"Has someone in your family had this condition?"

"Not that I'm aware of."

He washes his hands, drying them with brown paper towels, wiping down each finger. "If you like, we can schedule a CT scan, just to be sure. In the meantime, I suggest you avoid stress and take any medications as prescribed."

"Certainly."

* * *

I suppose I should've scheduled a CT scan. Don't know why I didn't.

If they find an aneurysmal subarachnoid hemorrhage, that means he's real.

I'm still gambling this is all a result of the acid I dropped before a Pink Floyd show in grad school. I knew there was a risk of flashbacks, just didn't think they'd be scheduling appointments and giving me money.

I stop outside the front doors, where the sun reflects off concrete, sunlight that took eight minutes to get here, warming the earth. Warming my skin. The air feels more comfortable. The salvias in the flowerbeds seem brighter. Redder.

How many days were I given when I was born? Eighteen thousand? Was that what I had? How many days did I piss away in front of the TV? How many did I waste sleeping or drinking or jerking off?

The day feels different, now that it's got a number. Even though nothing's changed, it's different. Precious.

My phone buzzes. Twelve missed calls. Four voicemails. Ten texts.

My wife wants to know WHERE R U?

I didn't exactly post a note where I was going that morning. In fact, I got on my bike, intent on going to the office. Then I had a panic attack just north of Broad Street.

What if I DO only have two days left?

I head out for campus amongst the medical students and young interns, the doctors and administrators and patients and grounds crew... all about their business. Just another day. They mindlessly fritter away minutes and seconds because they have millions of them to spend. Right?

There are thousands of days left, right?

I'll hammer out this cigarette, watch this movie, get laid, catch a buzz, drink some coffee, run ten miles, read a book, get a new smart-phone... just kill some time.

Kill a few days, years. Kill my life.

The urban garden comes into view. An acre of crops is lined in raised beds and PVC hoops. The volunteers gather at the back shed. The coordinator has a clipboard, pointing out assignments. Maybe I can check off day two plugging the ground with broccoli.

Or maybe I can get drunk.

One volunteer is already out there, on his knees, bent over a patch of Swiss chard. His skin black as asphalt. He's not looking at me. He doesn't have to. He knows I'll come to him.

And I do.

* * *

"I KNOW why you're doing this." My shadow stretches over his back.

He plucks a clump of henbit from the soil.

"You feast on fear," I say. "I saw how you ramped up the terror, savored the taste of horror, bathed in it like a sick fuck until you destroyed them in the most depraved way possible. And you're doing the same to me, flashing that goddamn number at me like some sort of fucking weapon, watching me sweat and cringe. If I'm going to die, then let it be. I don't need to hear a countdown."

"Are you afraid of death, James?"

"I'm human."

"Why do you cling to life?"

I laugh loudly. The volunteers look at me. "Look," I say quietly, "you're not afraid because you can't die, you made that clear with that…"

I don't want to say *vision*.

I feel like an idiot. I'm scared shitless about dying; I've bought his whole story. But that's a lot different than admitting there's a goddamn immortal on his hands and knees WEEDING A FUCKING GARDEN.

"I will die," he says. "The universe will end. So will I."

"Great. You'll die fifty billion years from now. I'm so sorry—Jesus Christ, I can't believe I'm having this conversation!"

I stomp away with every intention of not returning. If that crazy little fuck wants to have a therapy session, then he can talk to the cabbage. I'm not going to stand in the middle of a garden and argue about who's more scared of dying—men or a vampire.

The phone buzzes.

I turn it off.

I stop. I want to leave. I do. I really do. But, shit. I can't.

And then he says, "Pull weeds with me, James."

"Why are you doing this to me?"

"I'm not doing this to you any more than I'm making the sun set."

I stifle the urge to laugh like a maniac again. The volunteers have spread out. A pair of them are only two beds over, repairing drip tubing. I drop on my knees—they sink in the soft earth—and lean over the bed, grabbing a handful of betony.

"I'm not talking about death," I say.

He shakes the soil off the roots of another handful of weeds and gently places it on a green pile. Reaches for more.

"I'm talking about the visions. Why show me that? Just give me the number and be gone, I know what you are. Maybe you fool most people, but I know you're a disguised beast. You are Death incarnate."

I grab a fistful of soil, my fingers scratching stone beneath the ground.

"You feed on fear and death."

Another clutch of dirt and weeds and another hidden stone, my fingers numb as they scratch the cold, hard surface.

"And now that you're ten thousand years old or whatever the ridiculous number is, you've sophisticated your approach into psychological torture, raping my mind instead of my body. Like you did to the barmaid."

I pull away the soil and see the rounded stones piled at the bottom of the planter.

I lean my weight on the cold granite, getting close to Drayton's sweatless, darkened features.

"I hope you burn in hell."

And the stones grind into my knees.

Drayton dissolves into black night. The weeds, the soil, the vegetables transform into the pale face of a child, his lips parted. The taste of his blood lingers on my lips. His essence is light and tender. Delicate.

Innocent.

I like it.

I stand on the cobblestone street, the pavement pressing unevenly on my boots. There's fog above. The moon hidden. I relish the secret delight, a pleasant surprise as I've been wandering the streets in the late hours. I was not hungry, not looking for anything in particular, but my curiosity piqued when I felt the boy moving inside the building. I leaned against the wall, closed my eyes, and felt him toss in his bed, struggling with a bad dream. Despite the barriers between us, I tasted his essence like vapor.

I called him outside. Yes, I put a thought in his mind to get out of bed, to open the door and come to me. He did. Man, woman or child, they all do.

And I was not disappointed.

I lean him against the wall, crossing his hands on his lap so the nibble on his wrist does not immediately show. How could I ruin such an innocent face? I took his blood from the radial artery. My incisors sharpened to points for puncturing, not tearing. A single, surgical hole opened his circulatory system to my desire.

I dab my mouth with a handkerchief.

His mother is moving inside the apartment. I'm halfway down the narrow street, almost euphoric with delight. A child's essence. Oh, dear. I quiver with excitement. Ecstasy follows me—

I catch myself against the wall.

A dagger of grief stabs my loins.

I've sensed this emotion in others, but never have I felt it so intimately. Grief and remorse have never gripped my soul with their sharpened claws. Until now. I've always fed on the dregs of humanity, the lost souls, the tainted men and women that care less for others than they do for themselves. There was grief, but never like this. The wailing echoes along the walls, shrieks of a mother's agony. The father bellows, wrapping his arms around mother and child. Rocking back and forth. Back and forth.

Whatever pleasure touched me rots like fruit caught in early winter. Each cry drives a stake deeper into my belly. Never have I felt such torment. Such loss. I slide down the wall. The neighbors' lights come on. Men and women cross the street. I have felt loss before, only a faint glimmer. Never something as profound as a child.

His blood curdles in my stomach. I roll to my hands and knees, convulsing.

I splash the pavement red.

"Sir?"

A hand on my shoulder.

A woman stands back. Blue sky above her. Drool puddles below me.

"Are you all right?" she asks.

There's a pile of weeds across from me. Drayton is gone.

All that's left is the harrowing emptiness of guilt and remorse.

The woman watches me sit.

Watches me weep.

I STAY in bed until my wife's gone. She doesn't know about the hospital. She knows something's wrong; I tell her I'm not feeling well. She knows I'm lying, but I can't tell her the truth.

Tomorrow, I'll be dead.

Ritual is the armor against insanity. When the house is empty, I make coffee and stretch. I make a lap around the backyard, inspecting the plants for insects or disease, pulling a few weeds. When my cup is empty, I go into the back room and set up for meditation.

There's a low table against the wall with a flower vase and a stone bowl with sand. I bow, stab three sticks of incense into the sand and light them. One more bow and I adjust the meditation bench, tucking my legs beneath it. There's no use in waiting for calm to begin.

There's the story of the Zen master that's chased to a cliff by a man-eating tiger. The Zen master clings to a tiny branch just out of the tiger's reach, and as it slowly begins to break loose, he spots a strawberry growing from the crevice. "What a lovely gift," he says, plucking it from the vine.

I bang the tiny bell chime and fold my hands.

Having a thought, fuck strawberries.

I listen to the traffic. A container ship is passing through the harbor, blaring its horn. The house settles around me. All so peaceful. Just another day.

Inside, sensations linger. Fear and remorse. An entire universe of emotions roil like a bubbling cauldron. I sit with it, allow it to brew. Allow it space. I feel like a balloon at its limits.

Ash falls from the middle stick of incense. It lands on the rim of the stone bowl. The bowl my daughter, Hillary, gave me.

I'm going to die.

That thought is accompanied by a cold shiver. My bones liquefy. I remain sitting. I allow space for the thought and the sensation. Will it help if they know Daddy's going to die tomorrow? Should I tell them so we can... what? Hang out? Get closer? How do I explain that I'm treating a vampire and he informed me of an impending lethal stroke? My wife will commit me to an institution. At least she should.

I would.

Ash falls from the other two sticks almost simultaneously.

I've embraced insanity. I believe Drayton. I believe he's been alive for thousands of years, that he's viciously murdered countless people, drank their blood and feasted on their fear. I believe in monsters.

I do. I do.

He is the definition of a monster. How could those actions be categorized as anything else? But what's it like to be alive for eight thousand years? He started as an animal, abusing power in self-centered fashion. Has he developed empathy? Is there a spiritual evolution of the soul that takes place? Does he have a soul? He doesn't know, at least that's what he'll say if I ask. If I ask him what he is, he'll answer it like a koan: I don't know what I am.

I am this.

Are any of us different?

Humans don't live long enough. Few of us truly transform on a fundamental level. But, hell, give me a couple thousand years and unlimited power and maybe I'll be cool with picking strawberries from the cliff.

If Drayton was an animal, what is he now? *Every galaxy has a black hole.*

The incense withers into a pile of ash. The last bit of smoke slithers up the wall, vanishing somewhere near the ceiling.

Sit.

Label thoughts.

Allow space for the moment.

For the tiger and the strawberry.

* * *

I'M NUKING coffee number three when the doorbell rings. I watch the plate spinning inside the microwave and wait for the countdown to reach zero. Stir in creamer and sip once before going to the front door.

"May I enter?"

"Do I have a choice?"

I know the answer. I step aside, hoping he doesn't infect the house with death, that my family will not catch it like a virus. It doesn't work that way. Then again, vampires are only in the movies, so how the fuck am I supposed to know how it works. Maybe death works exactly like a virus.

He stands in the front room, facing the cold fireplace. His reflection looks back from the mirror above the mantel. I don't care anymore about reflections and holy water. Honestly, I don't think I care. And that worries me a bit.

I go to the kitchen and make tea. When I return, he's still standing there. He accepts the cup and saucer with a slight bow and sits on the couch. I go to the window and watch a yacht sail through the harbor. The sail flutters in the hesitant wind, finally catching on the starboard side.

"I'm an overpaid, mediocre therapist," I say. "Why choose me? Of all the people in the world, why come tell me how much time I have left? I didn't ask for this."

I shake my head.

"Doesn't matter, I guess. I believe you. Maybe I'm dead already and dreaming you up. Maybe I'm a ghost in this house, waiting for a reason to leave. That would make a whole hell of a lot more sense than believing a vampire is sipping tea in my front room."

He's sitting quite still, cup in hand. He blinks slowly. Not looking at me, but listening. Always hearing.

"I don't care, Drayton. I don't care if you're a monster, saint, or whatever you are. You know why?"

I sit in the chair across from him, the low table between us.

"Because the sun doesn't need me to believe. It will rise without me."

I cross my legs, cup balanced on my knee. Drayton looks up, his eyes large and calm. We sit this way for quite some time. The traffic goes by and the clock ticks on the wall. Our drinks turn cold. Drayton hardly moves, sitting as still and solid as if he's petrified. His patience emanates like sound waves, penetrating me, filling me. My head buzzes. I am no longer agitated. I'm just here. He's here.

Sitting.

The breeze blows through the room. My hair flutters.

The front door is open. Terraces have replaced the harbor. Wheat waves along the hillsides, golden and heavy with seed. The sun is near the ridge, grazing the fields. A flock of blackbirds circle in the heat.

An old man lies on the ground, his skin dark from decades in the sun, weathered like leather. His graying, frizzled hair sprays from the wide-brim hat crumpled behind his head. His brown eyes look through me, his cracked lips gaping. His heart is giving up. He labors for breath.

I know this man. He didn't always look this way. He was younger and stronger, spry and zestful. Time chipped that away, chiseled him down like marble. I have known him most of his life.

The life that's coming to an end this day.

Decades ago, he lost his wife to childbirth. I was with him for that.

We buried her behind the house and laid a stone near the grave, her name chiseled into the surface. His son was born with complications. He died years later. I was there for that, too. We buried him next to his mother. I dug the hole while the man looked on. He wept later, when he was alone. I wasn't with him, but I felt it. I felt the depth of his grief, the remorse that softens the girders that hold up one's life, threatening to bring it all down. Turns it to dust.

Together, we worked the fields, sold his crop. Some years were good, others bad. He never paid me, only provided food and shelter, neither of which I need. He never questioned where this dark-skinned lad had come from, or why he stayed. He never asked why—when his body ached and bent to time's will—I never aged. Some days he just thanked his good fortune.

Other times, he cursed it.

For thirty years, I worked alongside Redmond O'Gallchoir. During that time, I abstained from taking blood. The craving sometimes burned, other times ached. After eons, thirty years is but a small slice. The craving never disappeared, but it ebbed. It transformed.

I had transformed.

No longer the lusting beast, I found space for the craving to exist. Somehow, I had become more and the craving became less. No longer did I chase something that could not be possessed, for the craving would always be that. It would always be empty, never be satisfied.

The old man stiffens. The last breath leaks from him.

His eyes plead. He doesn't have the strength for words, but I feel them inside. *Thank you,* he says. And he bestows upon me a gift.

His body becomes light as if charged with particles.

I touch his neck and feel the something escape from him. It is light and silky. An essence that once infused his blood now drains into me. It is not good or bad, not pleasurable nor offensive.

It is filling.

Without taking his life, I find peace.

His body is as light as a sack of dry sticks. I carry him behind the house, where I bury him between two large stones. I roll a third to the head of his grave and rest while the sun sets.

No more bloodshed.

No beginning. No end.

Just this moment.

The stone softens, the darkness lifts, and I'm sitting on a chair in my house. Drayton is gone, of course. Whatever fear he once instilled has transformed into something else.

Something that fills me.

* * *

WHAT DO you do with your last day? Climb a mountain? Parachute out of a plane? Do you go do something that's absolutely insane, something you didn't have the courage to do until now—now that life is almost over?

Is life about filling the bucket? Is it about finding happiness?

Don't ask me. I know, I know… I'm a licensed psychologist, I help people with their problems. I have all the answers. But who says problems are supposed to be solved?

Who says they're even problems?

What do I do with my last day? I do something crazy, all right. I call my clients and apologize for not coming to our scheduled appointments. Three of them reschedule for next week (I don't tell them I won't be coming to that one, either, but they'll understand). Ms. Kampman schedules that afternoon because she's got a real problem that just can't wait (I say yes, of course), and Mr. Cullough says *fuck you*. Well, not really fuck you, he used other words like *I'll be finding another psychologist*. His tone, though, that definitely says *fuck you*.

I understand.

So that afternoon, I ride my bike to the office. That's right. With one day left, I mount up, grab coffee, and meet Ms. Kampman at the office, savoring the bumps in the roads, the sound of the fountain, the squirrels wrestling seed from the bird feeder.

Before enlightenment, chop wood, carry water. After enlightenment, chop wood, carry water.

I'm not enlightened. Would I know it if I was? No self-respecting teacher ever claims to be enlightened, even when it appears obvious to his or her students. Maybe things have transformed, I don't know. I don't think about it, I just go about the daily business of life and wonder why I didn't do this every day of my life.

Sound boring?

It's wondrous.

* * *

BEFORE DINNER, I do the laundry and fold clothes. The carpets get a quick vacuum and the floors are swept. Everything's in order when I go out to the balcony with a glass of sweet tea and call my eighty-year-old father. We talk about the Braves, about my kids, and his next doctor's appointment. He can't talk long, he has to get down to the bank before it closes. I avoid saying things like *I'll be seeing Mom tomorrow, anything you want me to pass along?* I don't even say the predictable *I love you.*

I just say, "Thanks, Pop."

"All right," he says.

I finish the tea and watch the harbor through the branches of a live oak draped with Spanish moss—an oak that's perhaps a thousand years old. Still doesn't touch Drayton. So much history in the Lowcountry. My ancestors have been part of it since the beginning. Maybe that's why Drayton came to me.

Redmond O'Gallchoir. Gallagher.

Redmond O'Gallchoir is one of my ancestors, I feel certain. Maybe that was the moment of Drayton's enlightenment, although it seems odd to describe a vampire as enlightened. Let's call it transformation. The moment Drayton no longer took blood but rather absorbed human essence. The moment Drayton no longer took life to get it.

The moment Drayton was no longer an animal. But something else.

This.

Perhaps he's been tracking us O'Gallchoirs because he likes the taste. Maybe he's repaying a debt. Or giving us a gift. Did I want to know I was going to die? Has the last week been a wreck?

Yes. Yes.

Has it been a gift?

That night, when dinner is done, I make the kids put away their phones and play a stupid board game, and despite their best efforts to sabotage the night, they laugh. We laugh. When it's dark and quiet, I retire to the balcony again. No tea this time. Just sitting back, listening to the ships. The scent of pluff mud is thick.

My wife comes through the bedroom. "There you are? You all right?"

She stands next to me, hands on hips, firing the psychologist laser beam into my brain to suck out my thoughts. She remains solid, unmoving. Demanding an explanation for my peculiar behavior.

I push the chair back, take her hand and draw her close. We dance like we did on our wedding night, swaying back and forth. This time to the sounds of the tree frogs. She relaxes into my embrace, laying her head on my shoulder. The psychologist retires and it's just her. Just me.

We dance.

LAST DAY

WET AND NUMB.

I started the morning with a headache and came down to the pier. It all seems like a dream now. Everything.

I sense strangers trying to help me while my eyelids get heavy and the day gets brighter. Blood floods my brain. I don't really care.

Drayton stands over me like a shadow.

Sounds mesh, becoming garbled nonsense. The world continues to get brighter, like an overexposed photo. I close my eyes for a long beat. Drayton is still there, his dark form contrasting in the wash of daylight.

Every galaxy has a black hole.

He kneels next to me. He doesn't reach out, he just waits.

He doesn't know when he was born. Or when he will die. And then I realize he has no beginning, no end. The answer to a koan is manifest, kneeling in the grass. Perhaps I am dreaming. Does it matter?

The world is now light. Only light.

My eyelids are the only things that move, and even that is involuntary. I can't say the words, but he feels them, sees them form as thoughts.

He puts his hand on my chest.

He doesn't drain me. Rather, he fills me.

And then he dissolves into the light until there's nothing. And I don't know where I am. Or why.

I become nothing.

I become everything.

I am this.

And the sun will rise without me.

Discover the mystery of Drayton's beginnings and end in the full-length novel, *The Roots of Drayton*.
http://bertauski.com/drayton

REVIEW DRAYTON!

If you enjoyed this ride, please drop a review on your favorite vendor. It doesn't have to be long and complicated. Throw some stars on it and write *Loved it!* or *It was really, really okay!* or *Meh.*

bertauski.com/drayton
Reviews make the difference.

.

BERTAUSKI STARTER LIBRARY

Send me the free books

* * *

bertauski.com